DREAD GODS ™

VOLUME ONE

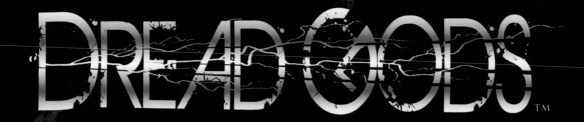

DREAD GODS™

WRITTEN BY
RON MARZ

ART BY
TOM RANEY

COLORS BY
NANJAN JAMBERI

LETTERS BY
A LARGER WORLDS STUDIOS' DAVE LANPHEAR AND TROY PETERI

COVER ART BY
TOM RANEY & NANJAN JAMBERI

DREAD GODS CREATED BY
BART SEARS

OMINOUS PRESS TEAM

SEAN HUSVAR · CHIEF EXECUTIVE OFFICER/PUBLISHER
BART SEARS · CHIEF CREATIVE OFFICER
RON MARZ · EDITOR-IN-CHIEF
ANDY SMITH · ART DIRECTOR
JASON SPOONER · SOCIAL MEDIA DIRECTOR
JAY PENN · CREATIVE ASSISTANT

OMINOUS SPECIAL THANKS

CHRIS SCIOLI, KIM REGANATO, BRITTANY BARNES, BUDDY BEAUDOIN

For international rights, contact **licensing@idwpublishing.com**

ISBN: 978-1-68405-202-8

21 20 19 18 1 2 3 4

IDW®

Greg Goldstein, President & Publisher • **John Barber**, Editor-in-Chief • **Robbie Robbins**, EVP/Sr. Art Director • **Cara Morrison**, Chief Financial Officer • **Matthew Ruzicka**, Chief Accounting Officer • **Anita Frazier**, SVP of Sales and Marketing • **David Hedgecock**, Associate Publisher • **Jerry Bennington**, VP of New Product Development • **Lorelei Bunjes**, VP of Digital Services • **Justin Eisinger**, Editorial Director, Graphic Novels & Collections • **Eric Moss**, Sr. Director, Licensing & Business Development

Ted Adams, IDW Founder

www.IDWPUBLISHING.com

Facebook: **facebook.com/idwpublishing** • Twitter: **@idwpublishing** • YouTube: **youtube.com/idwpublishing**
Tumblr: **tumblr.idwpublishing.com** • Instagram: **instagram.com/idwpublishing**

Originally published as DREAD GODS issues #1–4.

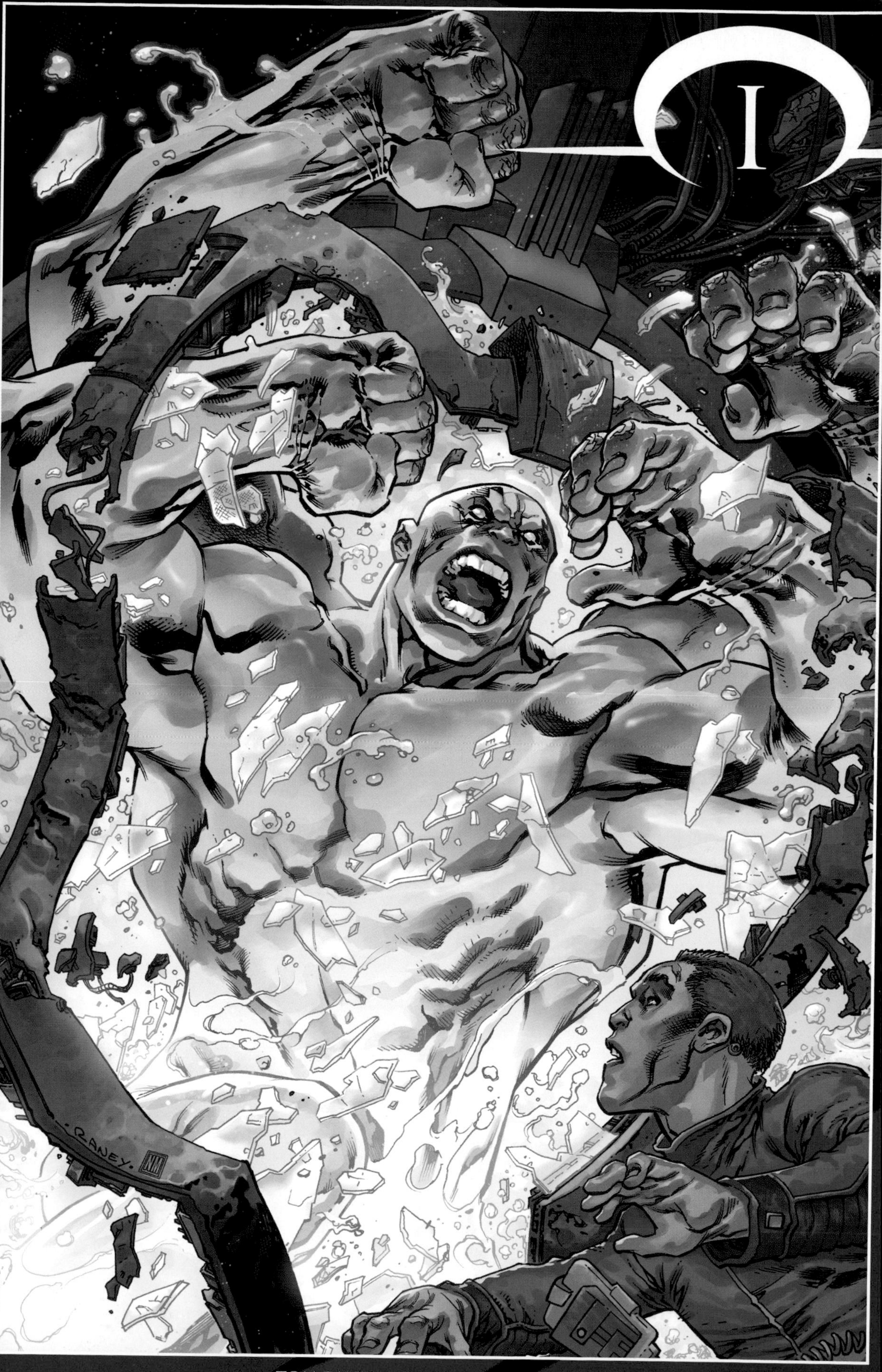
I
RANEY

ART BY **TOM RANEY** · COLORS BY **NEERAJ MENON**

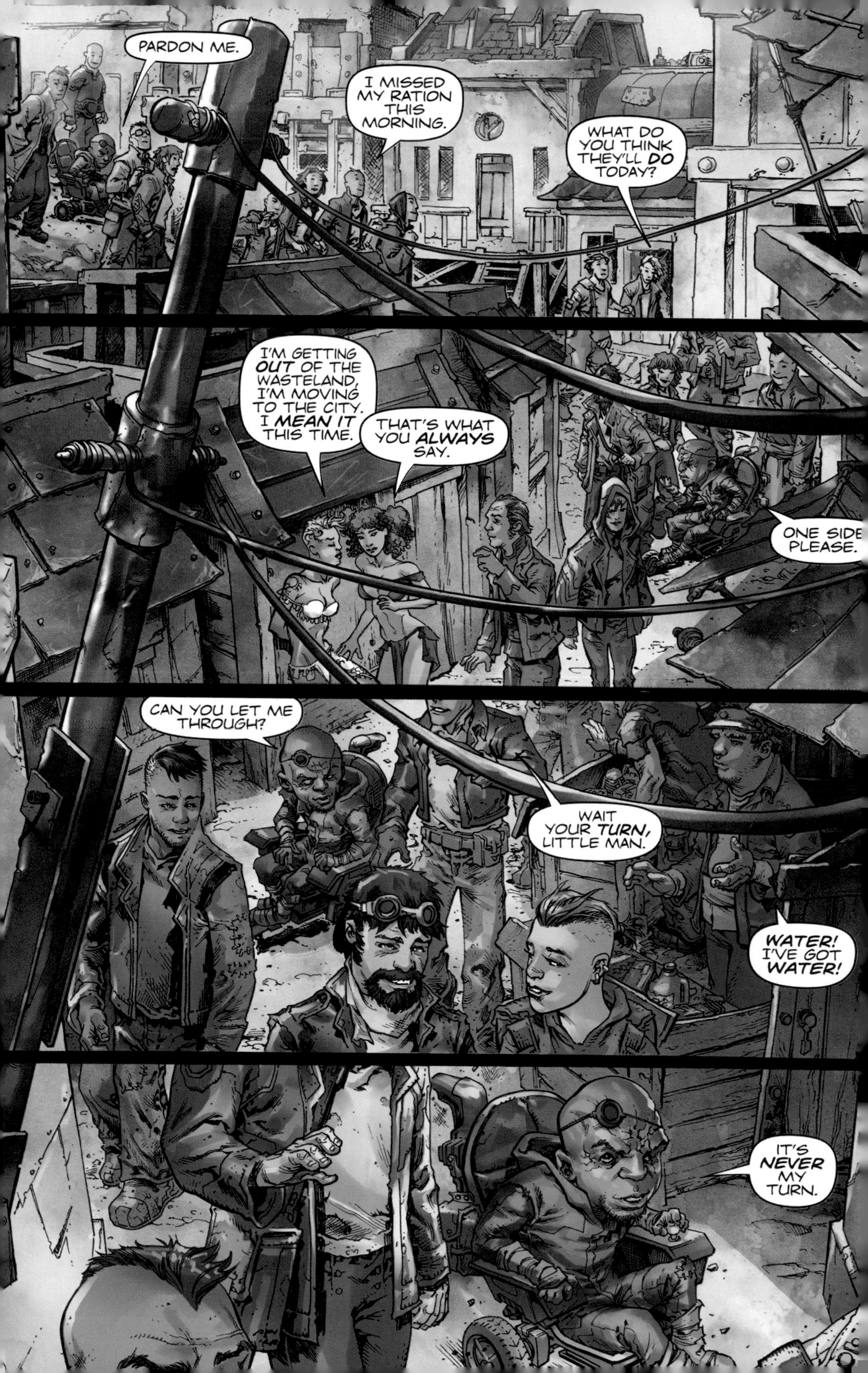
PARDON ME.
I MISSED MY RATION THIS MORNING.
WHAT DO YOU THINK THEY'LL DO TODAY?
I'M GETTING OUT OF THE WASTELAND, I'M MOVING TO THE CITY. I MEAN IT THIS TIME.
THAT'S WHAT YOU ALWAYS SAY.
ONE SIDE PLEASE.
CAN YOU LET ME THROUGH?
WAIT YOUR TURN, LITTLE MAN.
WATER! I'VE GOT WATER!
IT'S NEVER MY TURN.

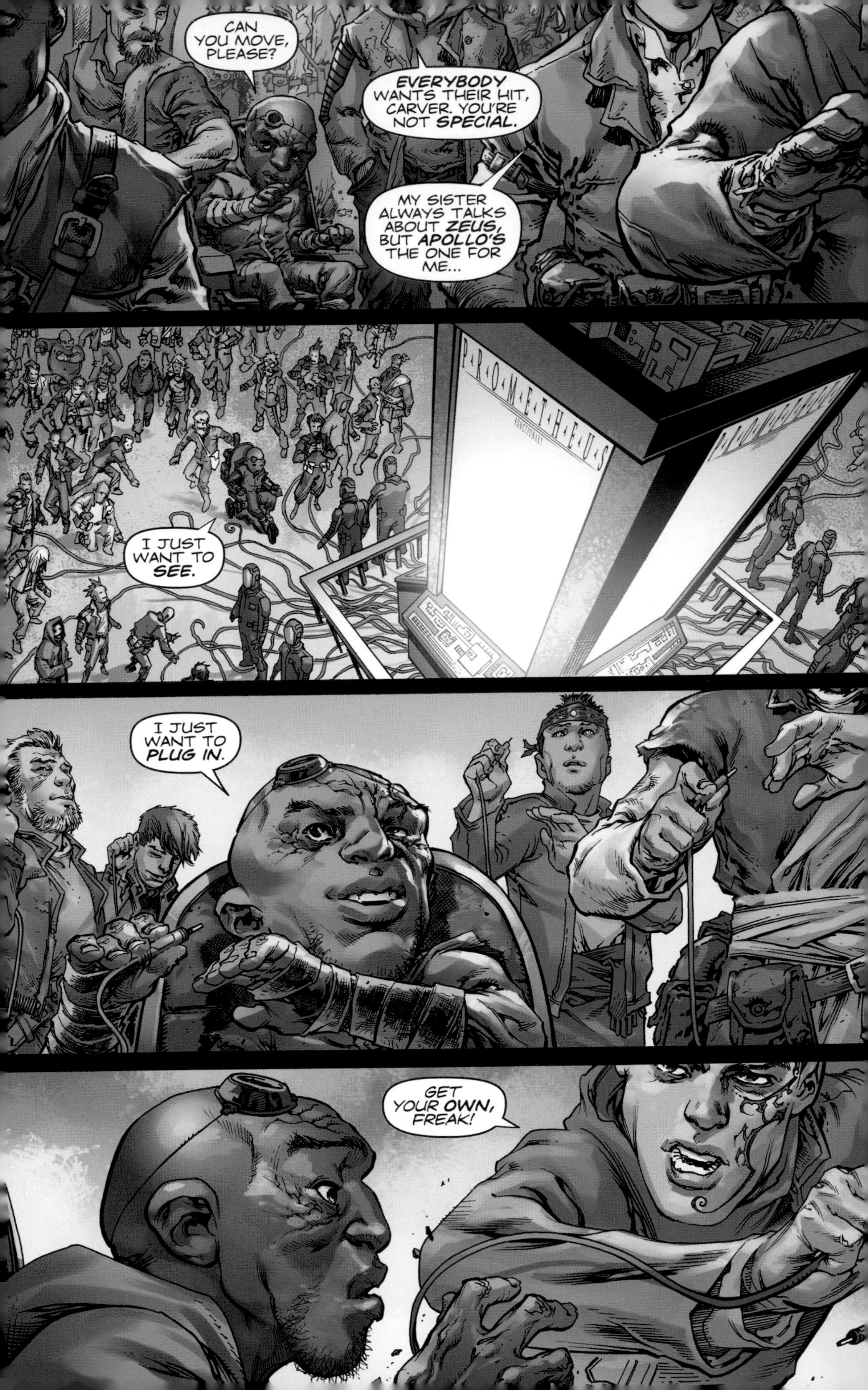
CAN YOU MOVE, PLEASE?
EVERYBODY WANTS THEIR HIT, CARVER. YOU'RE NOT SPECIAL.
MY SISTER ALWAYS TALKS ABOUT ZEUS, BUT APOLLO'S THE ONE FOR ME...
PROMETHEUS
I JUST WANT TO SEE.
I JUST WANT TO PLUG IN.
GET YOUR OWN, FREAK!

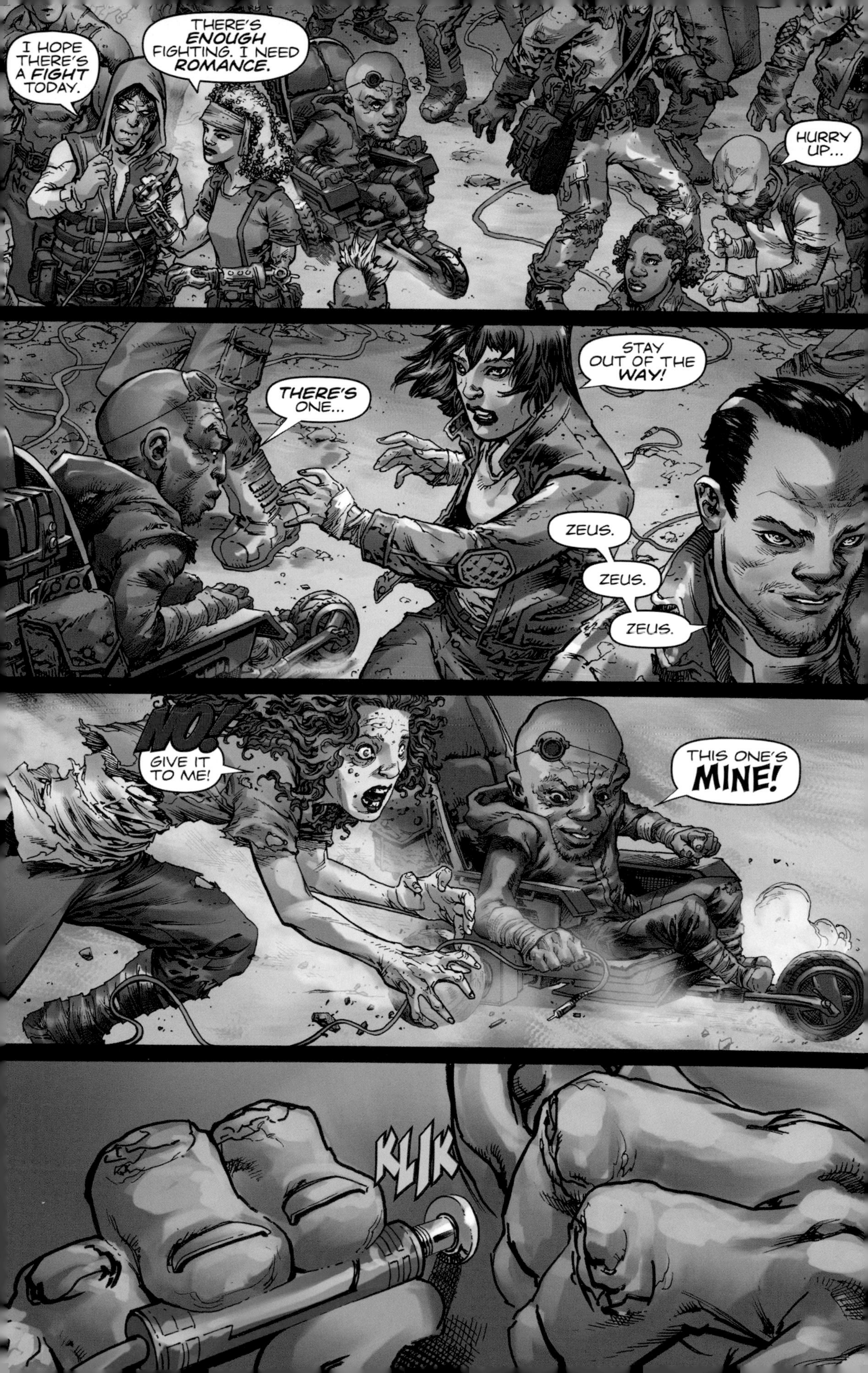

I HOPE THERE'S A FIGHT TODAY.
THERE'S ENOUGH FIGHTING. I NEED ROMANCE.
HURRY UP...
THERE'S ONE...
STAY OUT OF THE WAY!
ZEUS.
ZEUS.
ZEUS.
NO!
GIVE IT TO ME!
THIS ONE'S MINE!
KLIK

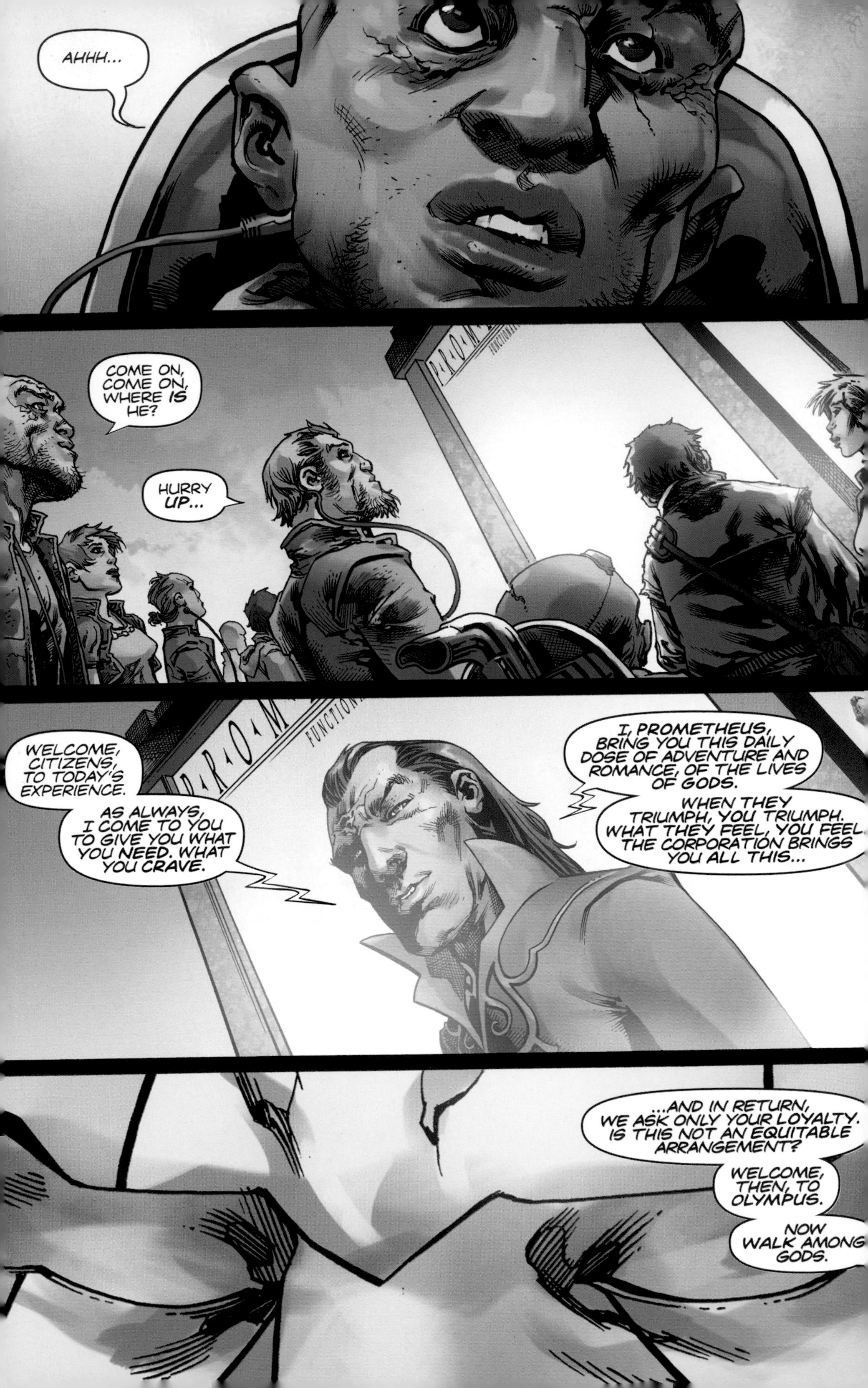
AHHH...
COME ON, COME ON, WHERE IS HE?
HURRY UP...
P·R·O·M
FUNCTION
WELCOME, CITIZENS, TO TODAY'S EXPERIENCE.
AS ALWAYS, I COME TO YOU TO GIVE YOU WHAT YOU NEED. WHAT YOU CRAVE.
I, PROMETHEUS, BRING YOU THIS DAILY DOSE OF ADVENTURE AND ROMANCE, OF THE LIVES OF GODS.
WHEN THEY TRIUMPH, YOU TRIUMPH. WHAT THEY FEEL, YOU FEEL. THE CORPORATION BRINGS YOU ALL THIS...
...AND IN RETURN, WE ASK ONLY YOUR LOYALTY. IS THIS NOT AN EQUITABLE ARRANGEMENT?
WELCOME, THEN, TO OLYMPUS.
NOW WALK AMONG GODS.

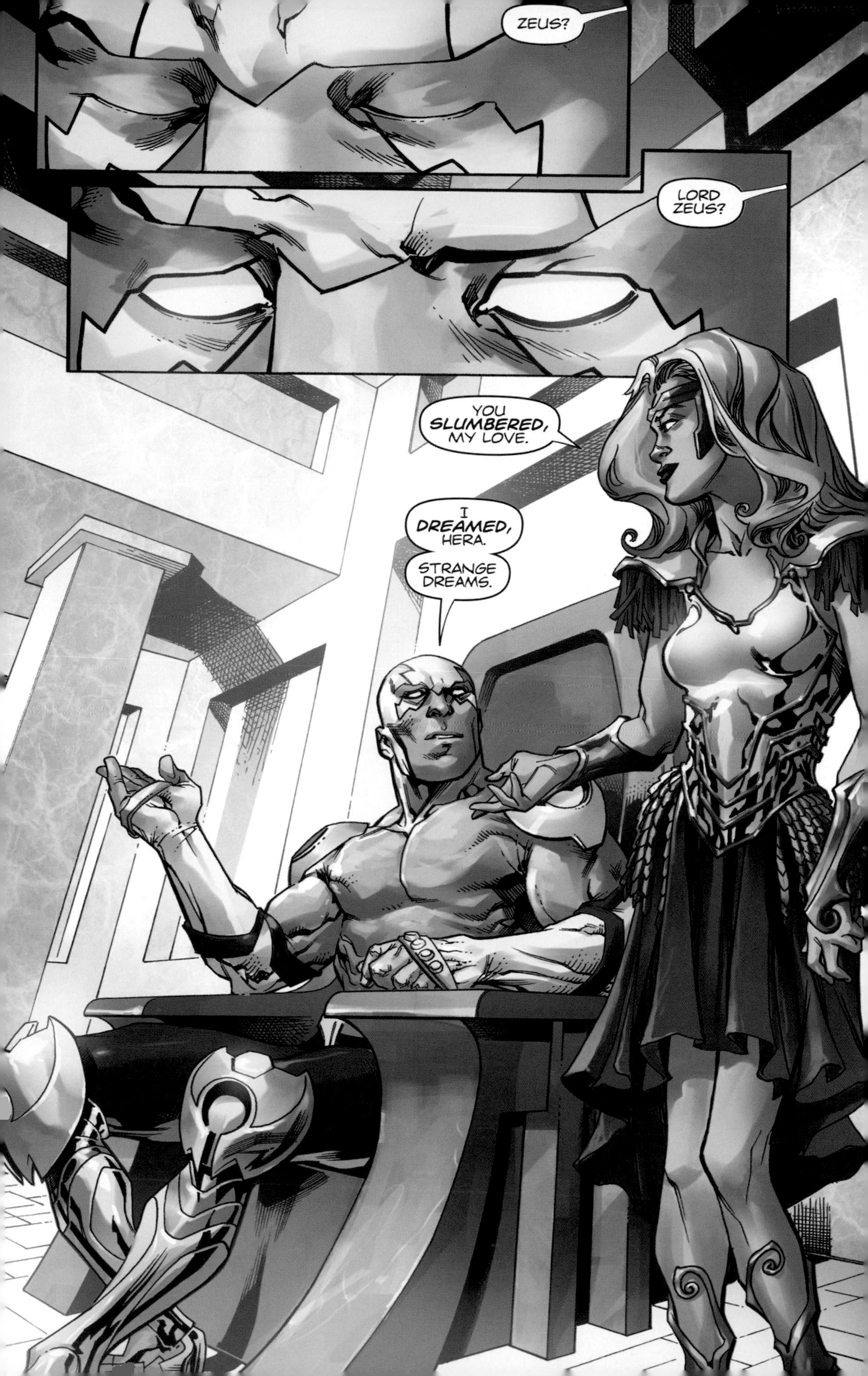
ZEUS?
LORD ZEUS?
YOU SLUMBERED, MY LOVE.
I DREAMED, HERA.
STRANGE DREAMS.

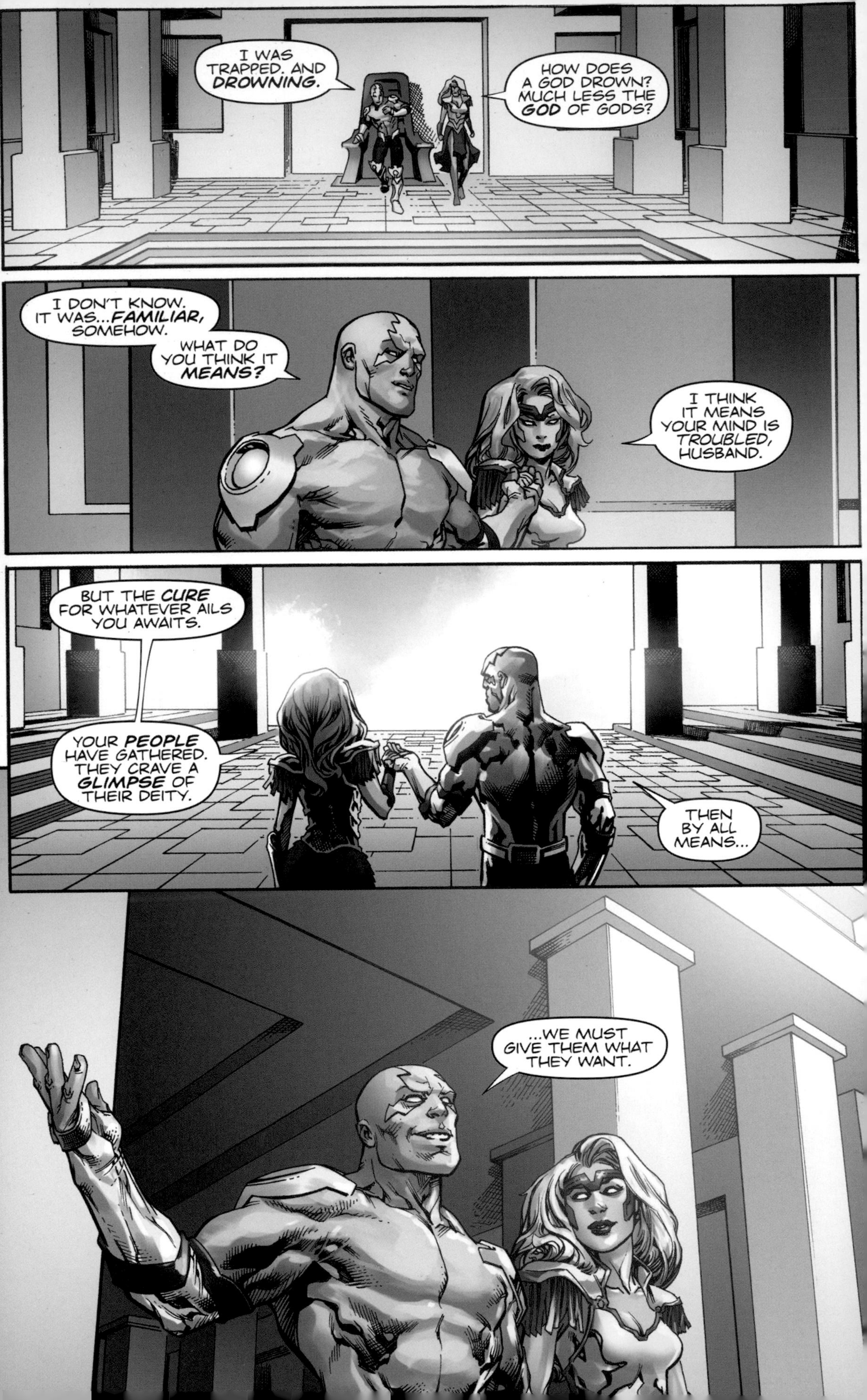
I WAS TRAPPED. AND DROWNING.
HOW DOES A GOD DROWN? MUCH LESS THE GOD OF GODS?
I DON'T KNOW. IT WAS...FAMILIAR, SOMEHOW.
WHAT DO YOU THINK IT MEANS?
I THINK IT MEANS YOUR MIND IS TROUBLED, HUSBAND.
BUT THE CURE FOR WHATEVER AILS YOU AWAITS.
YOUR PEOPLE HAVE GATHERED. THEY CRAVE A GLIMPSE OF THEIR DEITY.
THEN BY ALL MEANS...
...WE MUST GIVE THEM WHAT THEY WANT.

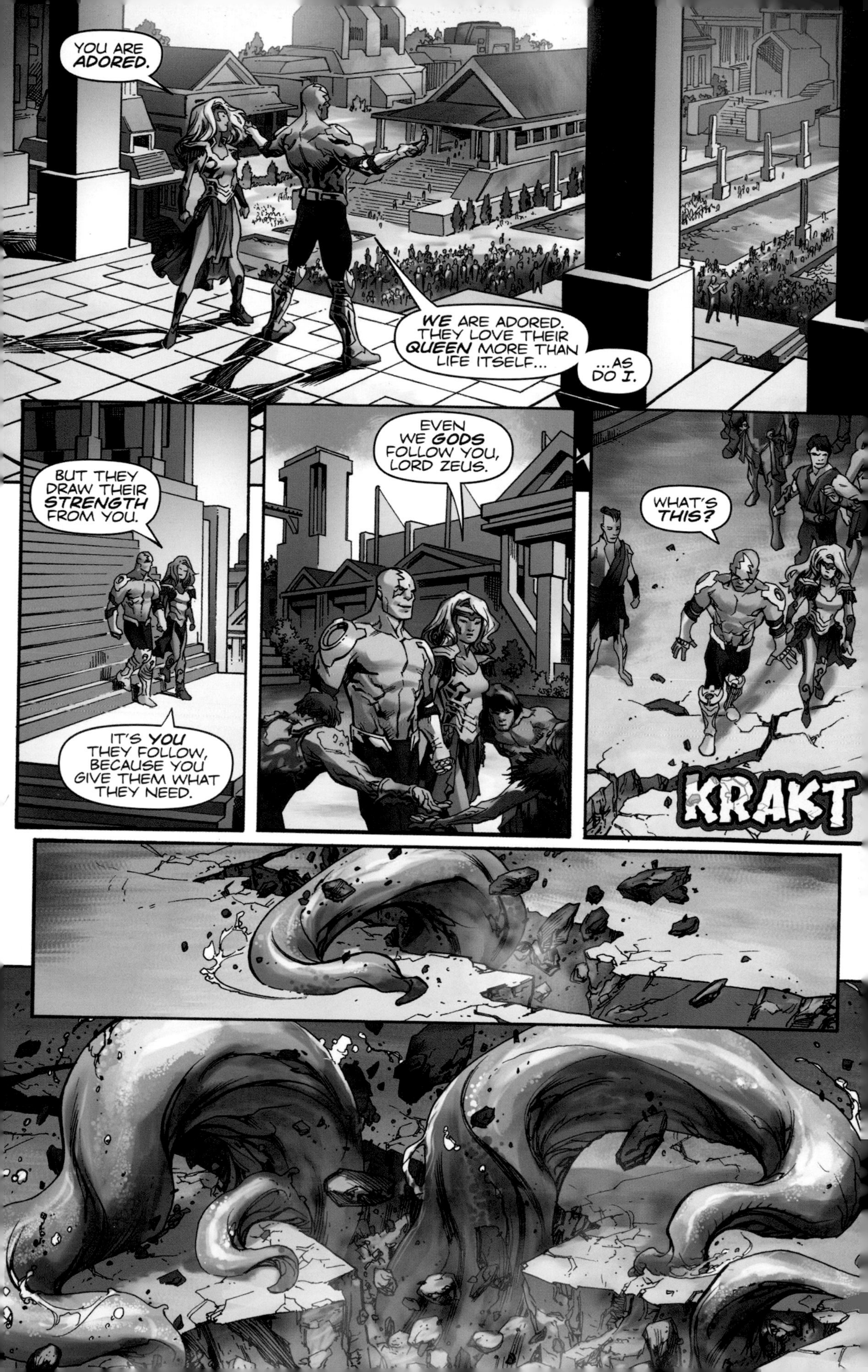

YOU ARE ADORED.
WE ARE ADORED. THEY LOVE THEIR QUEEN MORE THAN LIFE ITSELF...
...AS DO I.
BUT THEY DRAW THEIR STRENGTH FROM YOU.
IT'S YOU THEY FOLLOW, BECAUSE YOU GIVE THEM WHAT THEY NEED.
EVEN WE GODS FOLLOW YOU, LORD ZEUS.
WHAT'S THIS?
KRAKT

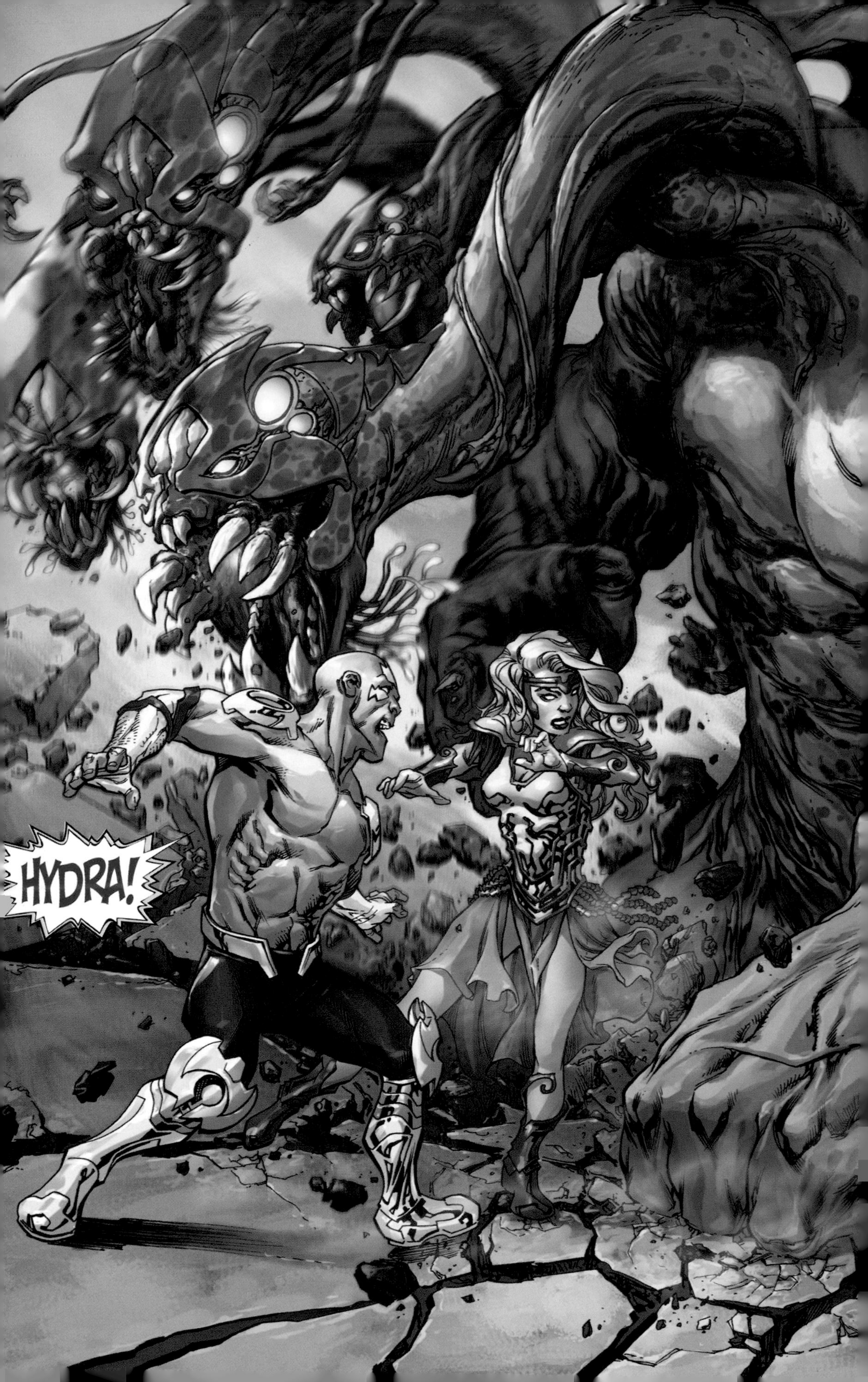
HYDRA!

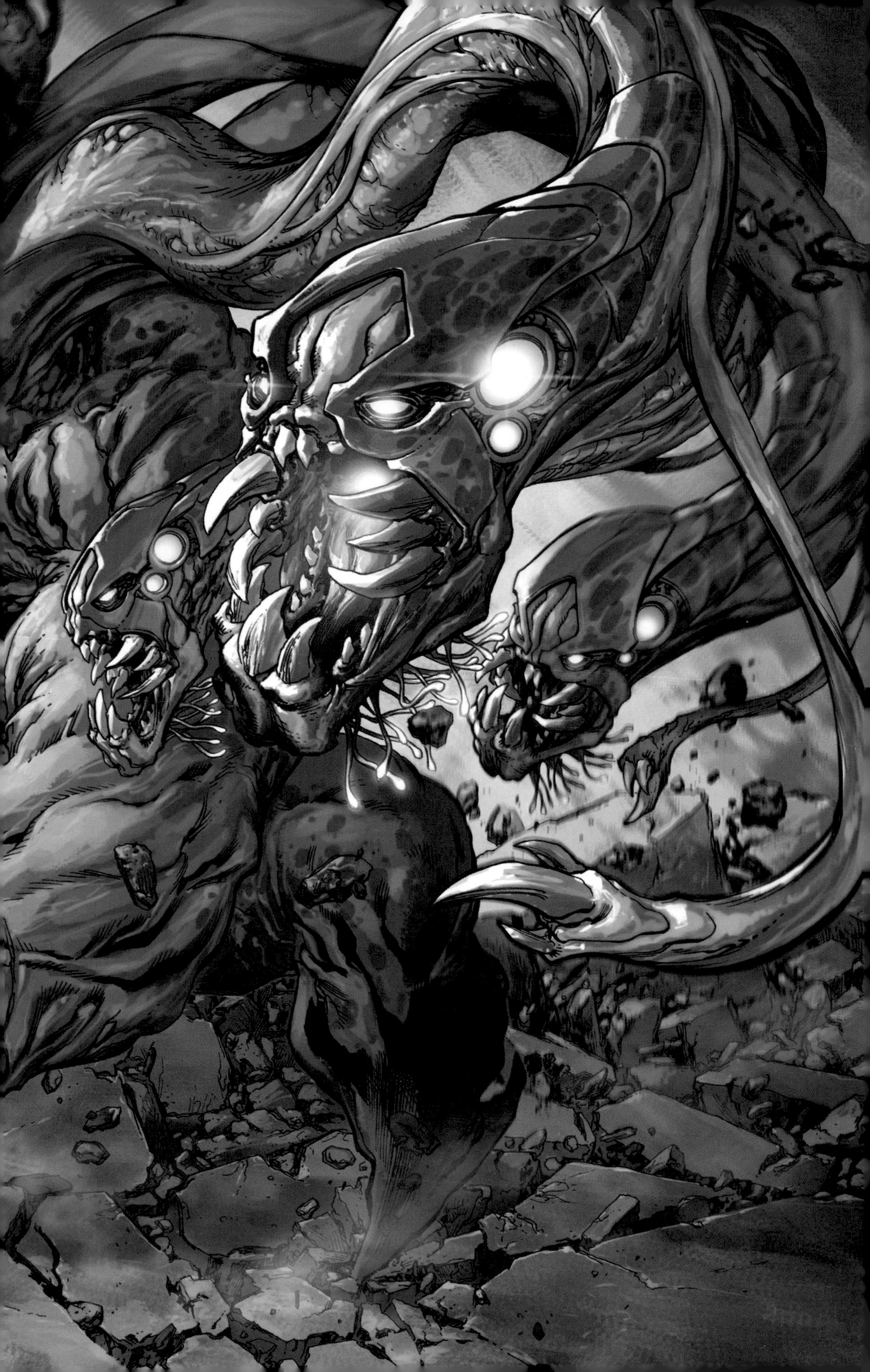

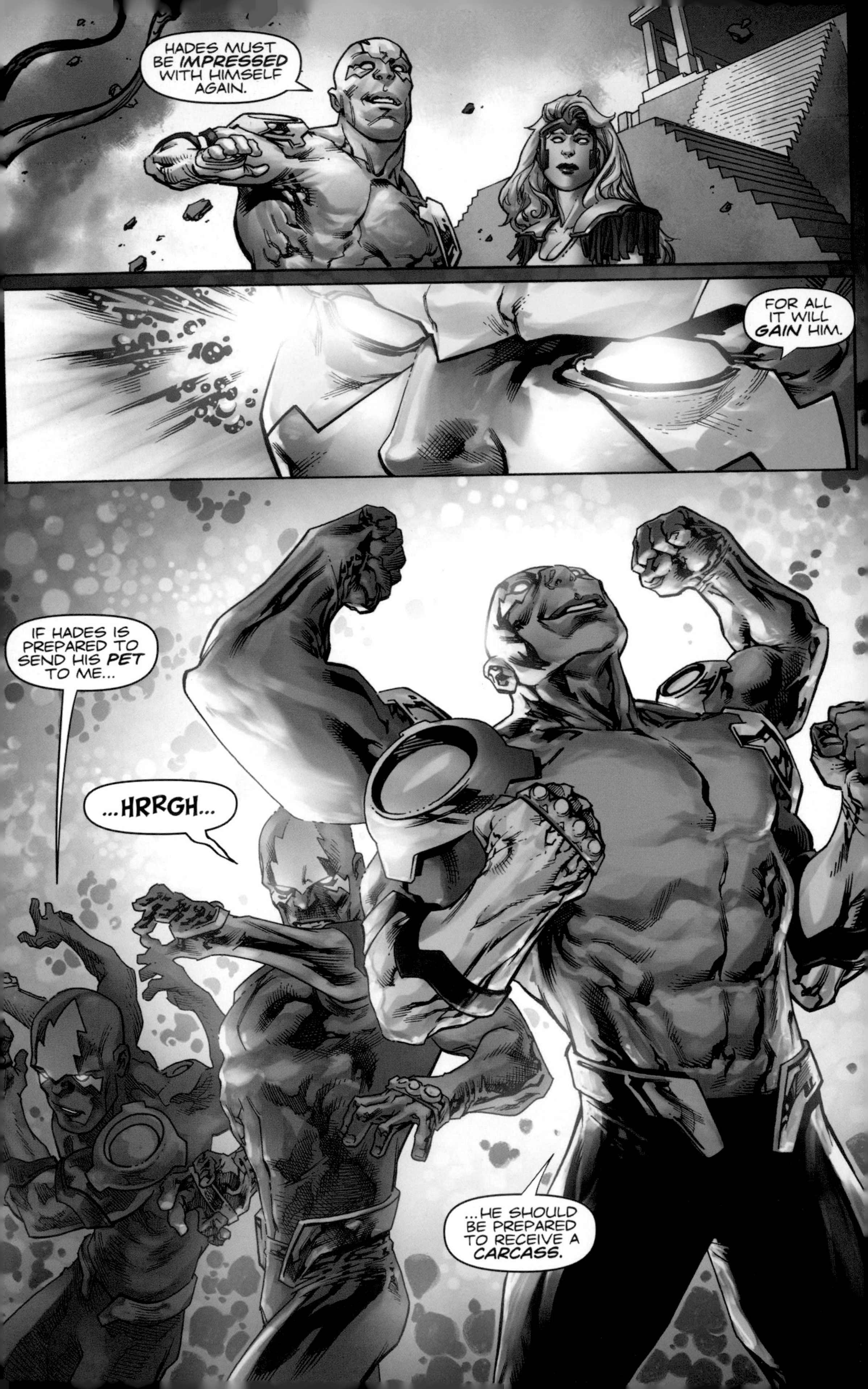
HADES MUST BE IMPRESSED WITH HIMSELF AGAIN.
FOR ALL IT WILL GAIN HIM.
IF HADES IS PREPARED TO SEND HIS PET TO ME...
...HRRGH...
...HE SHOULD BE PREPARED TO RECEIVE A CARCASS.

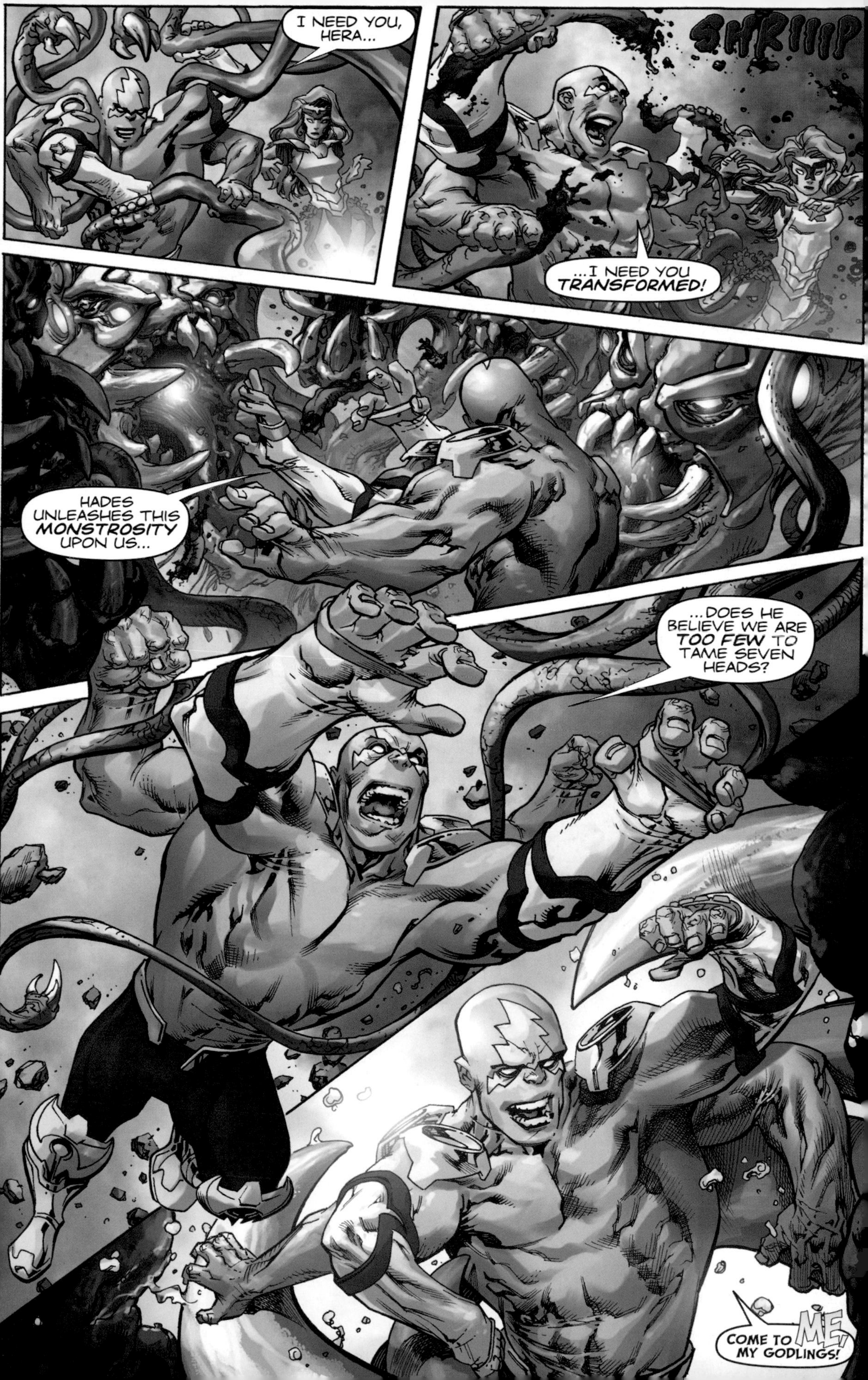

I NEED YOU, HERA...
SHRIIIP
...I NEED YOU TRANSFORMED!
HADES UNLEASHES THIS MONSTROSITY UPON US...
...DOES HE BELIEVE WE ARE TOO FEW TO TAME SEVEN HEADS?
COME TO ME, MY GODLINGS!

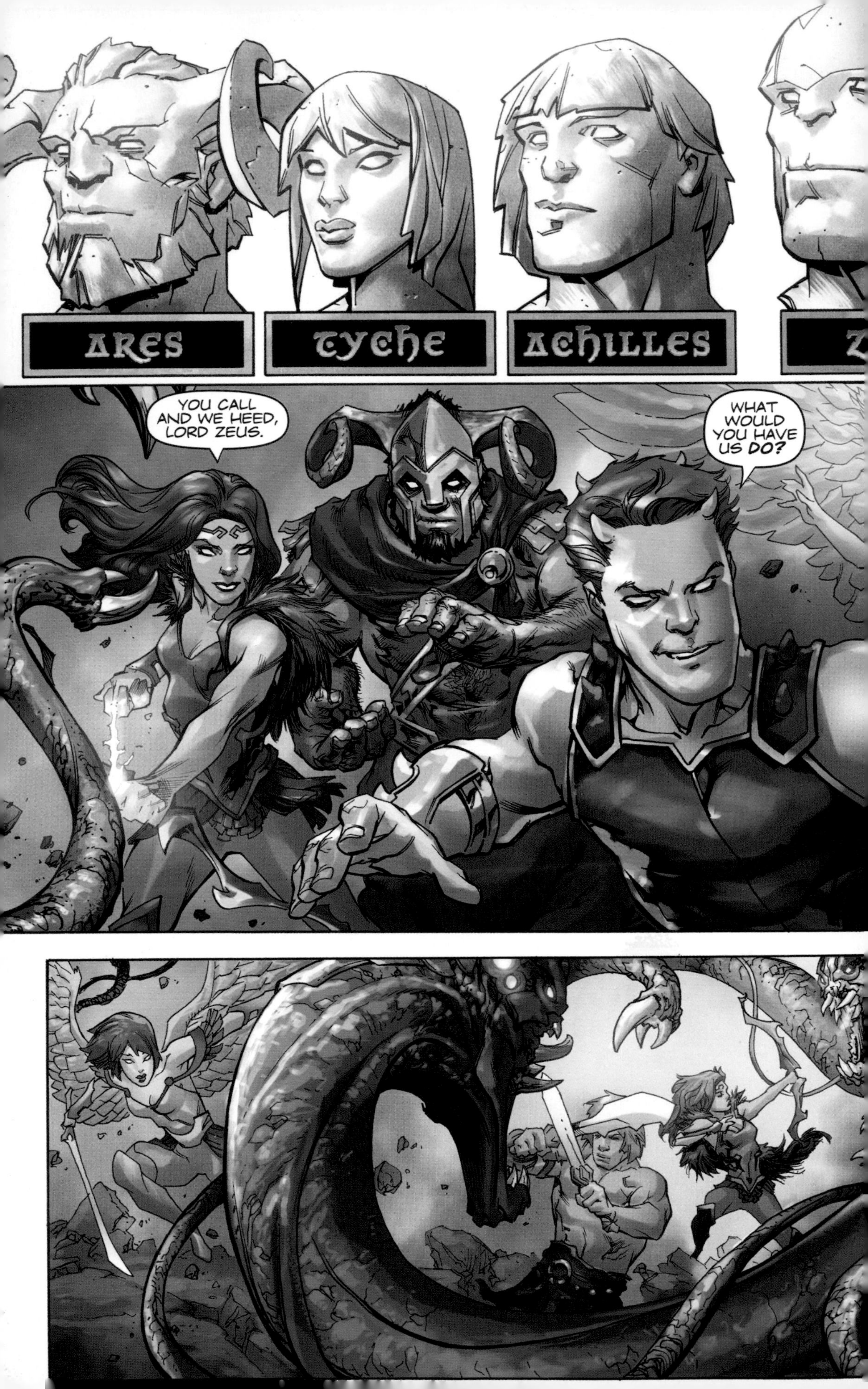
ARES
TYCHE
ACHILLES
YOU CALL AND WE HEED, LORD ZEUS.
WHAT WOULD YOU HAVE US **DO?**

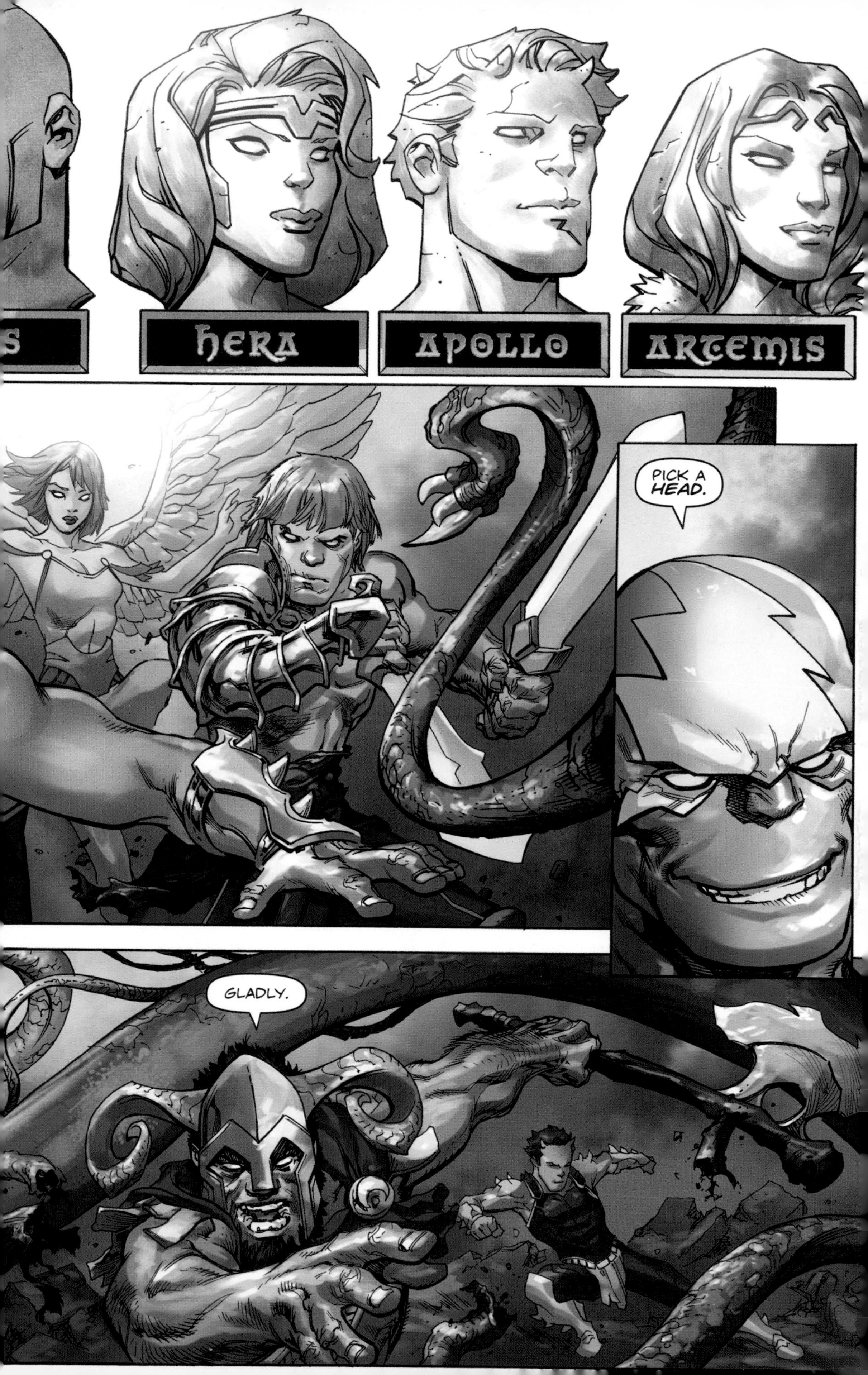
S
HERA
APOLLO
ARTEMIS
PICK A HEAD.
GLADLY.

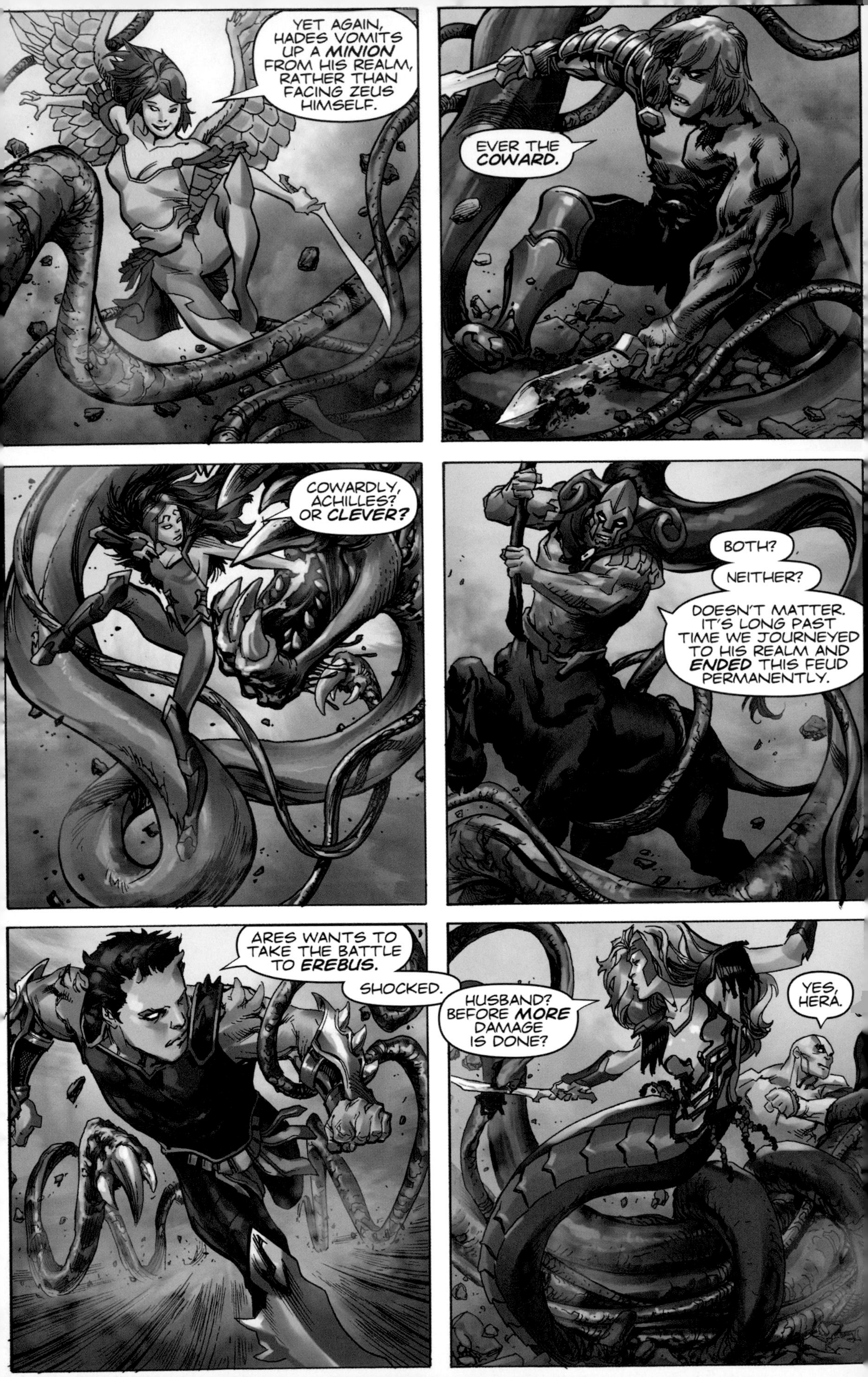
YET AGAIN, HADES VOMITS UP A **MINION** FROM HIS REALM, RATHER THAN FACING ZEUS HIMSELF.
EVER THE **COWARD.**
COWARDLY, ACHILLES? OR **CLEVER?**
BOTH?
NEITHER?
DOESN'T MATTER. IT'S LONG PAST TIME WE JOURNEYED TO HIS REALM AND **ENDED** THIS FEUD PERMANENTLY.
ARES WANTS TO TAKE THE BATTLE TO **EREBUS.**
SHOCKED.
HUSBAND? BEFORE **MORE** DAMAGE IS DONE?
YES, HERA.

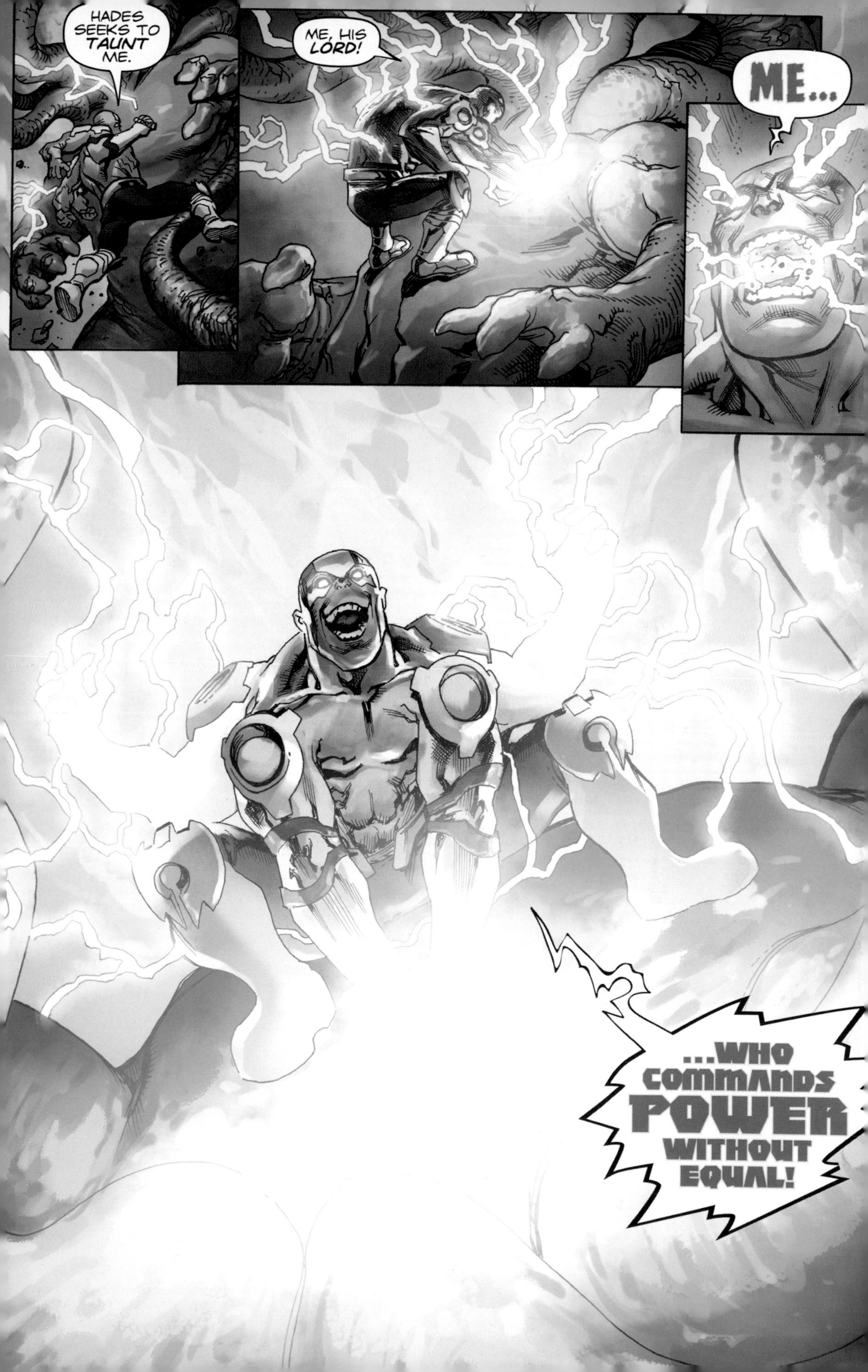
HADES SEEKS TO TAUNT ME.
ME, HIS LORD!
ME...
...WHO COMMANDS POWER WITHOUT EQUAL!

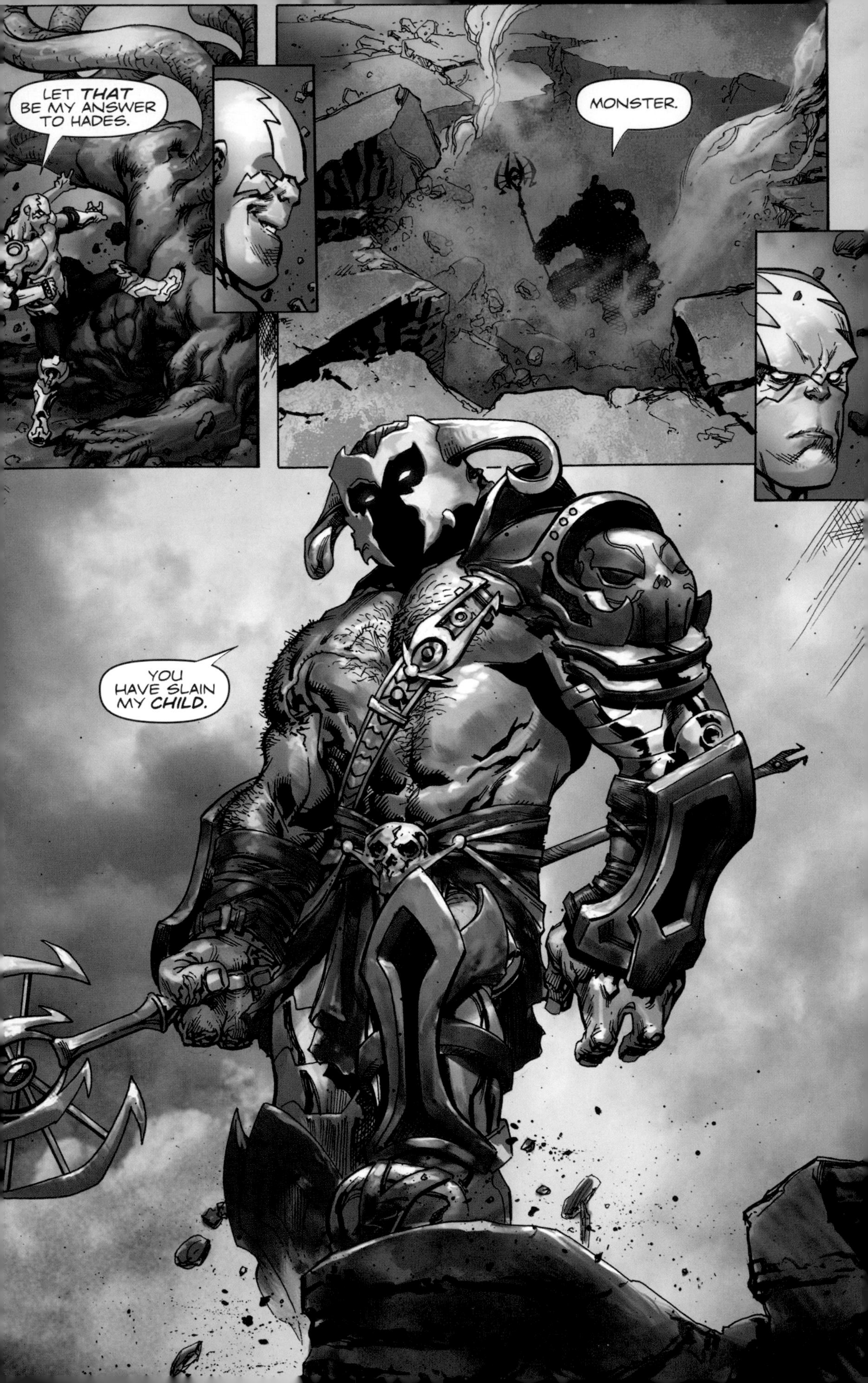
LET THAT BE MY ANSWER TO HADES.
MONSTER.
YOU HAVE SLAIN MY CHILD.

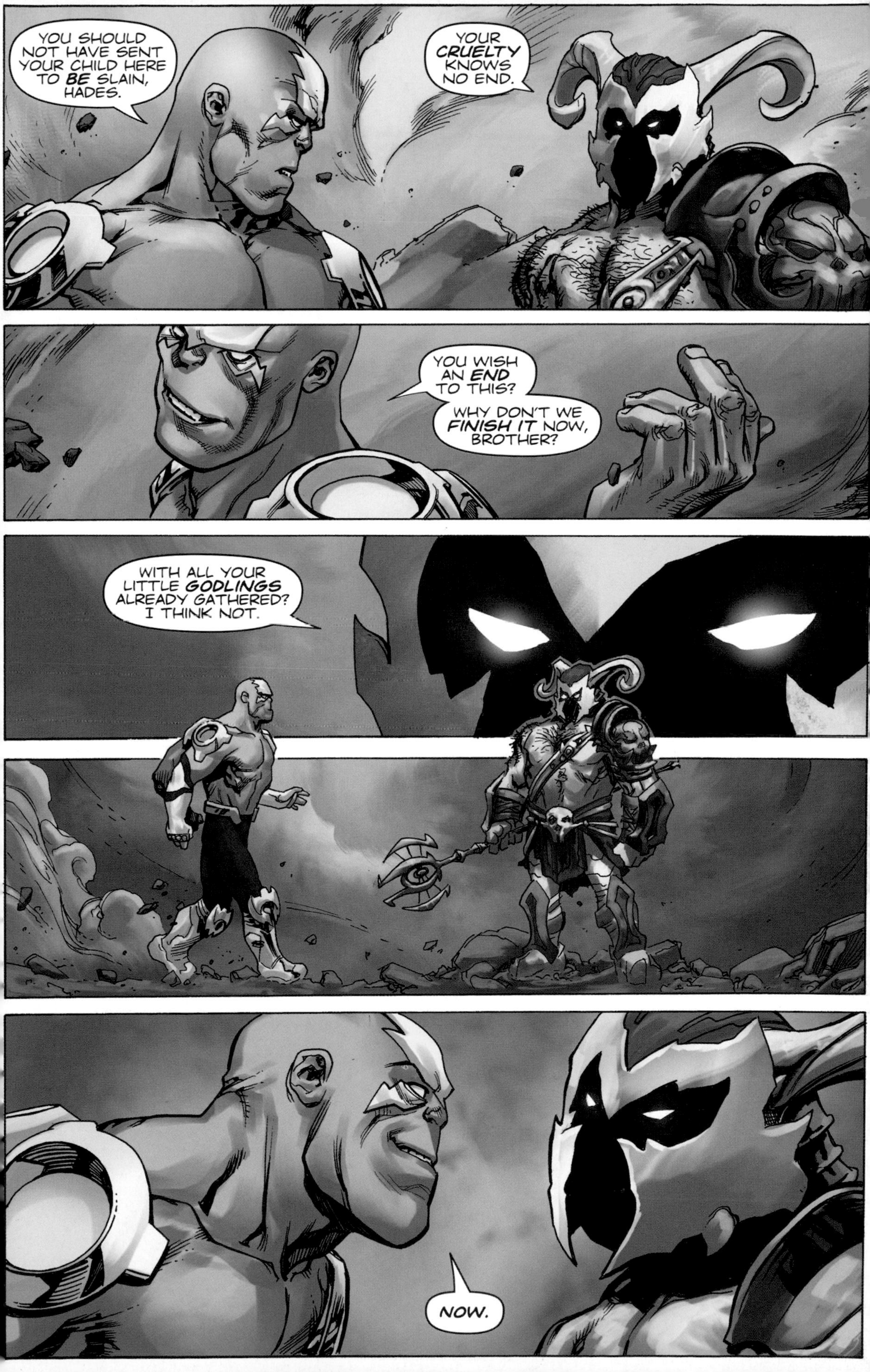
YOU SHOULD NOT HAVE SENT YOUR CHILD HERE TO BE SLAIN, HADES.
YOUR CRUELTY KNOWS NO END.
YOU WISH AN END TO THIS?
WHY DON'T WE FINISH IT NOW, BROTHER?
WITH ALL YOUR LITTLE GODLINGS ALREADY GATHERED? I THINK NOT.
NOW.

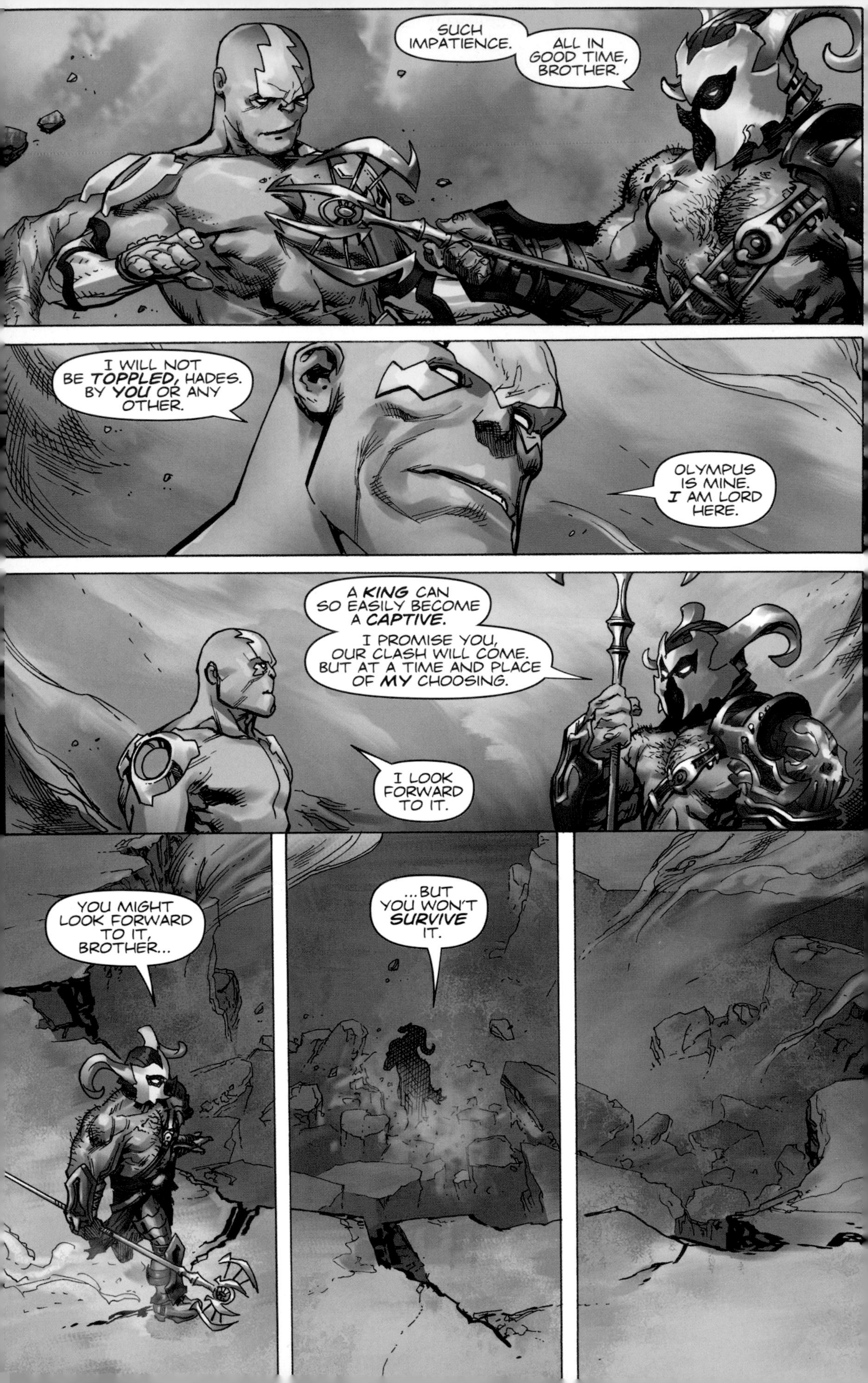

SUCH IMPATIENCE.
ALL IN GOOD TIME, BROTHER.
I WILL NOT BE TOPPLED, HADES. BY YOU OR ANY OTHER.
OLYMPUS IS MINE. I AM LORD HERE.
A KING CAN SO EASILY BECOME A CAPTIVE.
I PROMISE YOU, OUR CLASH WILL COME. BUT AT A TIME AND PLACE OF MY CHOOSING.
I LOOK FORWARD TO IT.
YOU MIGHT LOOK FORWARD TO IT, BROTHER...
...BUT YOU WON'T SURVIVE IT.

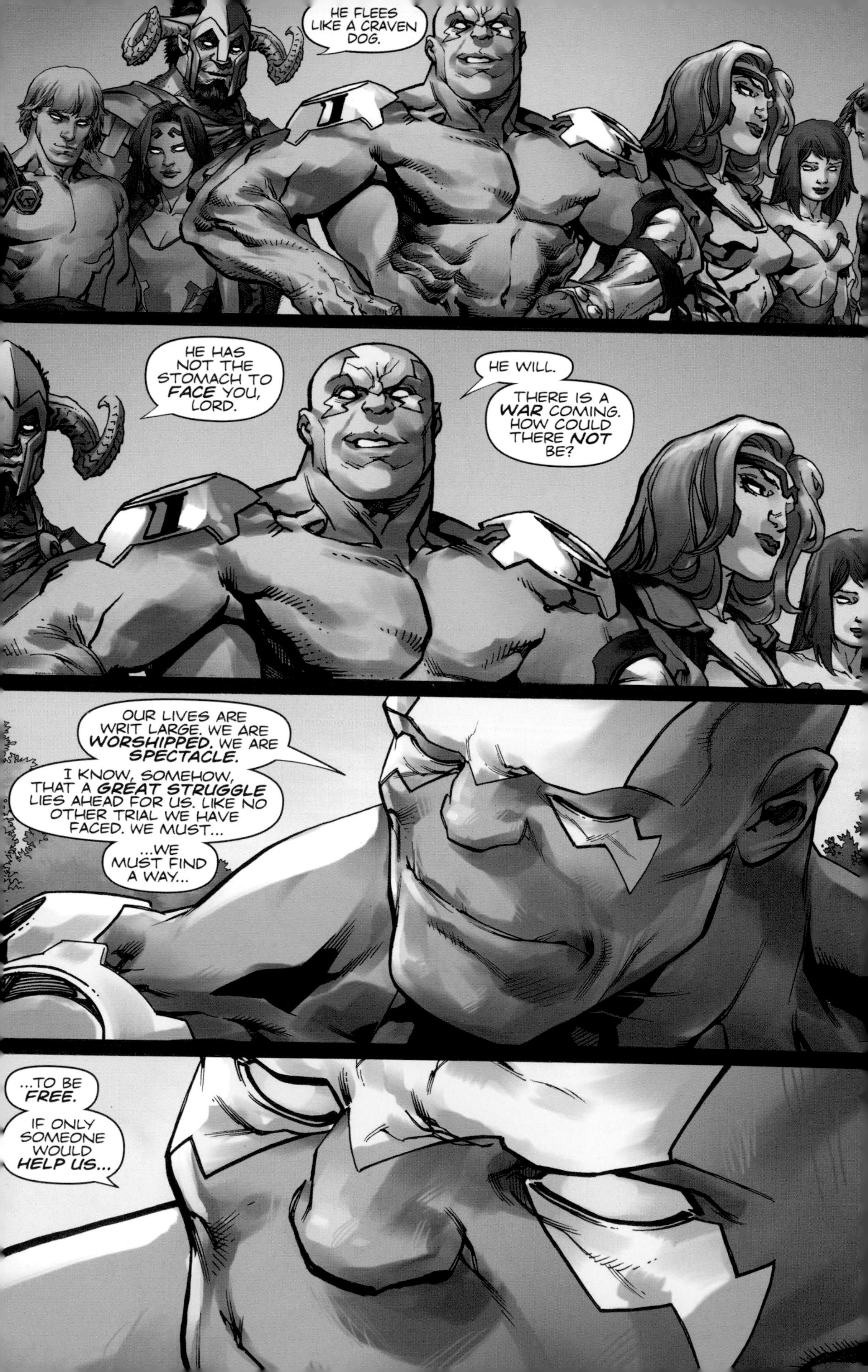

HE FLEES LIKE A CRAVEN DOG.
HE HAS NOT THE STOMACH TO FACE YOU, LORD.
HE WILL.
THERE IS A WAR COMING. HOW COULD THERE NOT BE?
OUR LIVES ARE WRIT LARGE. WE ARE WORSHIPPED. WE ARE SPECTACLE.
I KNOW, SOMEHOW, THAT A GREAT STRUGGLE LIES AHEAD FOR US. LIKE NO OTHER TRIAL WE HAVE FACED. WE MUST...
...WE MUST FIND A WAY...
...TO BE FREE.
IF ONLY SOMEONE WOULD HELP US...

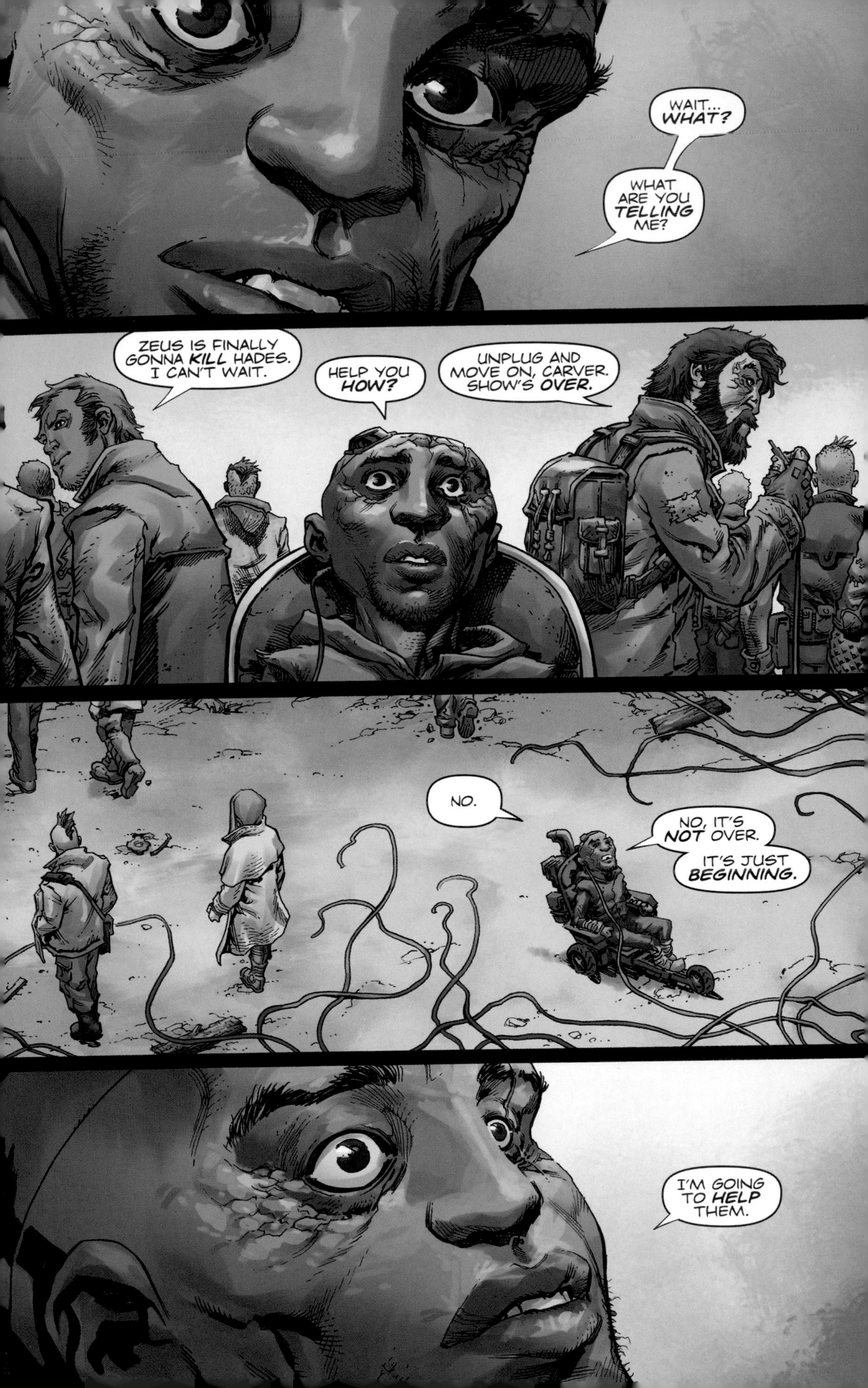
WAIT... **WHAT?**
WHAT ARE YOU **TELLING** ME?
ZEUS IS FINALLY GONNA **KILL** HADES. I CAN'T WAIT.
HELP YOU **HOW?**
UNPLUG AND MOVE ON, CARVER. SHOW'S **OVER.**
NO.
NO, IT'S **NOT** OVER.
IT'S JUST **BEGINNING.**
I'M GOING TO **HELP** THEM.

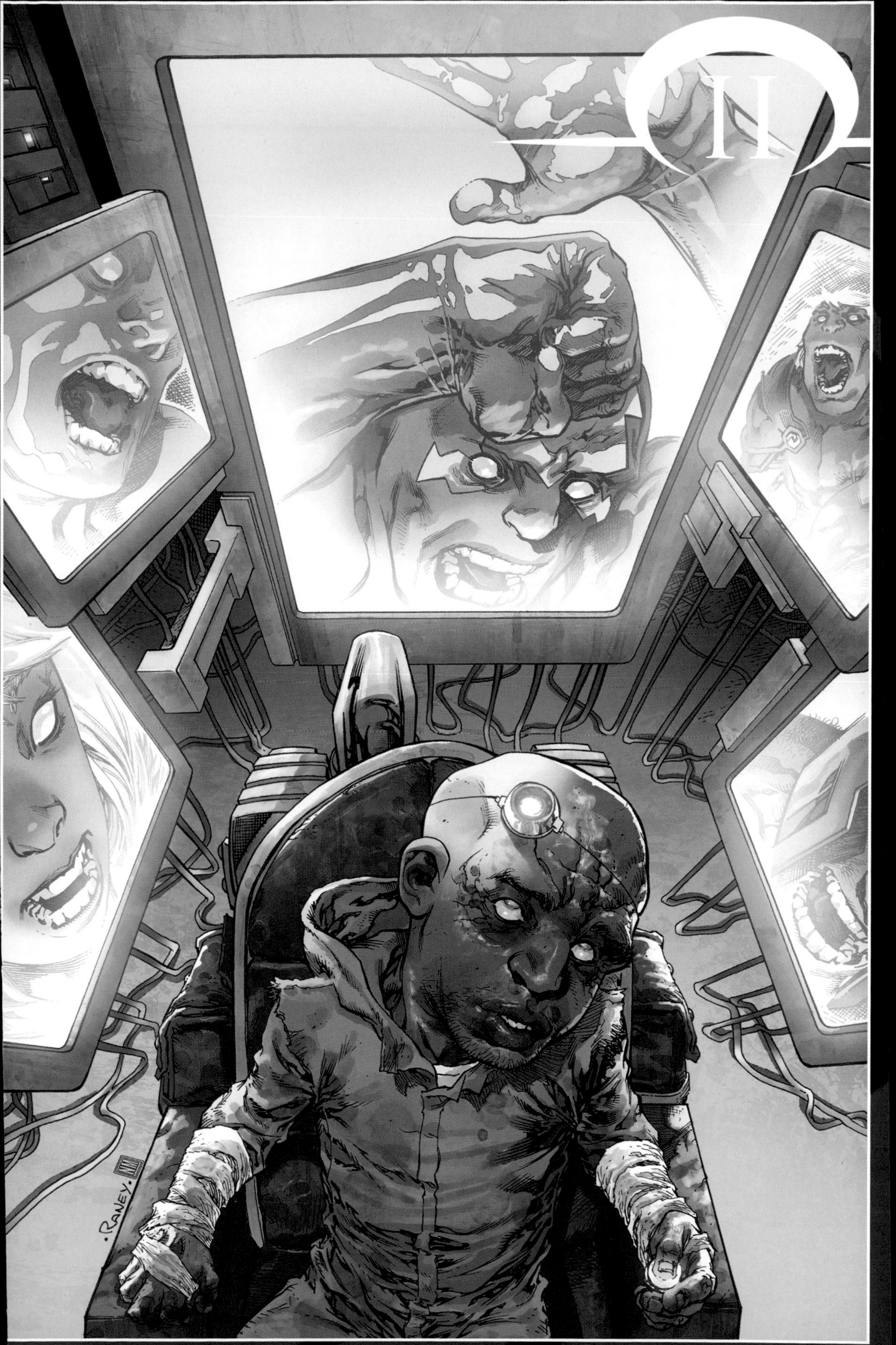
RANEY

ART BY TOM RANEY · COLORS BY NEERAJ MENON

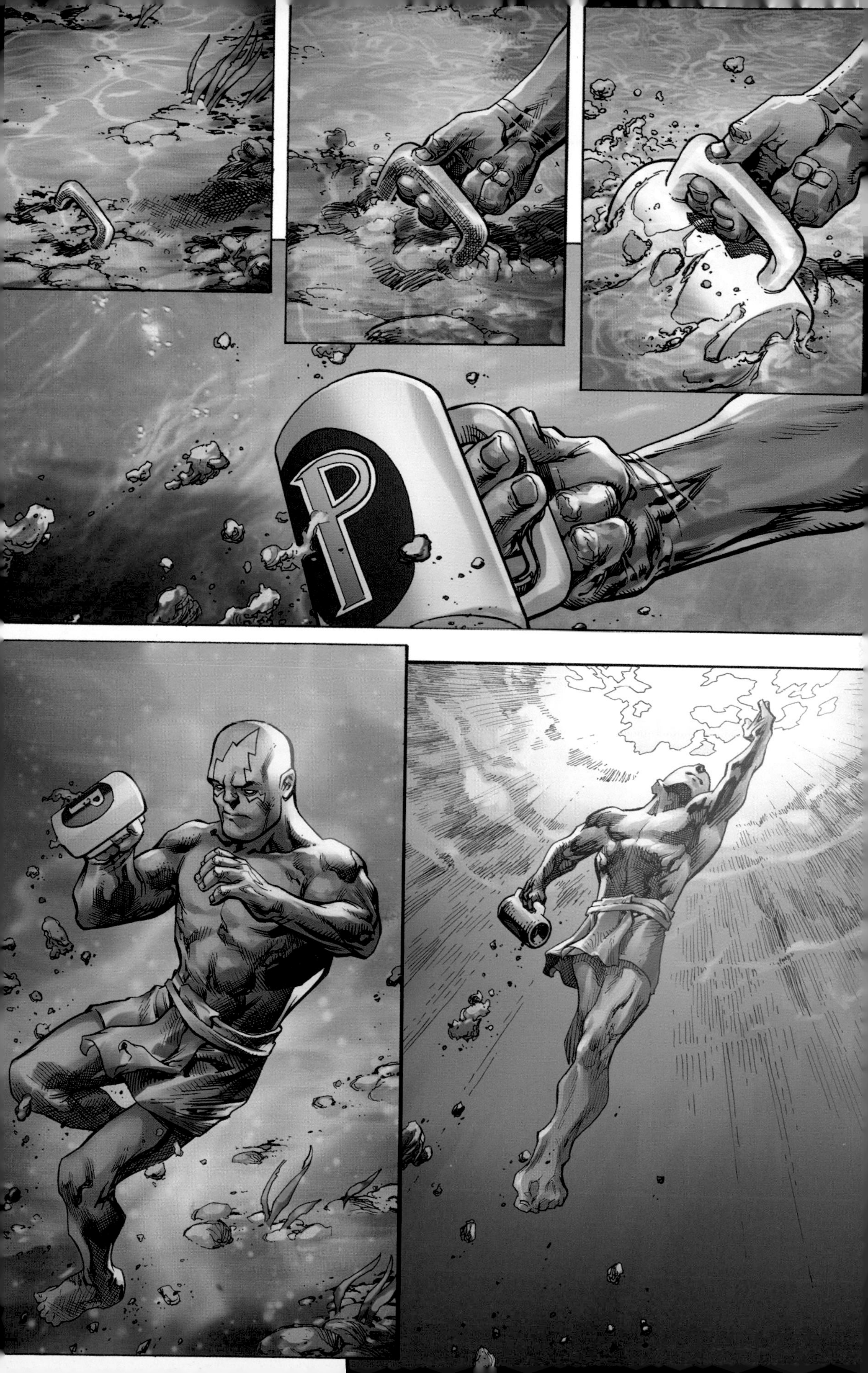

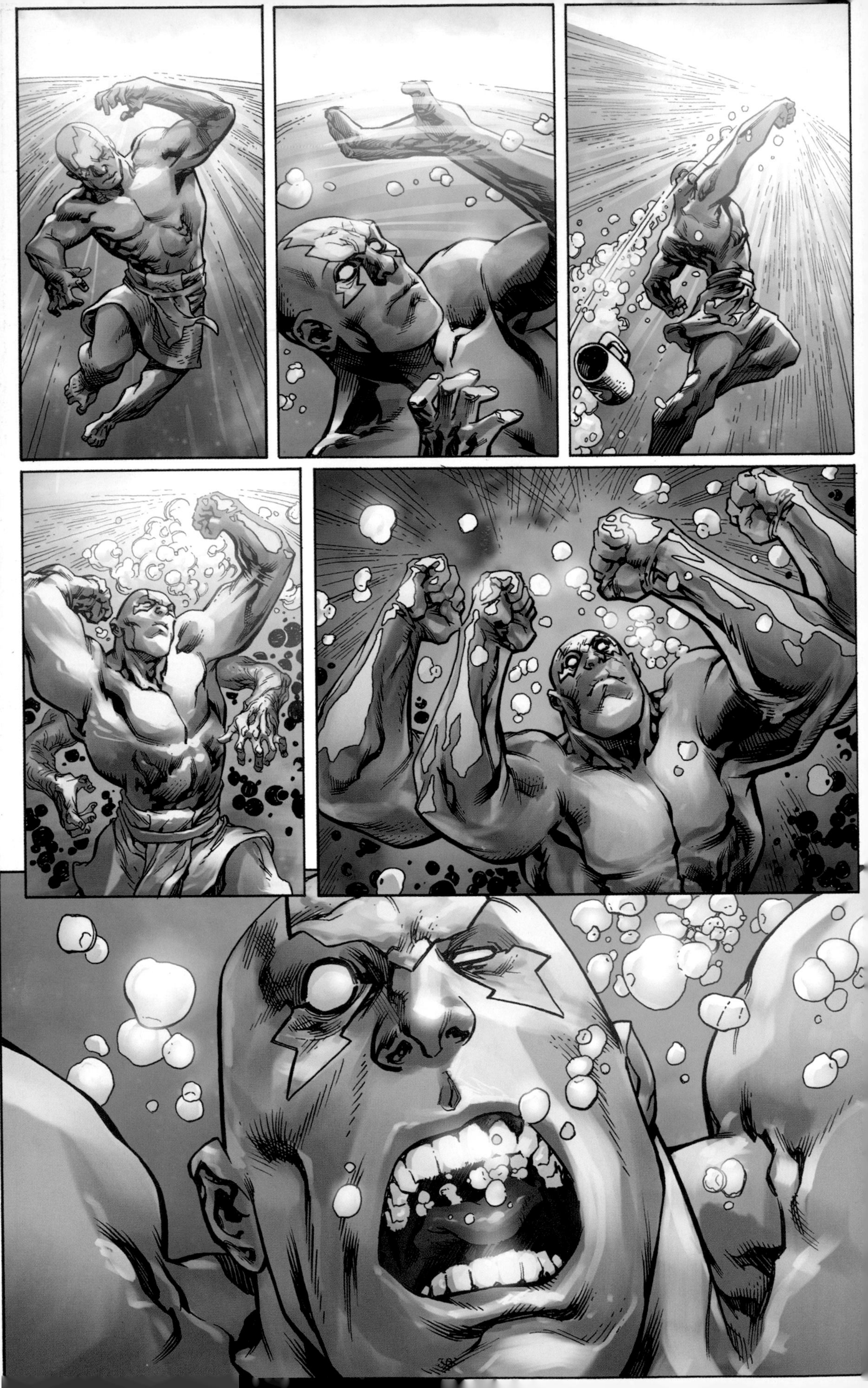

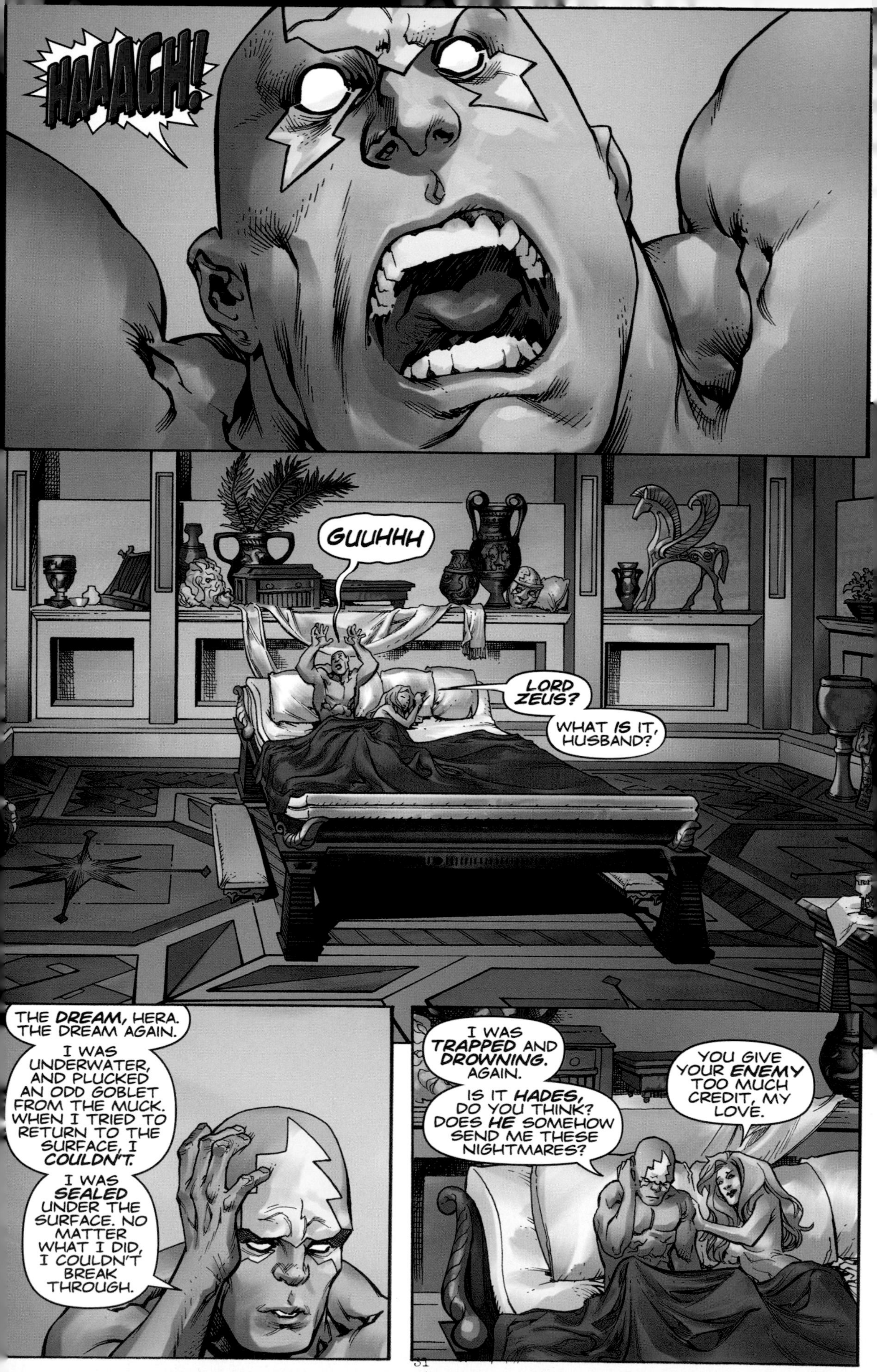
HAAAGH!
GUUHHH
LORD ZEUS?
WHAT IS IT, HUSBAND?
THE DREAM, HERA. THE DREAM AGAIN.
I WAS UNDERWATER, AND PLUCKED AN ODD GOBLET FROM THE MUCK. WHEN I TRIED TO RETURN TO THE SURFACE, I COULDN'T.
I WAS SEALED UNDER THE SURFACE. NO MATTER WHAT I DID, I COULDN'T BREAK THROUGH.
I WAS TRAPPED AND DROWNING. AGAIN.
IS IT HADES, DO YOU THINK? DOES HE SOMEHOW SEND ME THESE NIGHTMARES?
YOU GIVE YOUR ENEMY TOO MUCH CREDIT, MY LOVE.

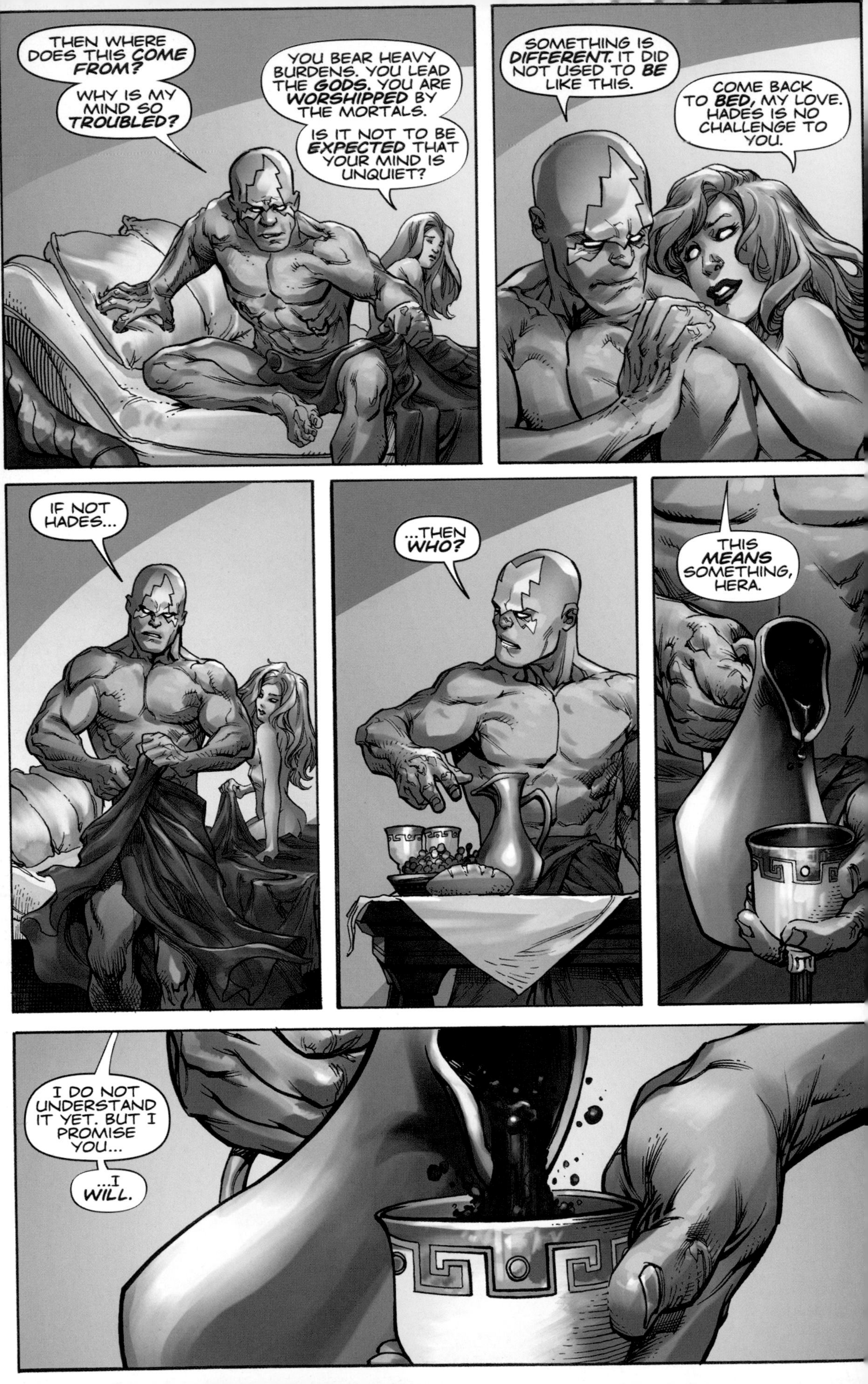
THEN WHERE DOES THIS COME FROM?
WHY IS MY MIND SO TROUBLED?
YOU BEAR HEAVY BURDENS. YOU LEAD THE GODS. YOU ARE WORSHIPPED BY THE MORTALS.
IS IT NOT TO BE EXPECTED THAT YOUR MIND IS UNQUIET?
SOMETHING IS DIFFERENT. IT DID NOT USED TO BE LIKE THIS.
COME BACK TO BED, MY LOVE. HADES IS NO CHALLENGE TO YOU.
IF NOT HADES...
...THEN WHO?
THIS MEANS SOMETHING, HERA.
I DO NOT UNDERSTAND IT YET. BUT I PROMISE YOU...
...I WILL.

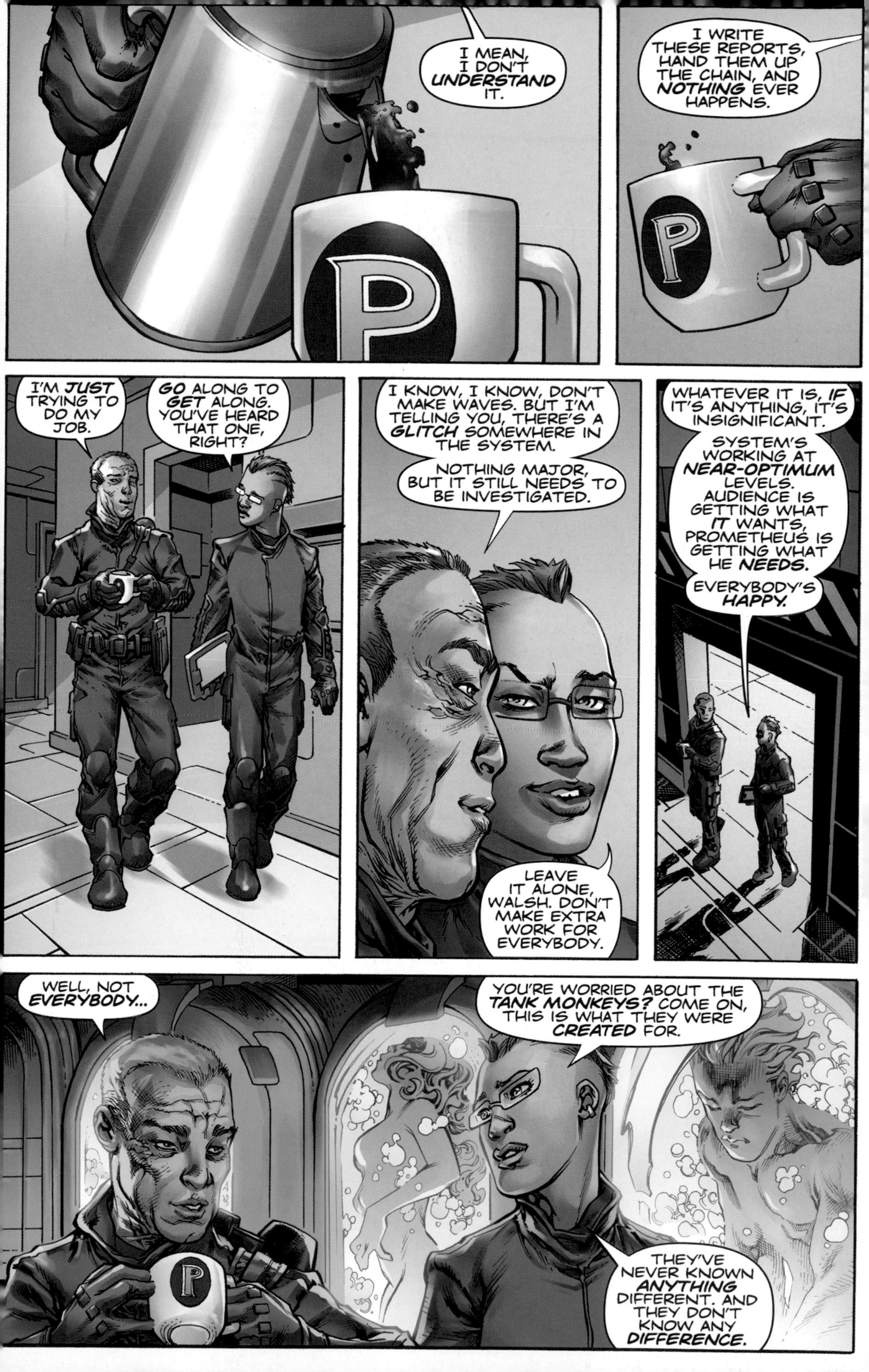
I MEAN, I DON'T UNDERSTAND IT.
I WRITE THESE REPORTS, HAND THEM UP THE CHAIN, AND NOTHING EVER HAPPENS.
I'M JUST TRYING TO DO MY JOB.
GO ALONG TO GET ALONG. YOU'VE HEARD THAT ONE, RIGHT?
I KNOW, I KNOW, DON'T MAKE WAVES. BUT I'M TELLING YOU, THERE'S A GLITCH SOMEWHERE IN THE SYSTEM.
NOTHING MAJOR, BUT IT STILL NEEDS TO BE INVESTIGATED.
LEAVE IT ALONE, WALSH. DON'T MAKE EXTRA WORK FOR EVERYBODY.
WHATEVER IT IS, IF IT'S ANYTHING, IT'S INSIGNIFICANT.
SYSTEM'S WORKING AT NEAR-OPTIMUM LEVELS. AUDIENCE IS GETTING WHAT IT WANTS, PROMETHEUS IS GETTING WHAT HE NEEDS.
EVERYBODY'S HAPPY.
WELL, NOT EVERYBODY...
YOU'RE WORRIED ABOUT THE TANK MONKEYS? COME ON, THIS IS WHAT THEY WERE CREATED FOR.
THEY'VE NEVER KNOWN ANYTHING DIFFERENT. AND THEY DON'T KNOW ANY DIFFERENCE.

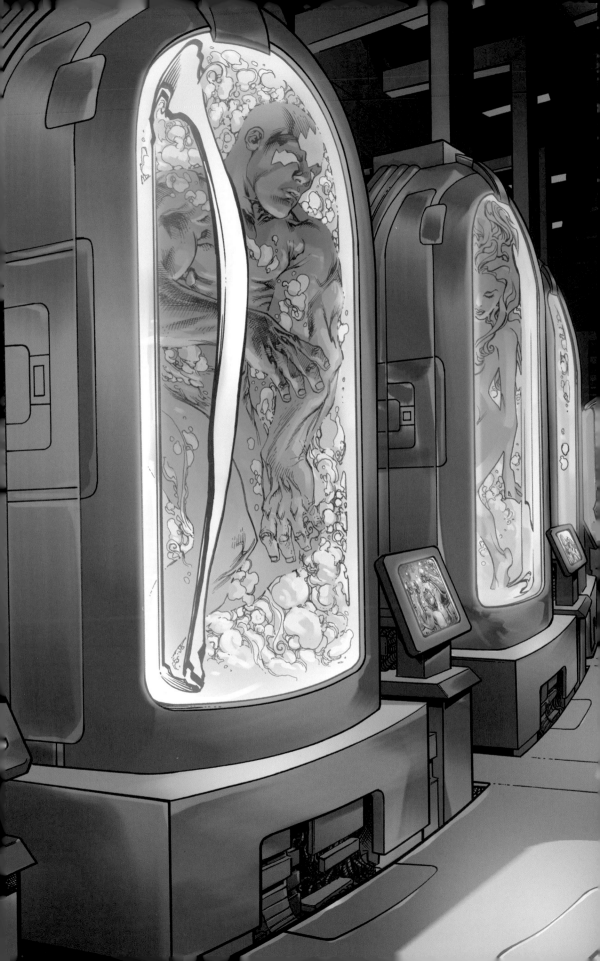

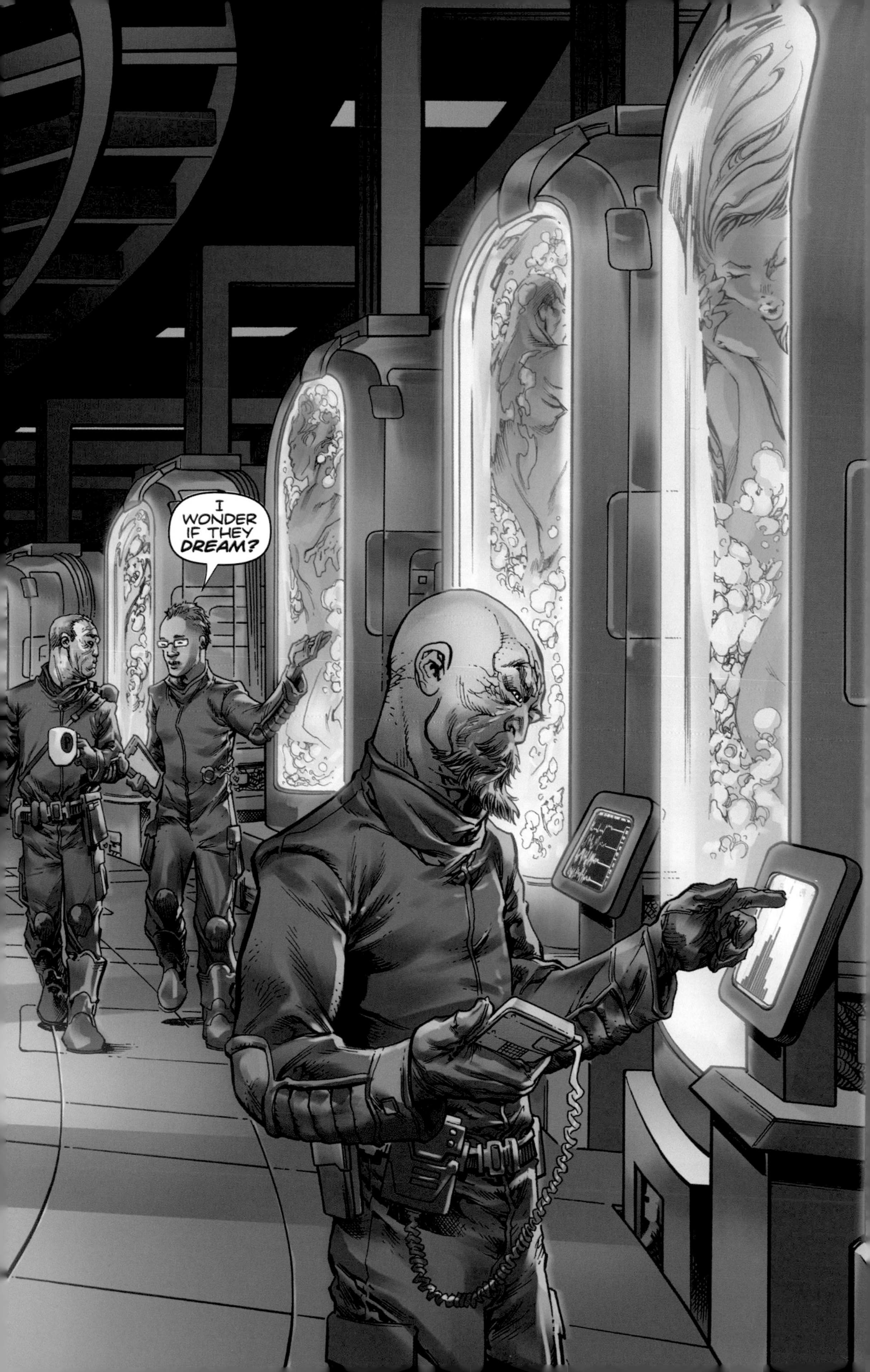
I WONDER IF THEY DREAM?

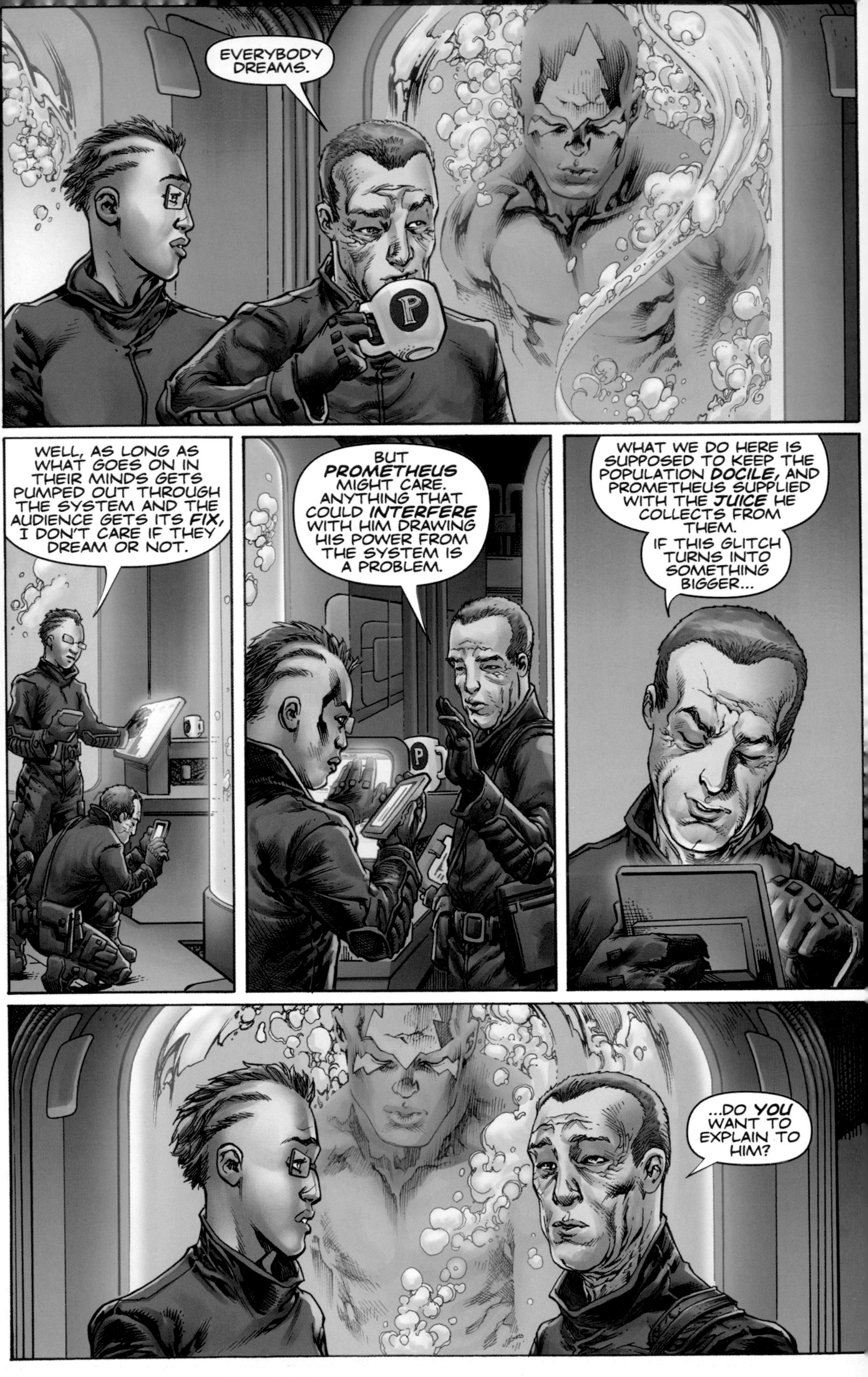
EVERYBODY DREAMS.
WELL, AS LONG AS WHAT GOES ON IN THEIR MINDS GETS PUMPED OUT THROUGH THE SYSTEM AND THE AUDIENCE GETS ITS FIX, I DON'T CARE IF THEY DREAM OR NOT.
BUT PROMETHEUS MIGHT CARE. ANYTHING THAT COULD INTERFERE WITH HIM DRAWING HIS POWER FROM THE SYSTEM IS A PROBLEM.
WHAT WE DO HERE IS SUPPOSED TO KEEP THE POPULATION DOCILE, AND PROMETHEUS SUPPLIED WITH THE JUICE HE COLLECTS FROM THEM.
IF THIS GLITCH TURNS INTO SOMETHING BIGGER...
...DO YOU WANT TO EXPLAIN TO HIM?

...DO *YOU* WANT TO EXPLAIN TO HIM?

HAVE THE WOMAN *FIRED*...

...AND *BANISHED* TO THE WASTELAND. I WON'T TOLERATE CARELESS BEHAVIOR FROM THOSE WHO SERVE ME.

AS YOU WISH, PROMETHEUS.

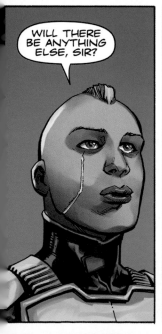

WILL THERE BE ANYTHING ELSE, SIR?

I WANT EACH OF THE STASIS TANKS THOROUGHLY ANALYZED FOR FAILURES AND DEFICIENCIES.

ESPECIALLY *ZEUS*.

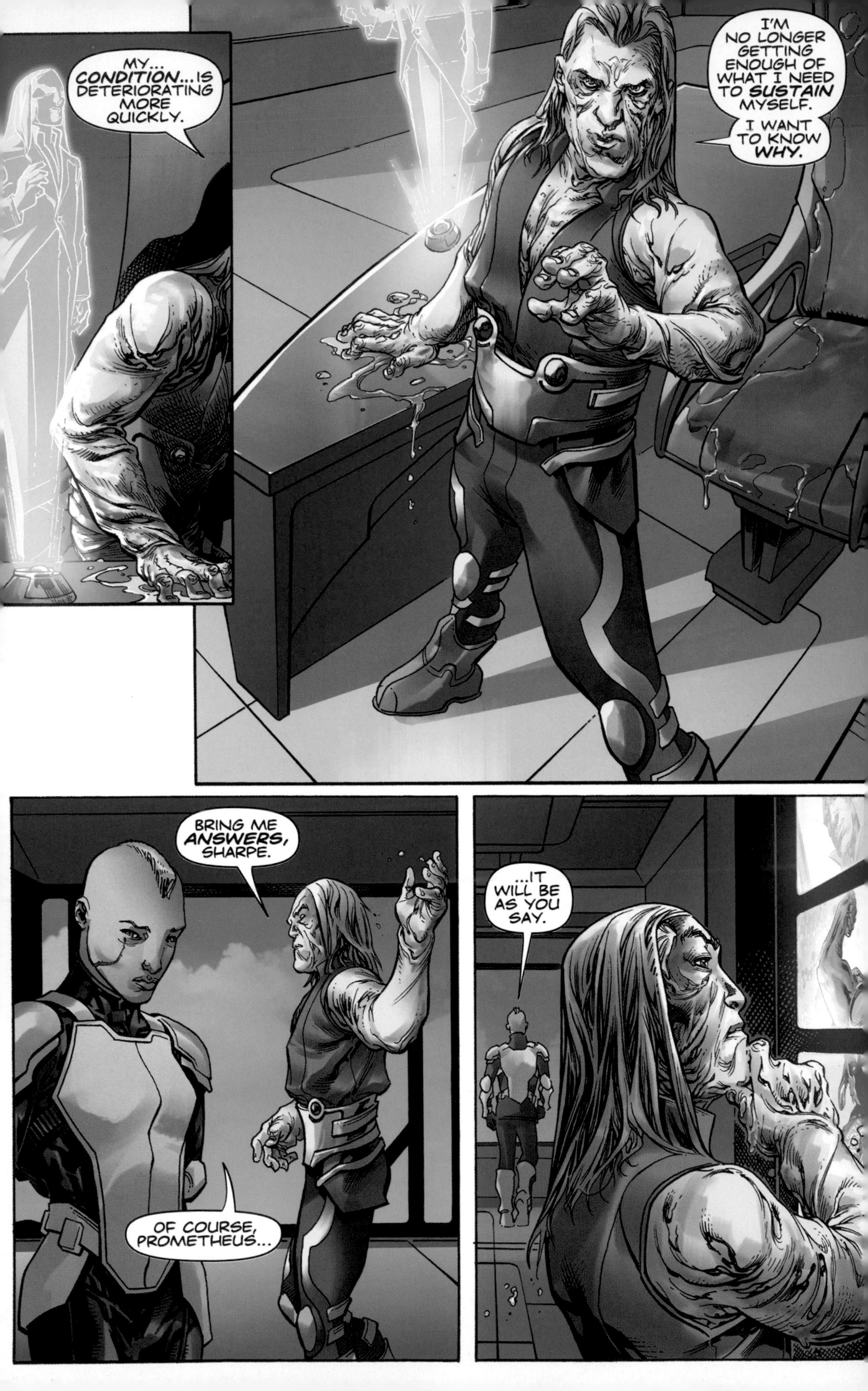
MY... CONDITION...IS DETERIORATING MORE QUICKLY.
I'M NO LONGER GETTING ENOUGH OF WHAT I NEED TO SUSTAIN MYSELF.
I WANT TO KNOW WHY.
BRING ME ANSWERS, SHARPE.
OF COURSE, PROMETHEUS...
...IT WILL BE AS YOU SAY.

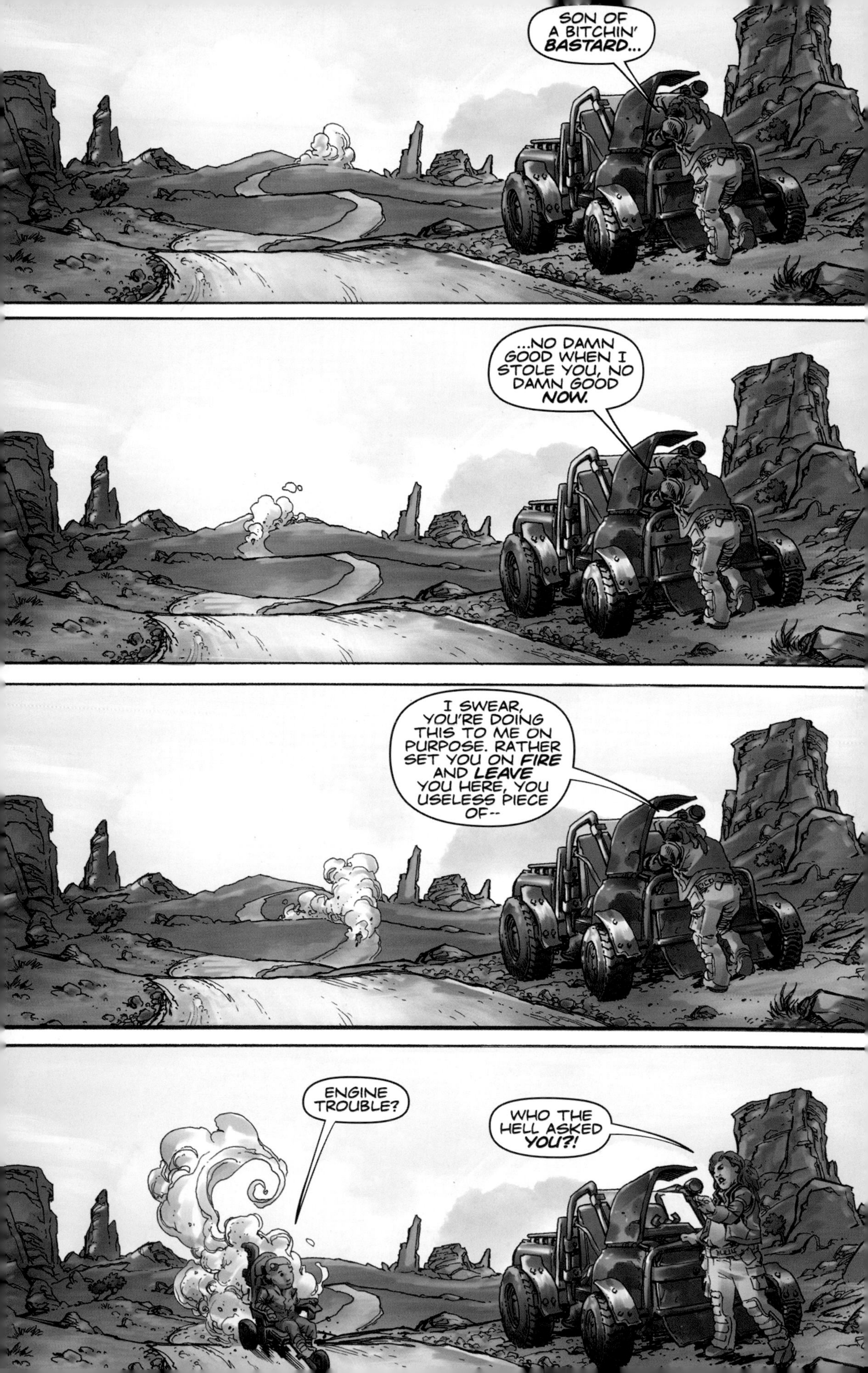
SON OF A BITCHIN' BASTARD...
...NO DAMN GOOD WHEN I STOLE YOU, NO DAMN GOOD NOW.
I SWEAR, YOU'RE DOING THIS TO ME ON PURPOSE. RATHER SET YOU ON FIRE AND LEAVE YOU HERE, YOU USELESS PIECE OF--
ENGINE TROUBLE?
WHO THE HELL ASKED YOU?!

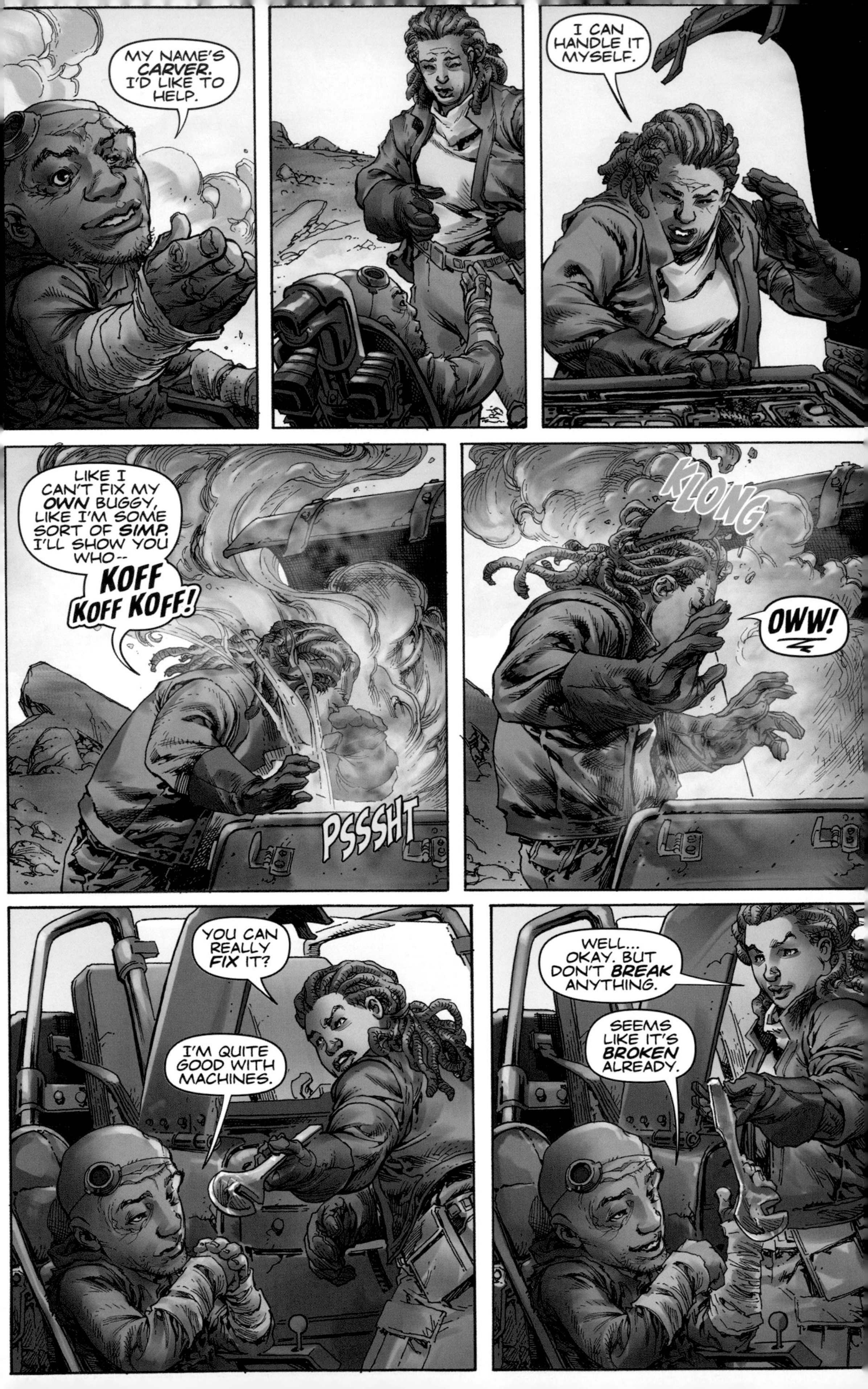
MY NAME'S CARVER. I'D LIKE TO HELP.
I CAN HANDLE IT MYSELF.
LIKE I CAN'T FIX MY OWN BUGGY, LIKE I'M SOME SORT OF SIMP. I'LL SHOW YOU WHO-- KOFF KOFF KOFF!
PSSSHT
KLONG
OWW!
YOU CAN REALLY FIX IT?
I'M QUITE GOOD WITH MACHINES.
WELL... OKAY. BUT DON'T BREAK ANYTHING.
SEEMS LIKE IT'S BROKEN ALREADY.

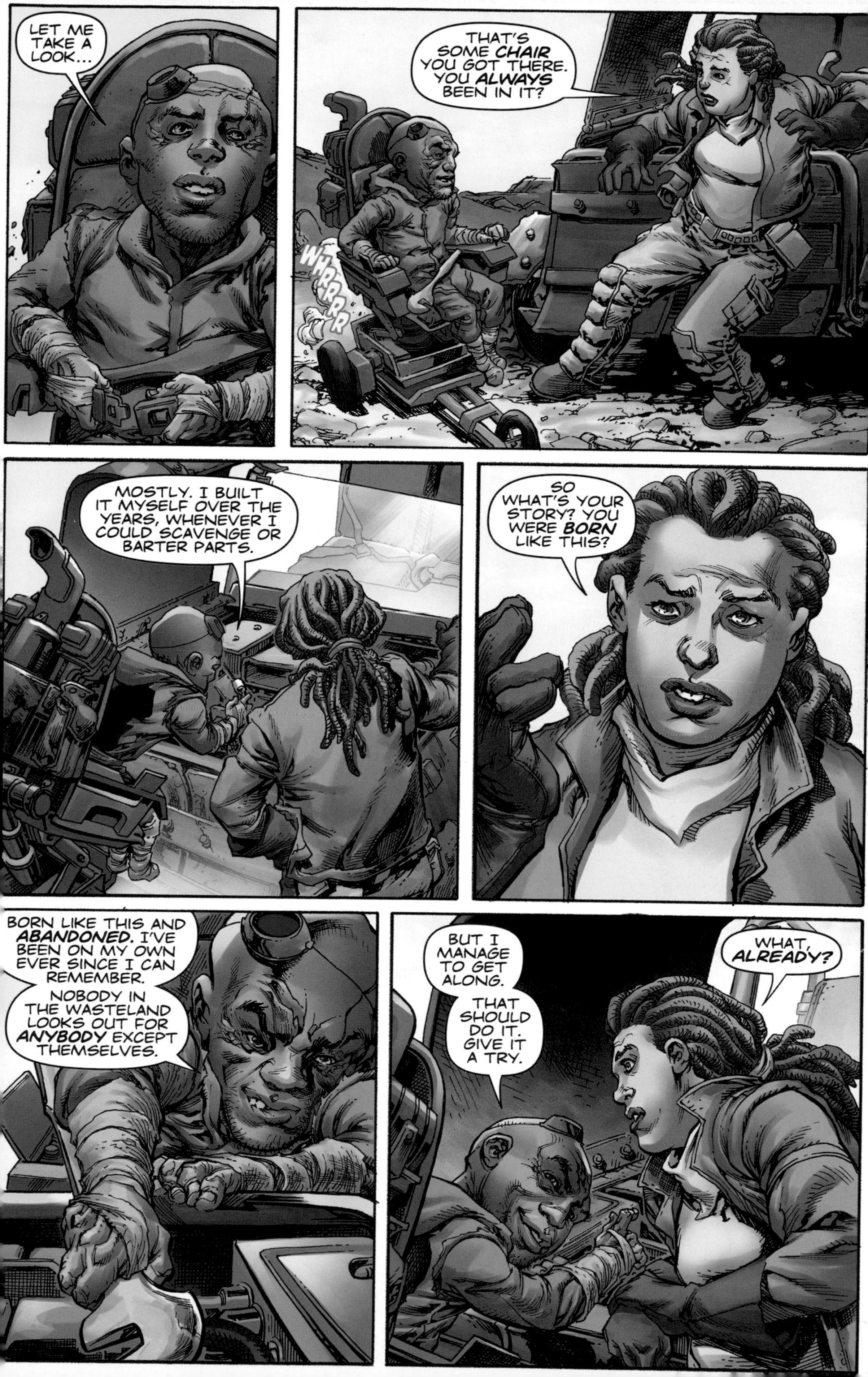
LET ME TAKE A LOOK...
THAT'S SOME **CHAIR** YOU GOT THERE. YOU **ALWAYS** BEEN IN IT?
WHRRRRR
MOSTLY. I BUILT IT MYSELF OVER THE YEARS, WHENEVER I COULD SCAVENGE OR BARTER PARTS.
SO WHAT'S YOUR STORY? YOU WERE **BORN** LIKE THIS?
BORN LIKE THIS AND **ABANDONED.** I'VE BEEN ON MY OWN EVER SINCE I CAN REMEMBER.
NOBODY IN THE WASTELAND LOOKS OUT FOR **ANYBODY** EXCEPT THEMSELVES.
BUT I MANAGE TO GET ALONG.
THAT SHOULD DO IT. GIVE IT A TRY.
WHAT, **ALREADY?**

I'M TELLING YOU RIGHT NOW, YOU *DIDN'T* FIX NO ENGINE THAT QUICK. I KNOW THIS ENGINE LIKE THE BACK OF MY HAND, AND IT AIN'T POSSIBLE FOR YOU TO--

IT... WORKS?

RRRRR

SEE? *TOLD YOU* I WAS GOOD WITH MACHINES.

THAT'S *BETTER* THAN GOOD. THAT'S *MAGIC* OR SOMETHING.

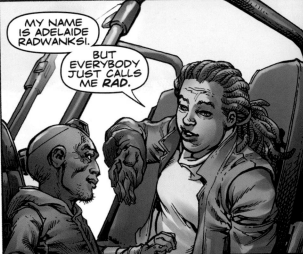

MY NAME IS ADELAIDE RADWANKSI.

BUT EVERYBODY JUST CALLS ME *RAD*.

I'M GLAD TO MEET YOU, RAD.

YOU, TOO, CARVER. SO, WHERE YOU *HEADED*?

PROMETHEUS CITY. I HAVE SOME BUSINESS THERE.

WELL, ME, TOO. WHY DON'T YOU HOP IN, AND WE'LL FIGURE OUT SOME WAY TO GET YOUR *CONTRAPTION* UP HERE.

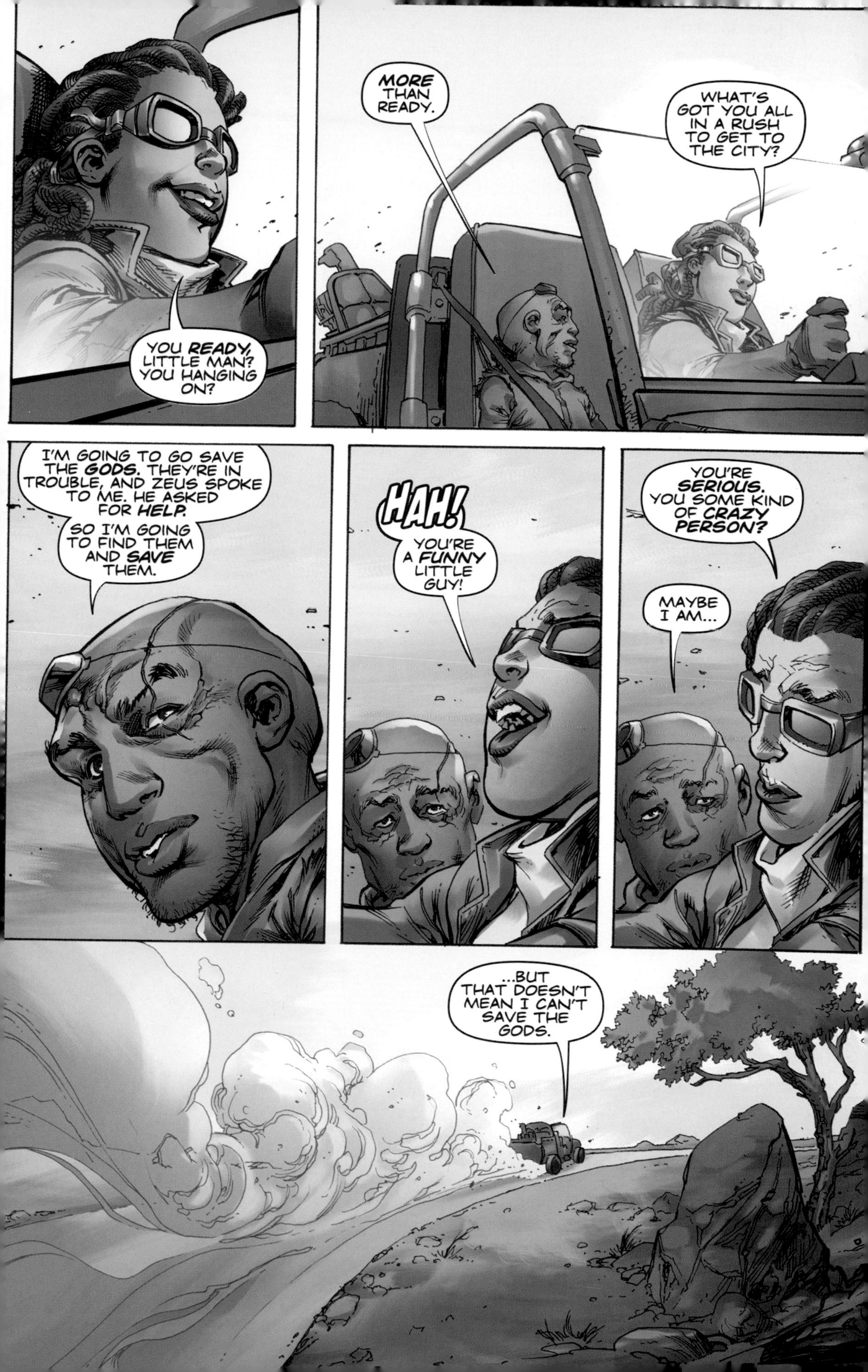
YOU **READY,** LITTLE MAN? YOU HANGING ON?
MORE THAN READY.
WHAT'S GOT YOU ALL IN A RUSH TO GET TO THE CITY?
I'M GOING TO GO SAVE THE **GODS.** THEY'RE IN TROUBLE, AND ZEUS SPOKE TO ME. HE ASKED FOR **HELP.**
SO I'M GOING TO FIND THEM AND **SAVE** THEM.
HAH!
YOU'RE A **FUNNY** LITTLE GUY!
YOU'RE **SERIOUS.** YOU SOME KIND OF **CRAZY PERSON?**
MAYBE I AM...
...BUT THAT DOESN'T MEAN I CAN'T SAVE THE GODS.

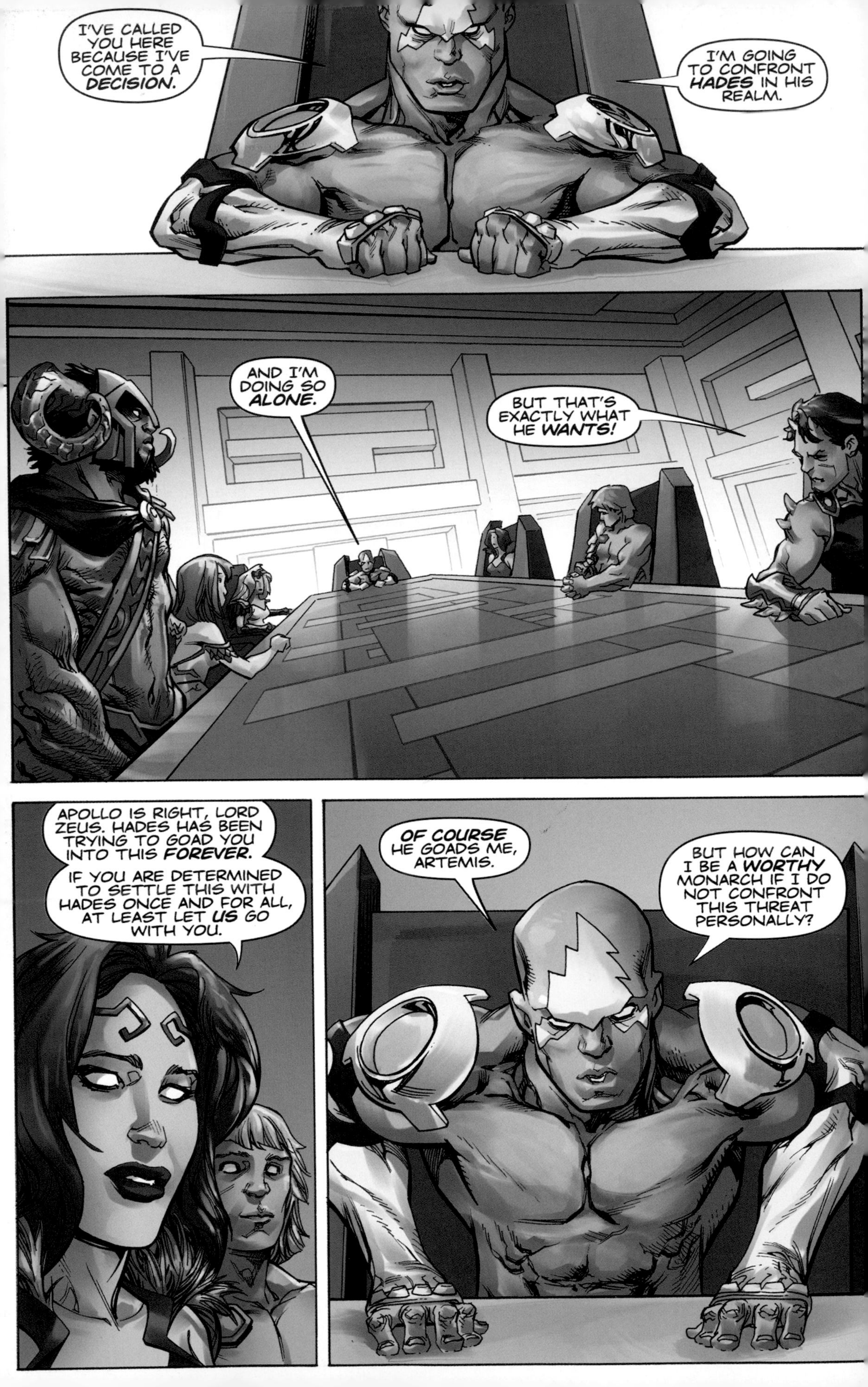
I'VE CALLED YOU HERE BECAUSE I'VE COME TO A DECISION.
I'M GOING TO CONFRONT HADES IN HIS REALM.
AND I'M DOING SO ALONE.
BUT THAT'S EXACTLY WHAT HE WANTS!
APOLLO IS RIGHT, LORD ZEUS. HADES HAS BEEN TRYING TO GOAD YOU INTO THIS FOREVER.
IF YOU ARE DETERMINED TO SETTLE THIS WITH HADES ONCE AND FOR ALL, AT LEAST LET US GO WITH YOU.
OF COURSE HE GOADS ME, ARTEMIS.
BUT HOW CAN I BE A WORTHY MONARCH IF I DO NOT CONFRONT THIS THREAT PERSONALLY?

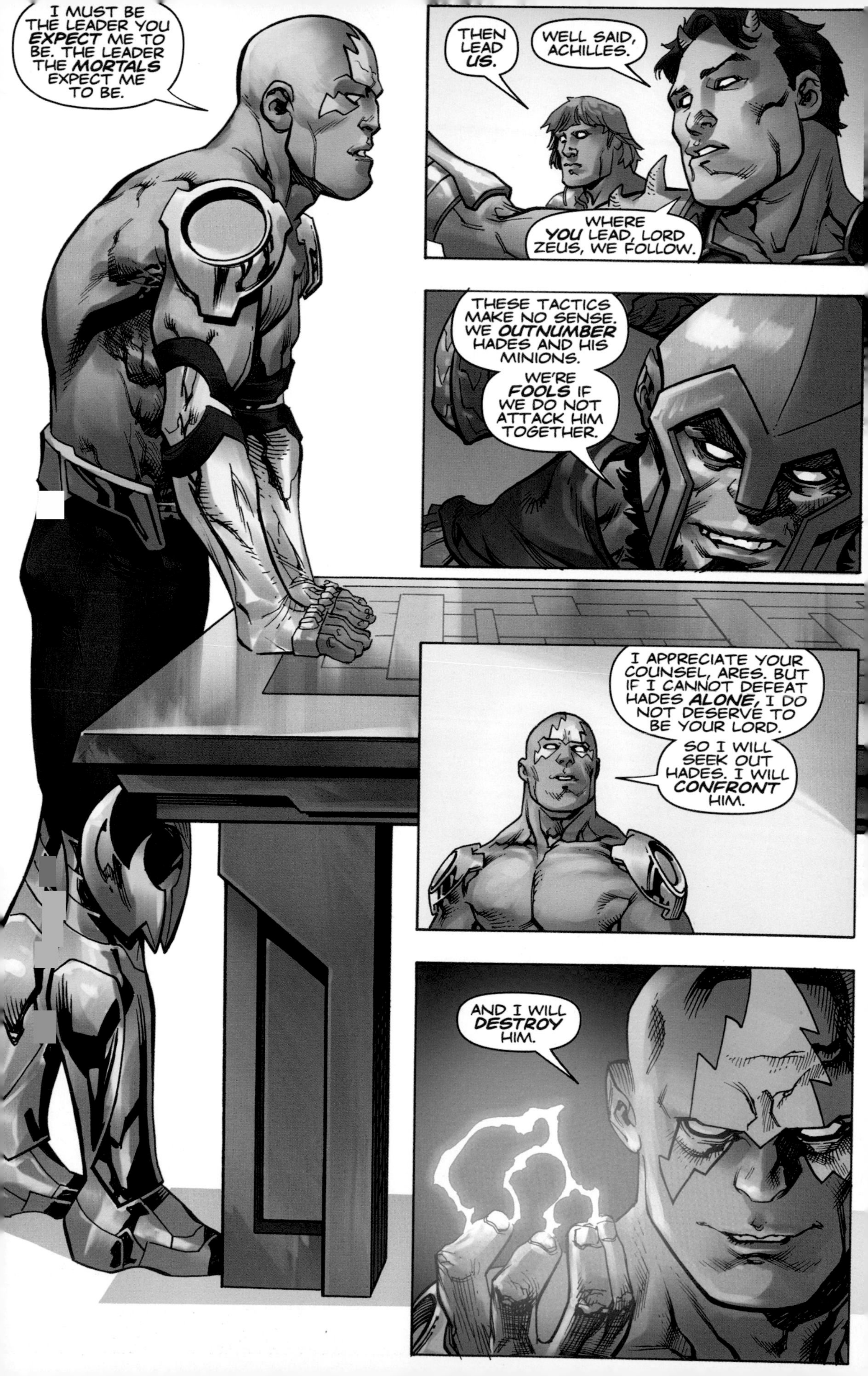
I MUST BE THE LEADER YOU EXPECT ME TO BE. THE LEADER THE MORTALS EXPECT ME TO BE.
THEN LEAD US.
WELL SAID, ACHILLES.
WHERE YOU LEAD, LORD ZEUS, WE FOLLOW.
THESE TACTICS MAKE NO SENSE. WE OUTNUMBER HADES AND HIS MINIONS.
WE'RE FOOLS IF WE DO NOT ATTACK HIM TOGETHER.
I APPRECIATE YOUR COUNSEL, ARES. BUT IF I CANNOT DEFEAT HADES ALONE, I DO NOT DESERVE TO BE YOUR LORD.
SO I WILL SEEK OUT HADES. I WILL CONFRONT HIM.
AND I WILL DESTROY HIM.

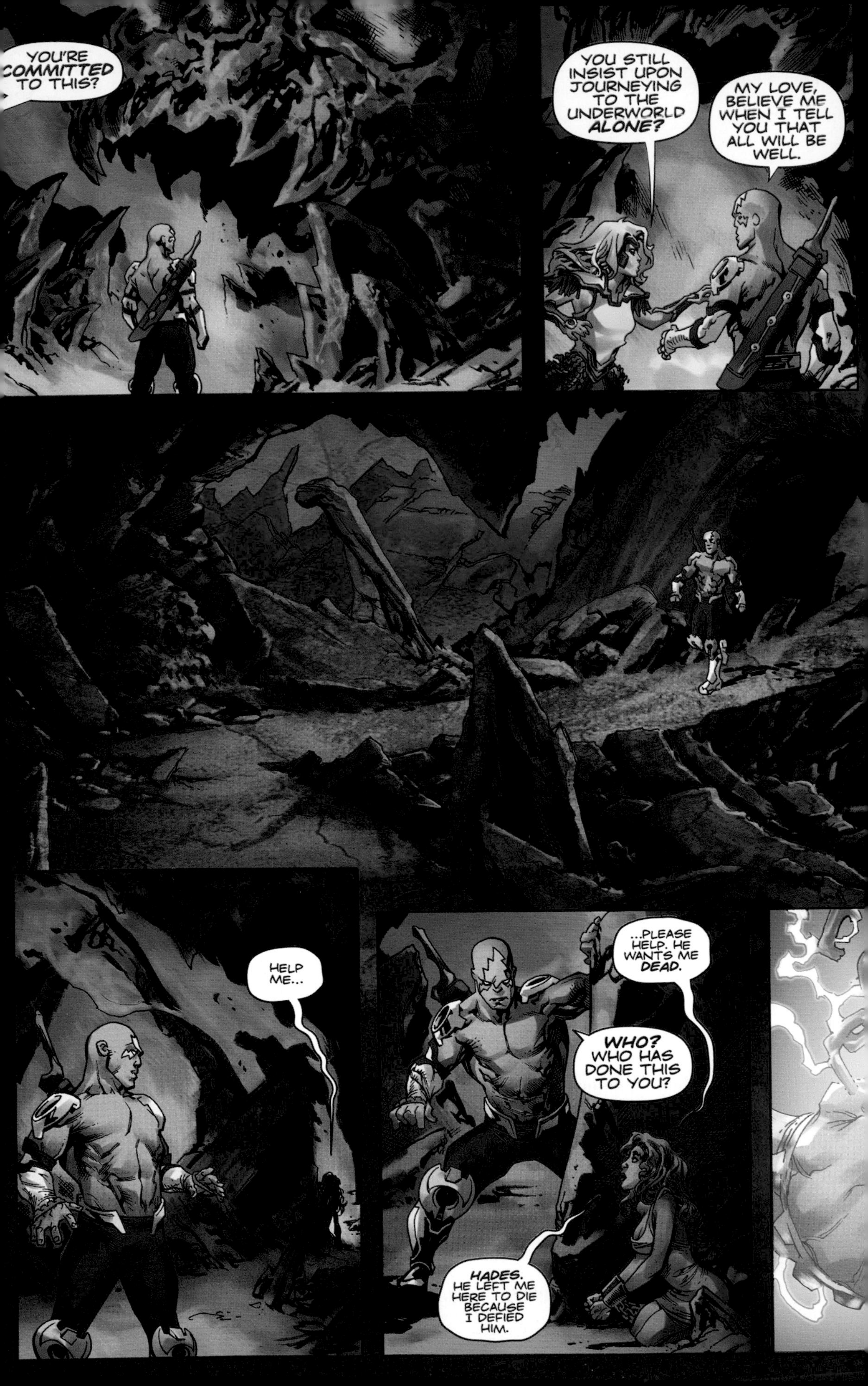
YOU'RE COMMITTED TO THIS?
YOU STILL INSIST UPON JOURNEYING TO THE UNDERWORLD ALONE?
MY LOVE, BELIEVE ME WHEN I TELL YOU THAT ALL WILL BE WELL.
HELP ME...
...PLEASE HELP. HE WANTS ME DEAD.
WHO? WHO HAS DONE THIS TO YOU?
HADES. HE LEFT ME HERE TO DIE BECAUSE I DEFIED HIM.

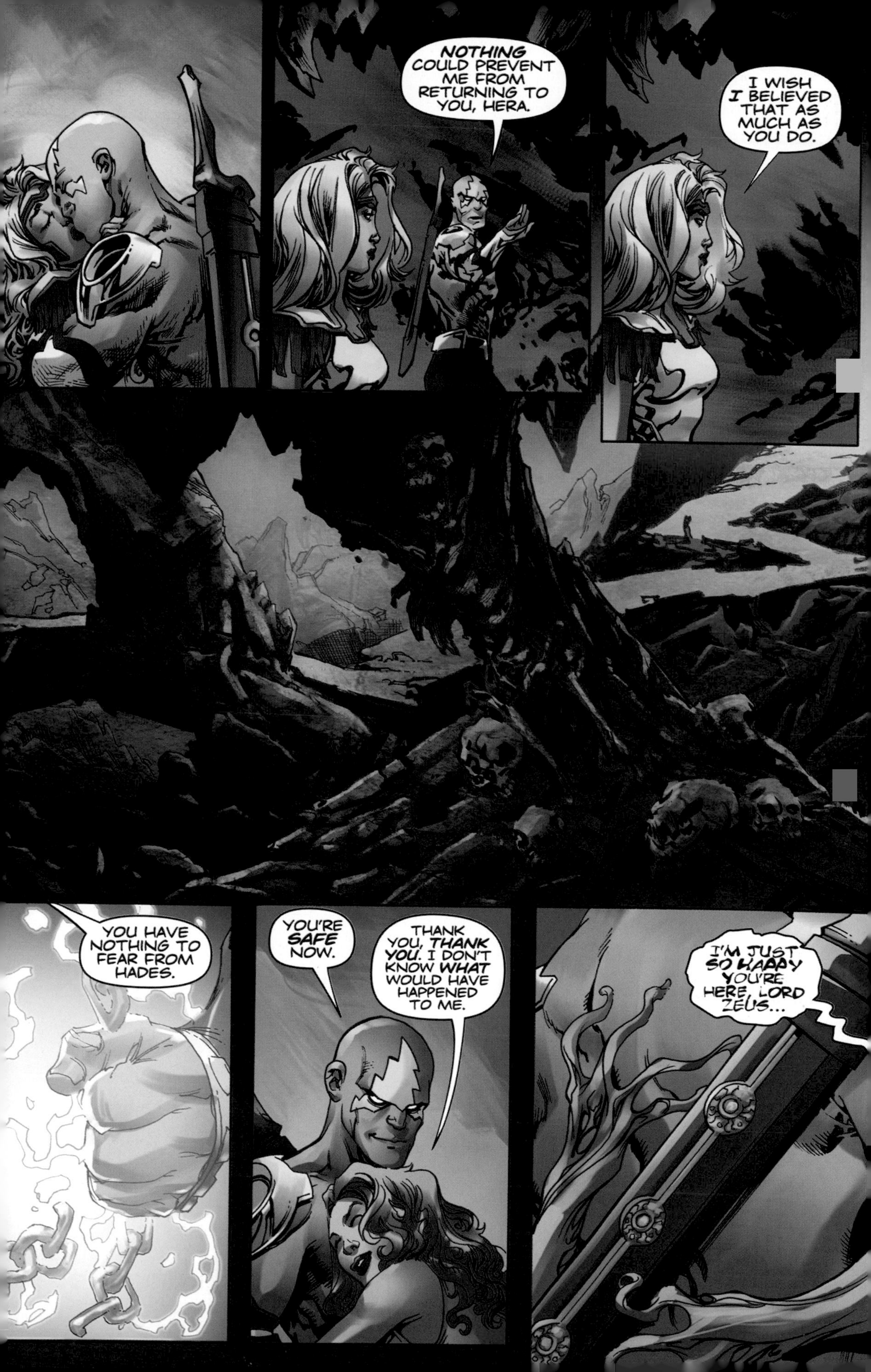
NOTHING COULD PREVENT ME FROM RETURNING TO YOU, HERA.
I WISH I BELIEVED THAT AS MUCH AS YOU DO.
YOU HAVE NOTHING TO FEAR FROM HADES.
YOU'RE SAFE NOW.
THANK YOU, THANK YOU. I DON'T KNOW WHAT WOULD HAVE HAPPENED TO ME.
I'M JUST SO HAPPY YOU'RE HERE, LORD ZEUS...

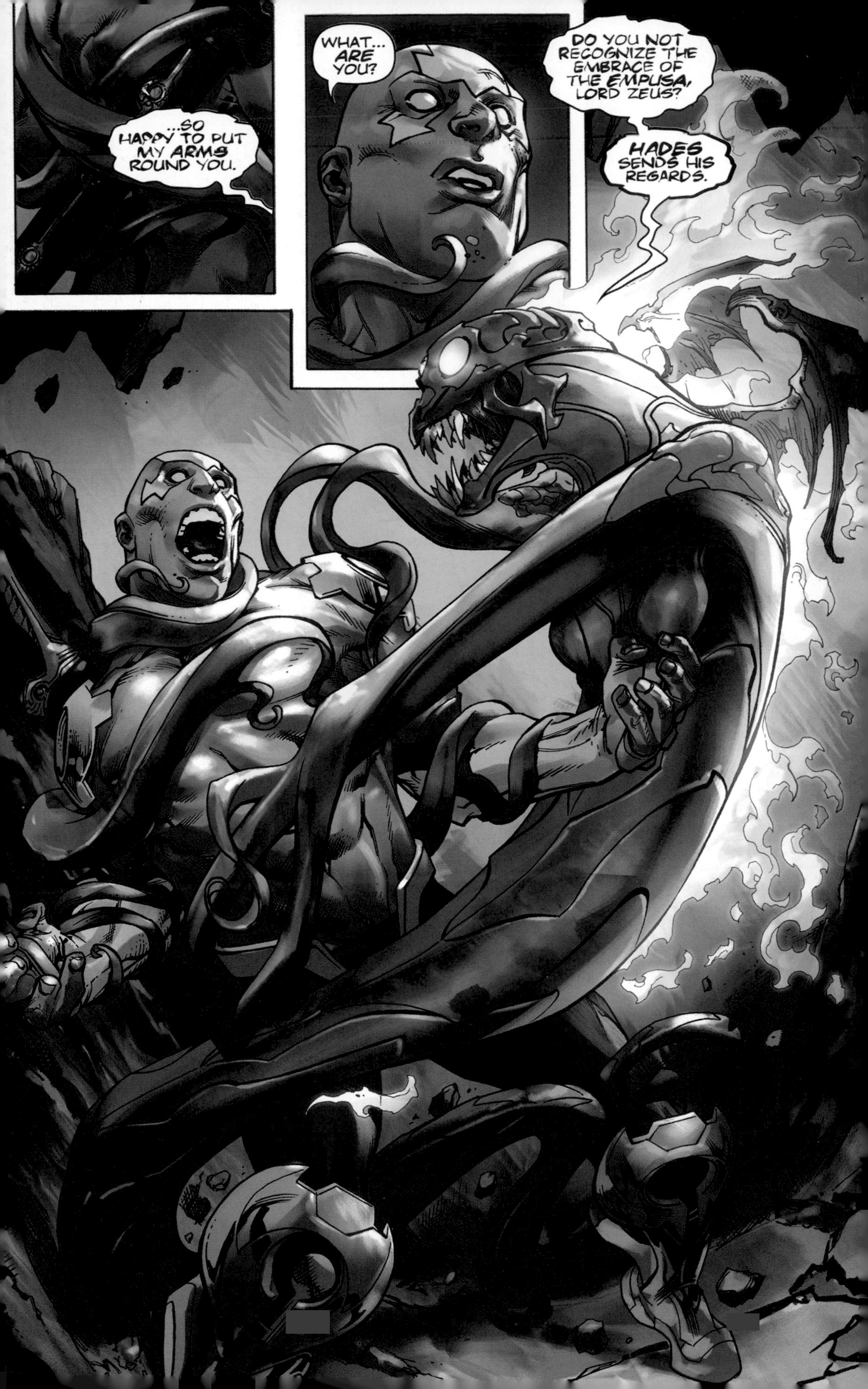
...SO HAPPY TO PUT MY ARMS ROUND YOU.
WHAT... ARE YOU?
DO YOU NOT RECOGNIZE THE EMBRACE OF THE EMPUSA, LORD ZEUS?
HADES SENDS HIS REGARDS.

III

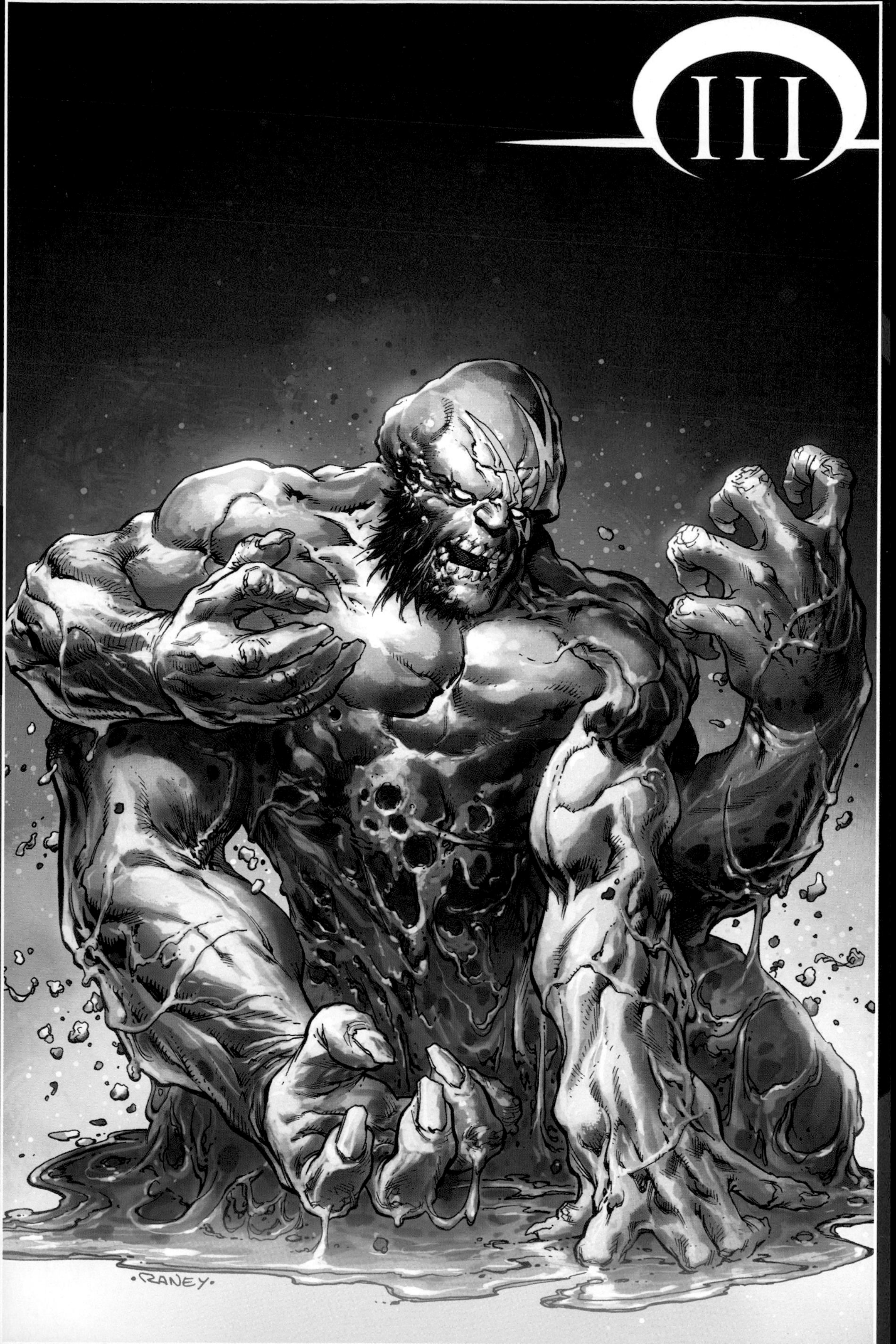
RANEY

ART BY **TOM RANEY** · COLORS BY **NANJAN JAMBERI**

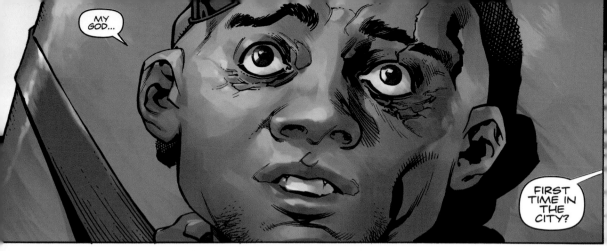

MY GOD...

FIRST TIME IN THE CITY?

YES. I'VE NEVER SEEN ANYTHING *LIKE* THIS, RAD.

I KNOW IT CAN BE A LITTLE *OVERWHELMING* THE FIRST TIME.

PEOPLE IN THE WASTELAND *TALK* ABOUT PROMETHEUS CITY, BUT THIS IS...

...THIS IS SO MUCH *MORE* THAN I IMAGINED. SO MANY *PEOPLE*.

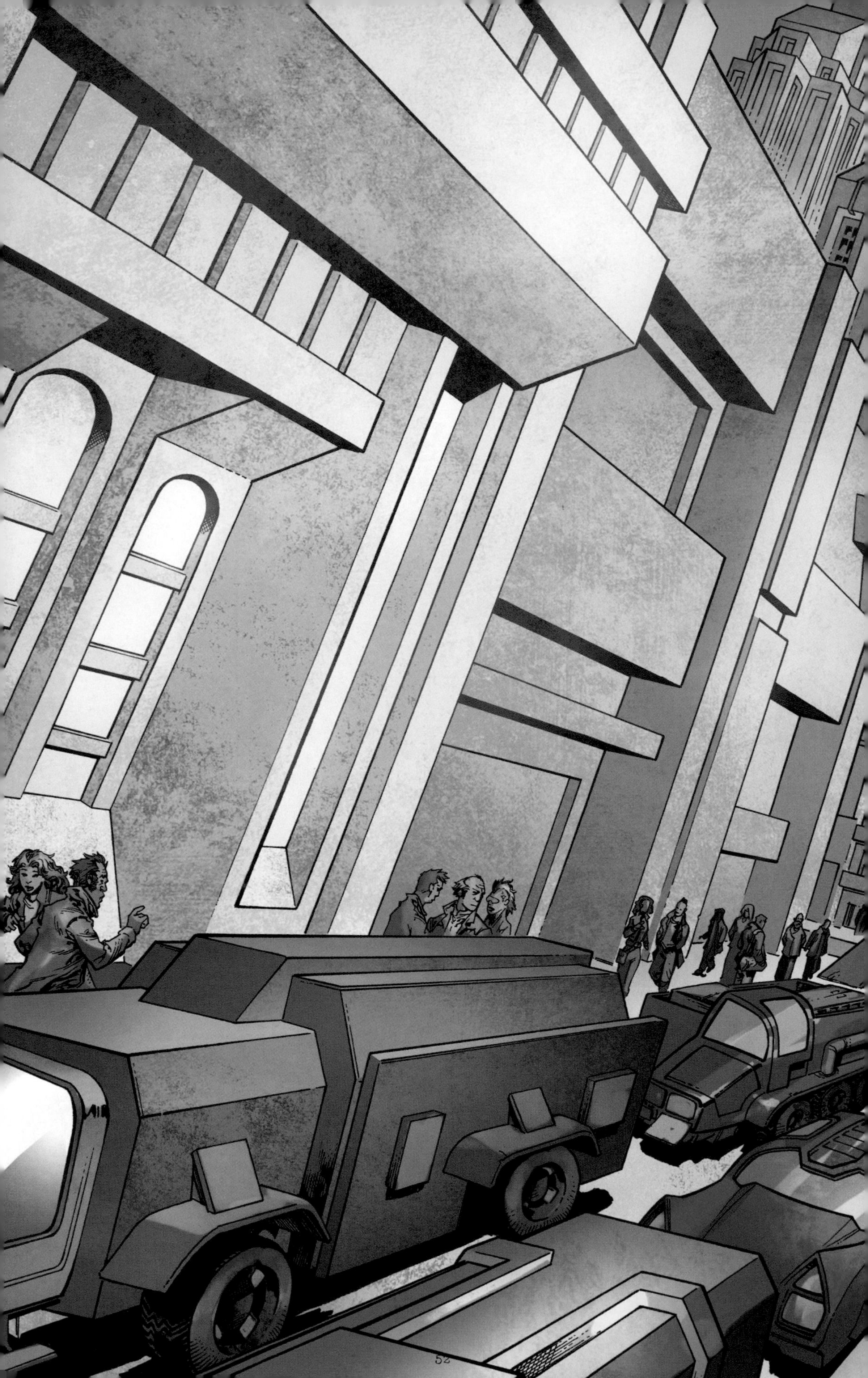

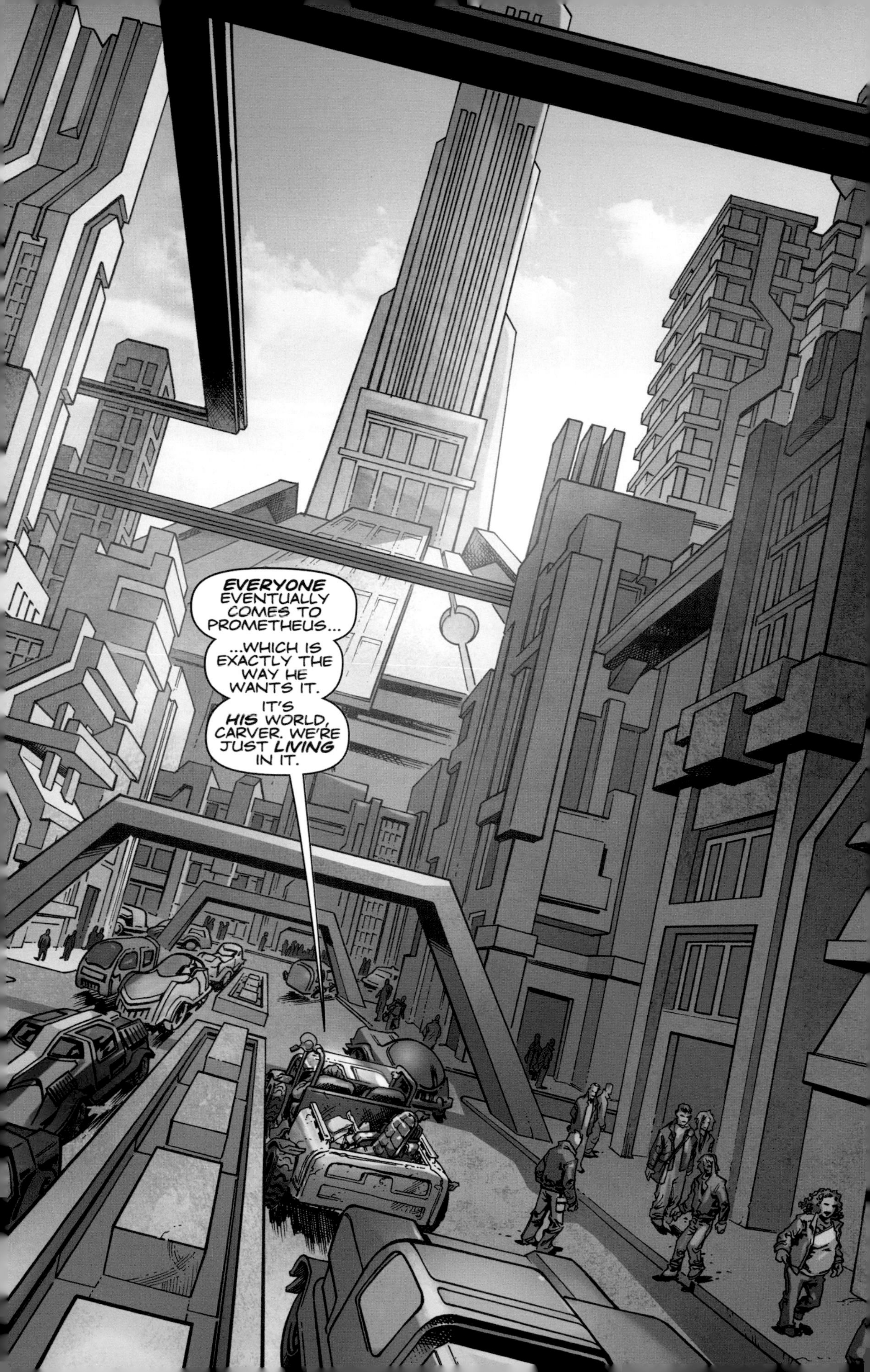

EVERYONE EVENTUALLY COMES TO PROMETHEUS...
...WHICH IS EXACTLY THE WAY HE WANTS IT.
IT'S **HIS** WORLD, CARVER. WE'RE JUST **LIVING** IN IT.

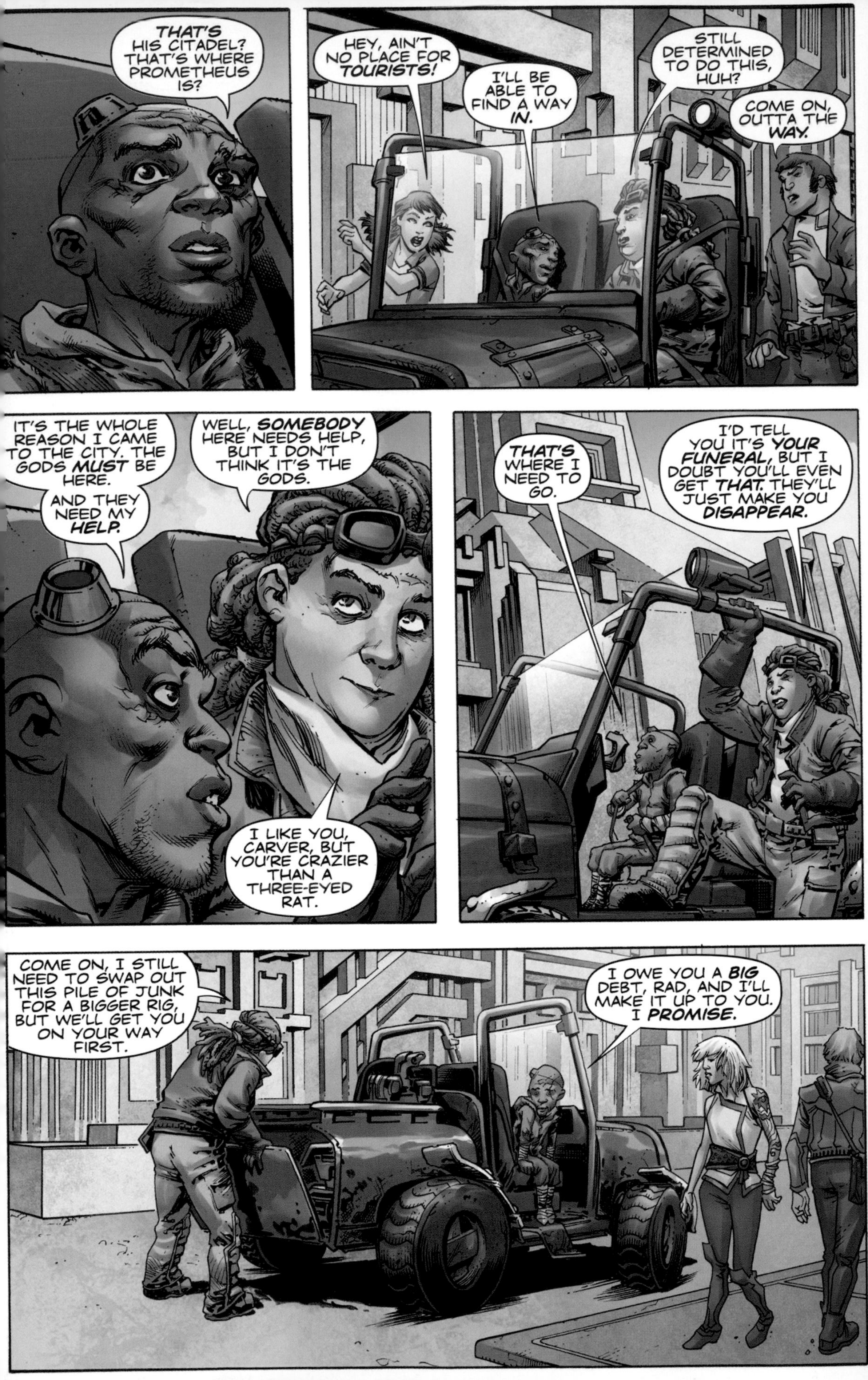
THAT'S HIS CITADEL? THAT'S WHERE PROMETHEUS IS?
HEY, AIN'T NO PLACE FOR TOURISTS!
I'LL BE ABLE TO FIND A WAY IN.
STILL DETERMINED TO DO THIS, HUH?
COME ON, OUTTA THE WAY.
IT'S THE WHOLE REASON I CAME TO THE CITY. THE GODS MUST BE HERE.
AND THEY NEED MY HELP.
WELL, SOMEBODY HERE NEEDS HELP, BUT I DON'T THINK IT'S THE GODS.
I LIKE YOU, CARVER, BUT YOU'RE CRAZIER THAN A THREE-EYED RAT.
THAT'S WHERE I NEED TO GO.
I'D TELL YOU IT'S YOUR FUNERAL, BUT I DOUBT YOU'LL EVEN GET THAT. THEY'LL JUST MAKE YOU DISAPPEAR.
COME ON, I STILL NEED TO SWAP OUT THIS PILE OF JUNK FOR A BIGGER RIG, BUT WE'LL GET YOU ON YOUR WAY FIRST.
I OWE YOU A BIG DEBT, RAD, AND I'LL MAKE IT UP TO YOU. I PROMISE.

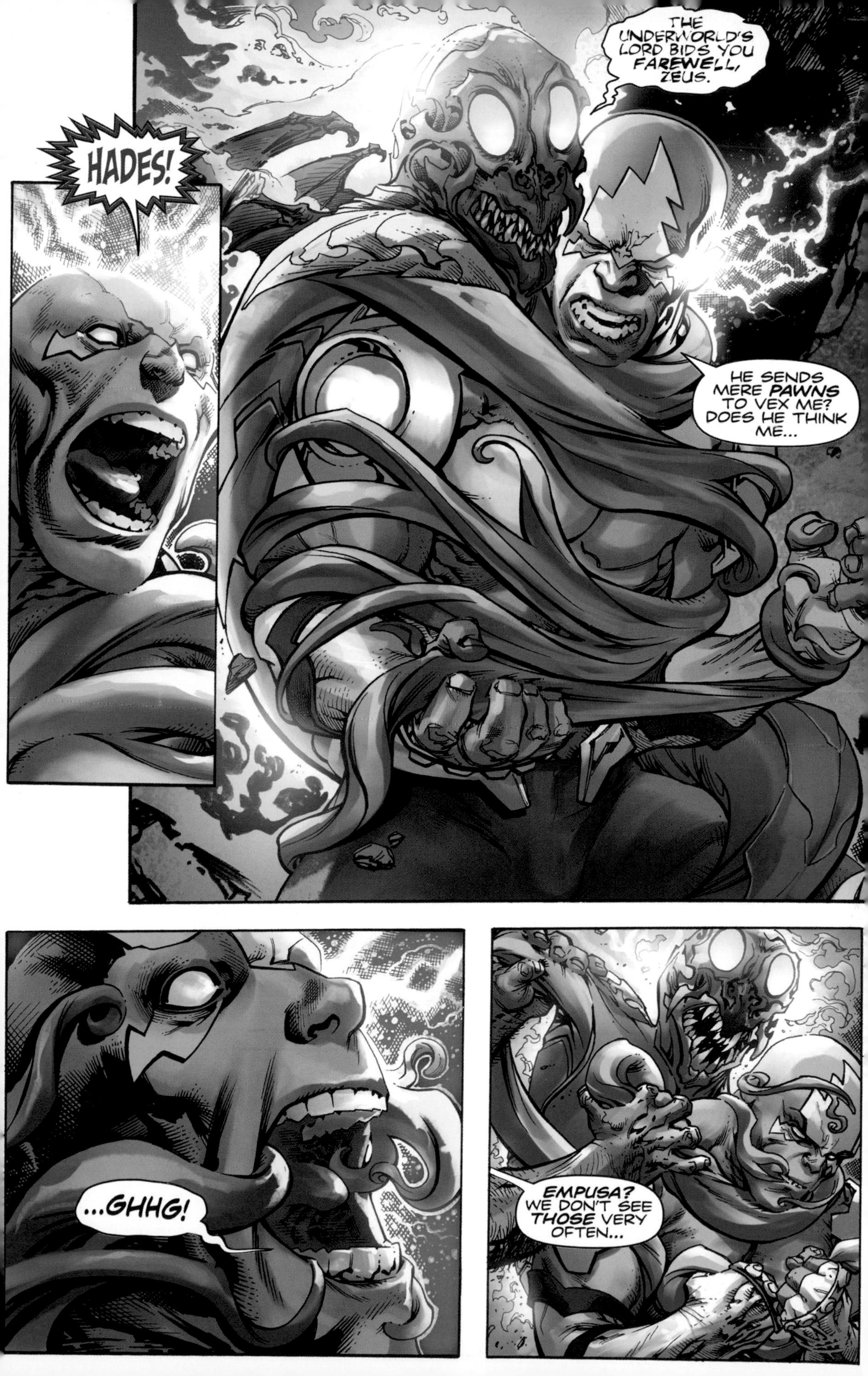
THE UNDERWORLD'S LORD BIDS YOU FAREWELL, ZEUS.
HADES!
HE SENDS MERE PAWNS TO VEX ME? DOES HE THINK ME...
...GHHG!
EMPUSA? WE DON'T SEE THOSE VERY OFTEN...

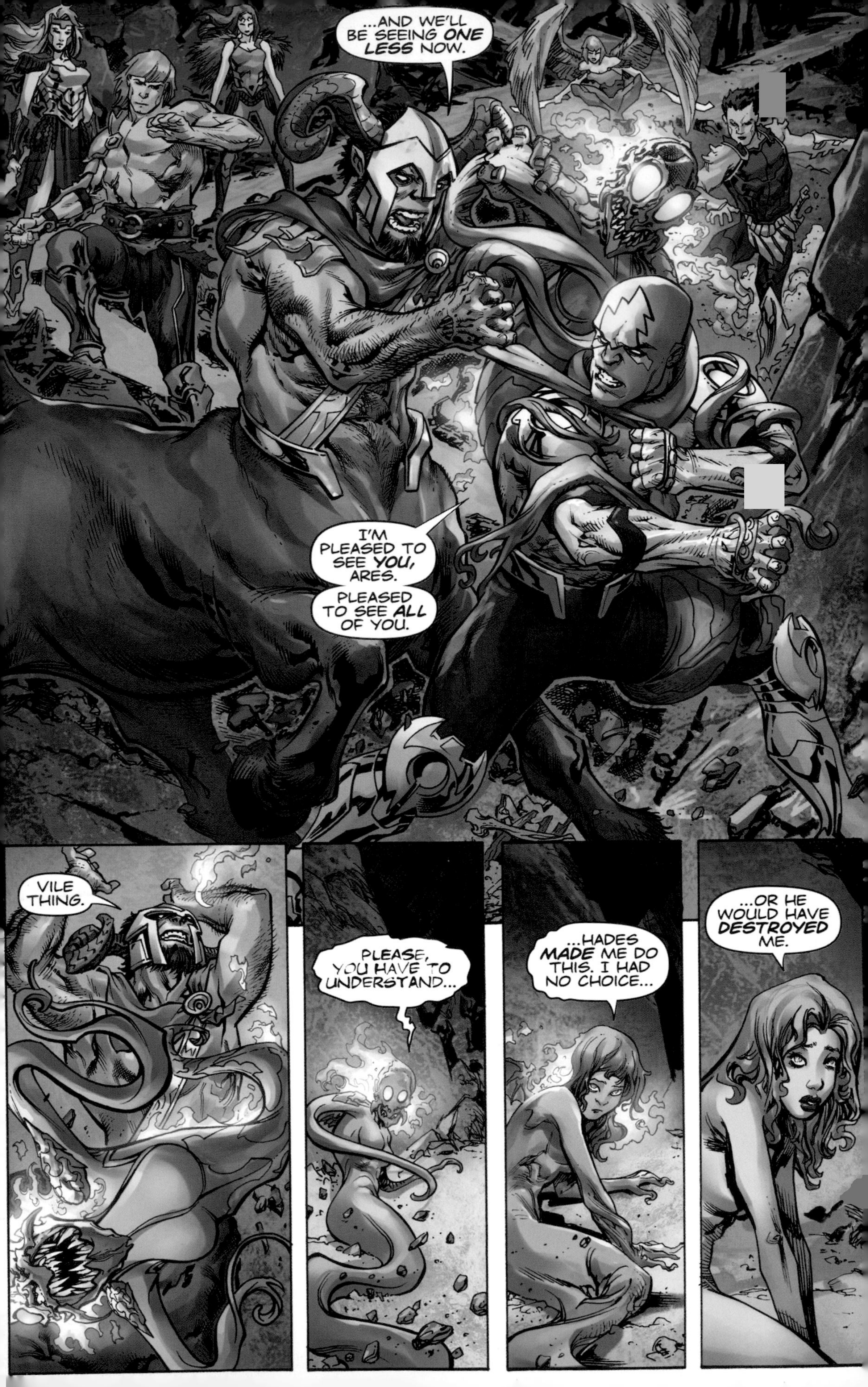
...AND WE'LL BE SEEING ONE LESS NOW.
I'M PLEASED TO SEE YOU, ARES.
PLEASED TO SEE ALL OF YOU.
VILE THING.
PLEASE, YOU HAVE TO UNDERSTAND...
...HADES MADE ME DO THIS. I HAD NO CHOICE...
...OR HE WOULD HAVE DESTROYED ME.

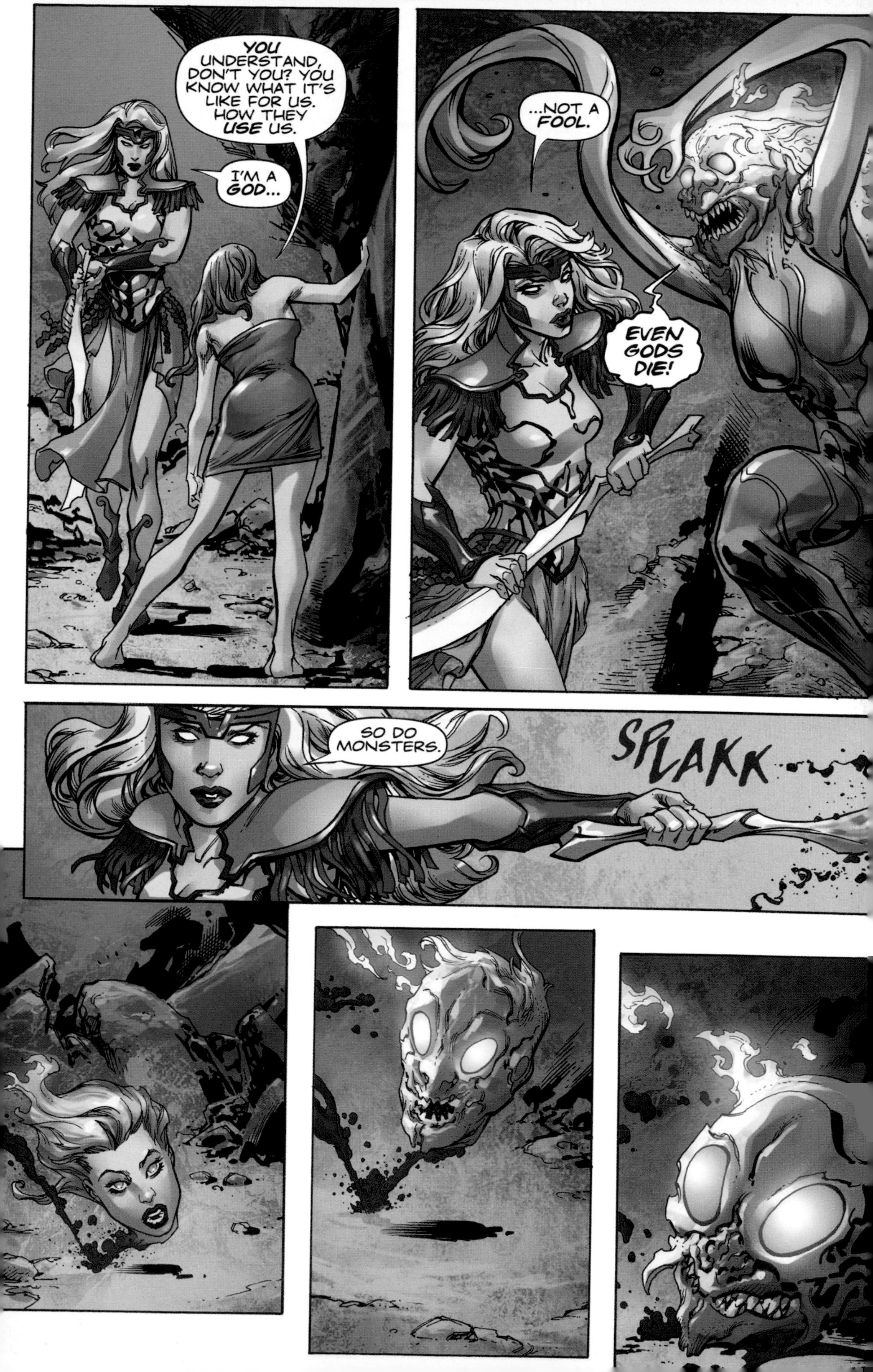
YOU UNDERSTAND, DON'T YOU? YOU KNOW WHAT IT'S LIKE FOR US. HOW THEY USE US.
I'M A GOD...
...NOT A FOOL.
EVEN GODS DIE!
SO DO MONSTERS.
SPLAKK

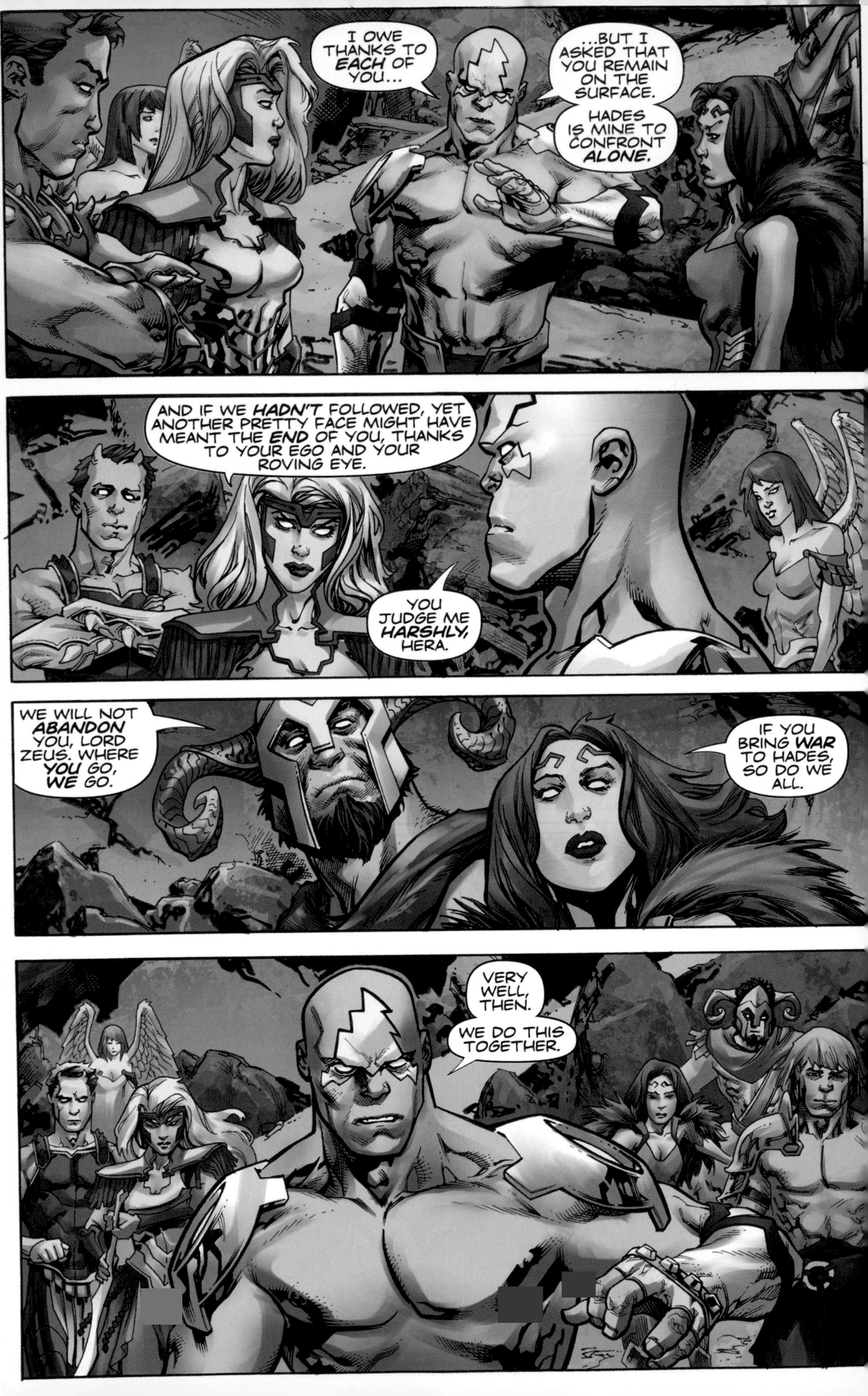
I OWE THANKS TO EACH OF YOU...
...BUT I ASKED THAT YOU REMAIN ON THE SURFACE.
HADES IS MINE TO CONFRONT ALONE.
AND IF WE HADN'T FOLLOWED, YET ANOTHER PRETTY FACE MIGHT HAVE MEANT THE END OF YOU, THANKS TO YOUR EGO AND YOUR ROVING EYE.
YOU JUDGE ME HARSHLY, HERA.
WE WILL NOT ABANDON YOU, LORD ZEUS. WHERE YOU GO, WE GO.
IF YOU BRING WAR TO HADES, SO DO WE ALL.
VERY WELL, THEN.
WE DO THIS TOGETHER.

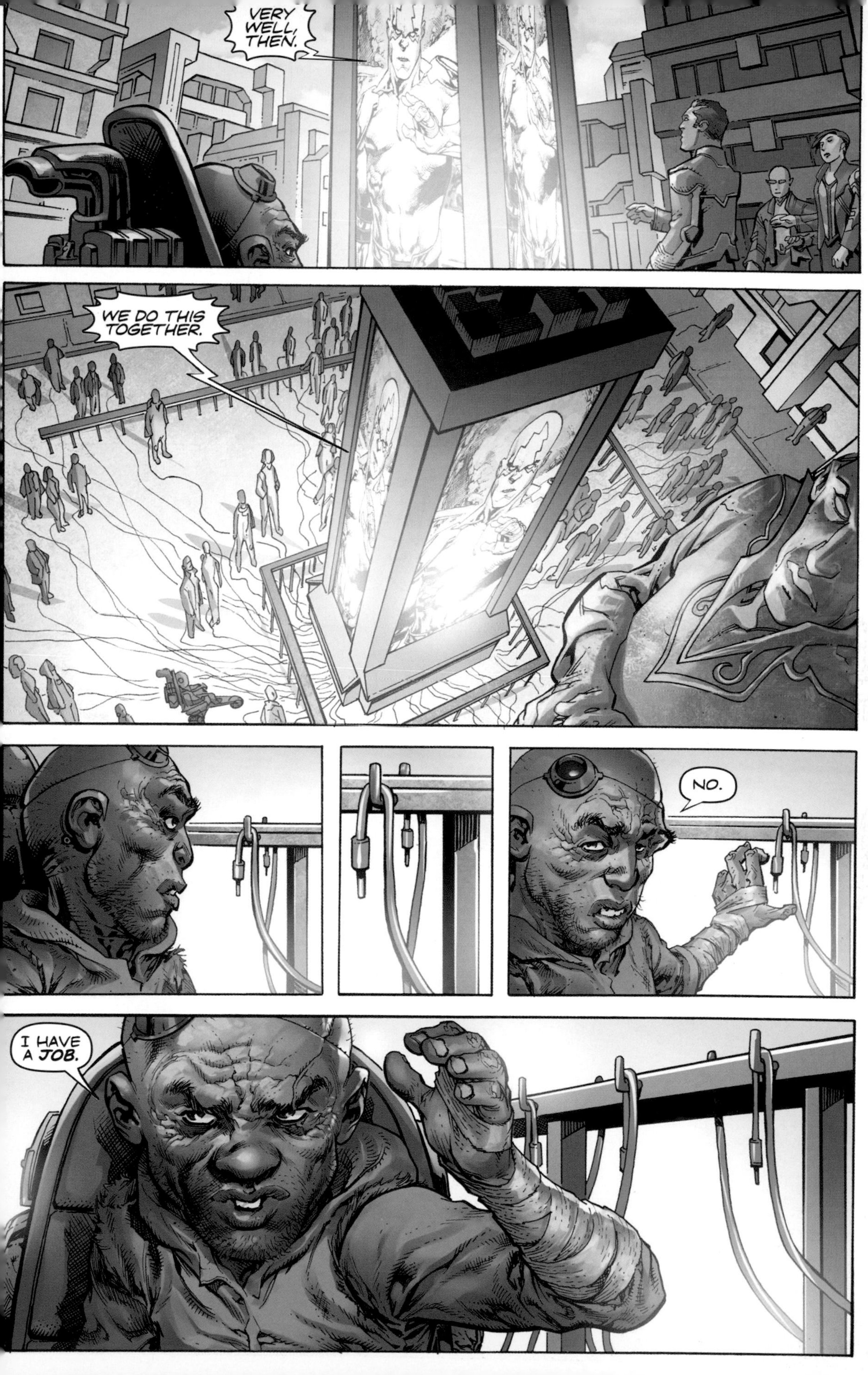
VERY WELL, THEN.
WE DO THIS TOGETHER.
NO.
I HAVE A JOB.

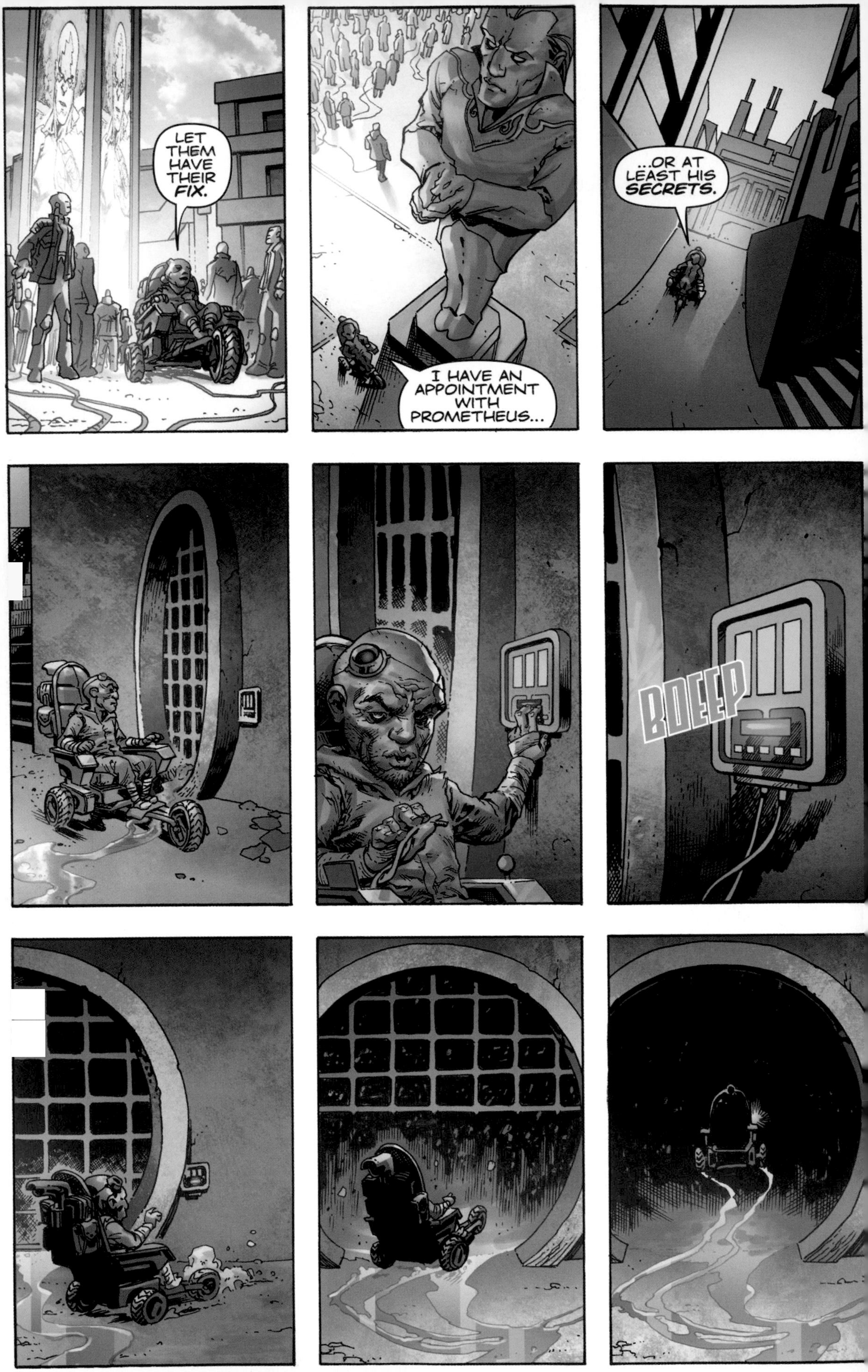
LET THEM HAVE THEIR FIX.
I HAVE AN APPOINTMENT WITH PROMETHEUS...
...OR AT LEAST HIS SECRETS.
BDEEP

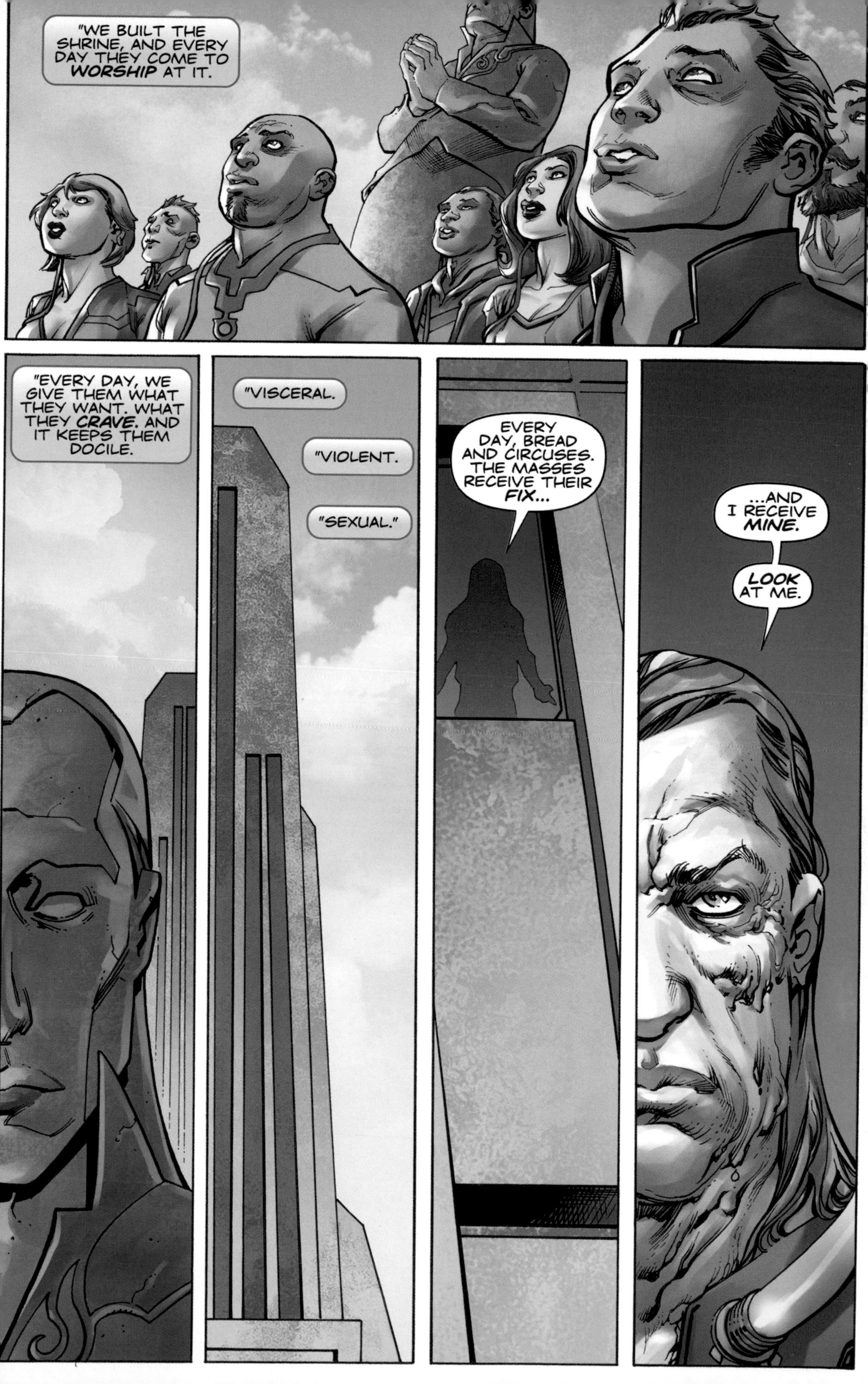
"WE BUILT THE SHRINE, AND EVERY DAY THEY COME TO WORSHIP AT IT.
"EVERY DAY, WE GIVE THEM WHAT THEY WANT. WHAT THEY CRAVE. AND IT KEEPS THEM DOCILE.
"VISCERAL.
"VIOLENT.
"SEXUAL."
EVERY DAY, BREAD AND CIRCUSES. THE MASSES RECEIVE THEIR FIX...
...AND I RECEIVE MINE.
LOOK AT ME.

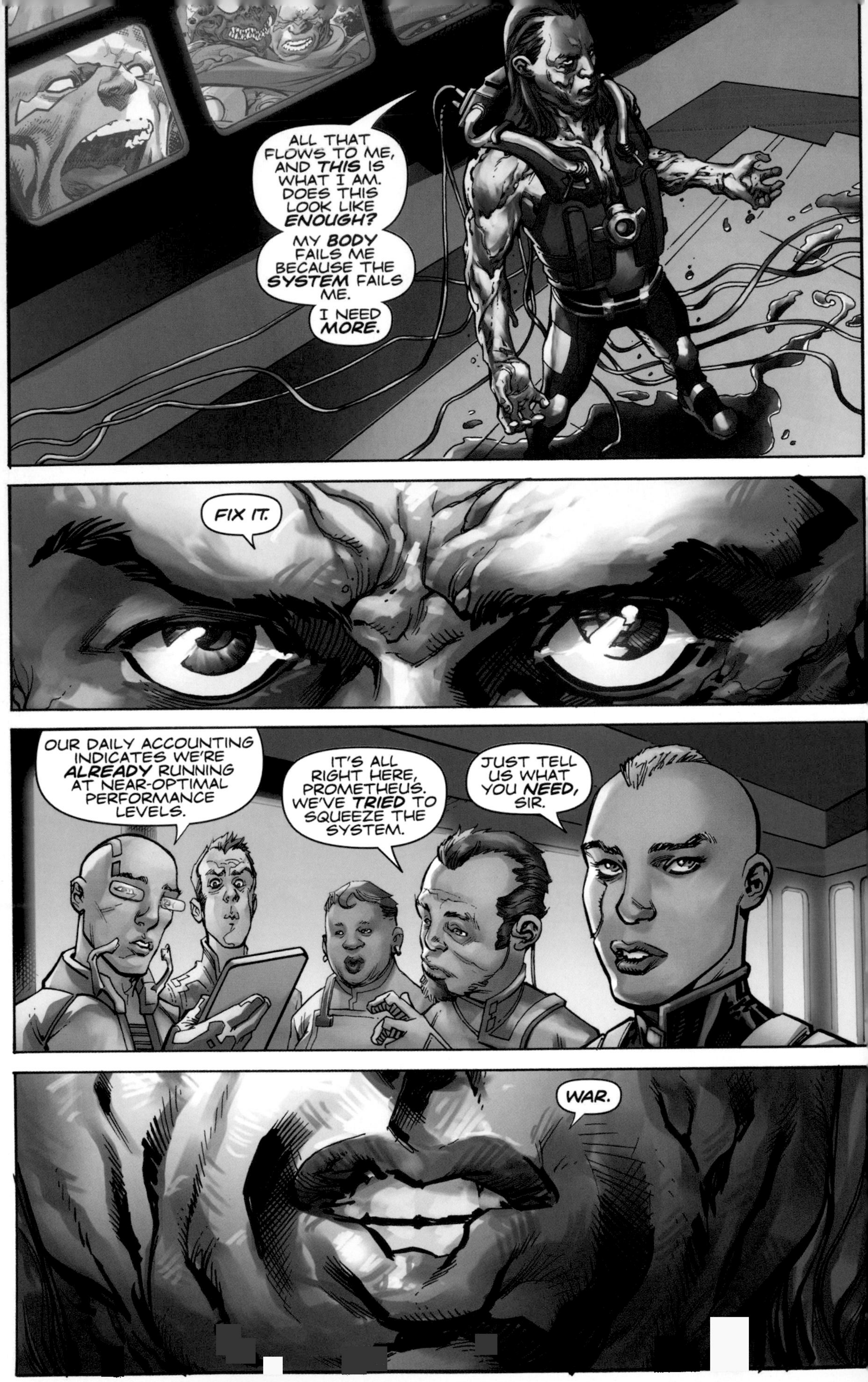
ALL THAT FLOWS TO ME, AND THIS IS WHAT I AM. DOES THIS LOOK LIKE ENOUGH?
MY BODY FAILS ME BECAUSE THE SYSTEM FAILS ME.
I NEED MORE.
FIX IT.
OUR DAILY ACCOUNTING INDICATES WE'RE ALREADY RUNNING AT NEAR-OPTIMAL PERFORMANCE LEVELS.
IT'S ALL RIGHT HERE, PROMETHEUS. WE'VE TRIED TO SQUEEZE THE SYSTEM.
JUST TELL US WHAT YOU NEED, SIR.
WAR.

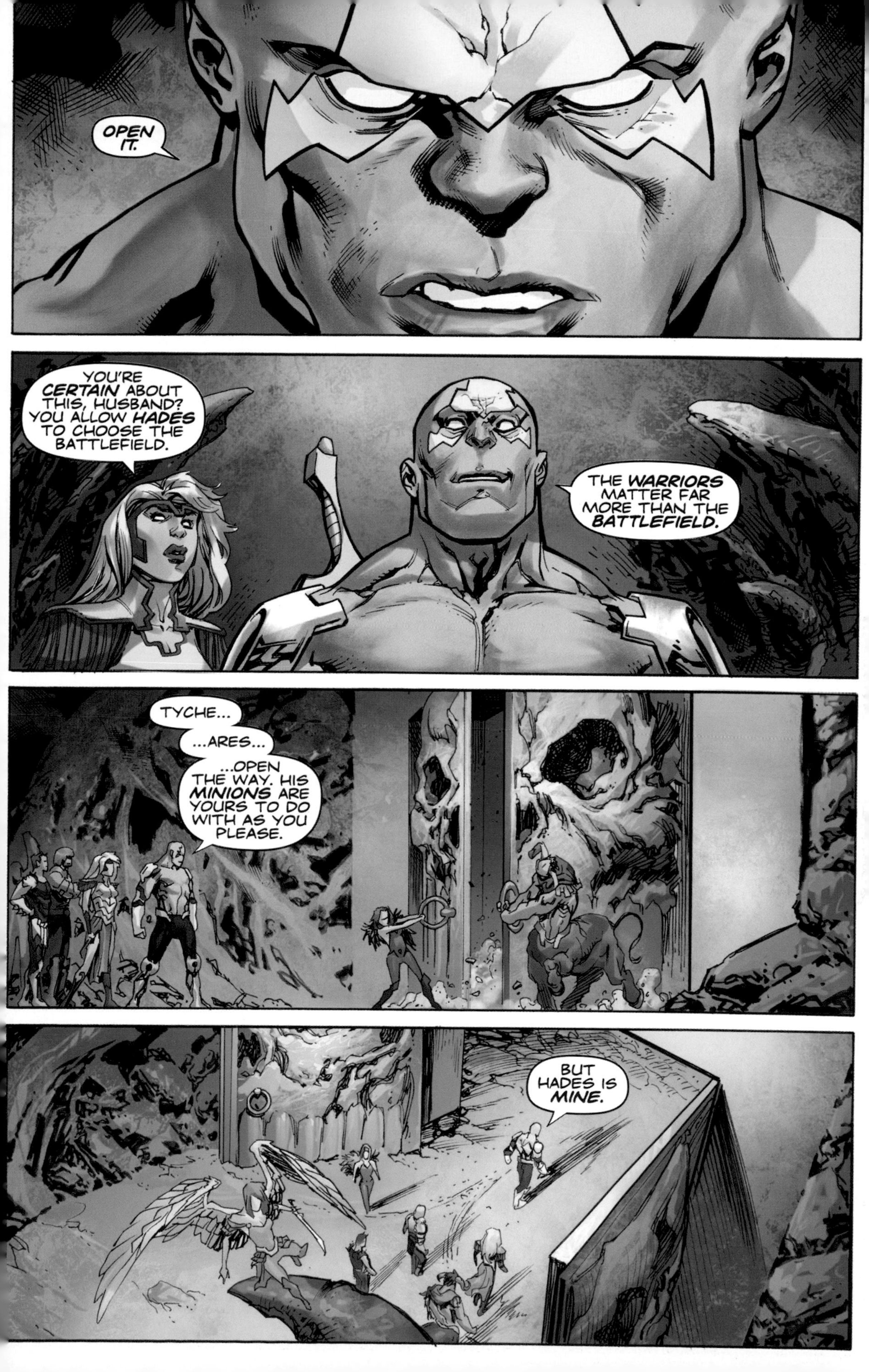
OPEN IT.
YOU'RE CERTAIN ABOUT THIS, HUSBAND? YOU ALLOW HADES TO CHOOSE THE BATTLEFIELD.
THE WARRIORS MATTER FAR MORE THAN THE BATTLEFIELD.
TYCHE...
...ARES...
...OPEN THE WAY. HIS MINIONS ARE YOURS TO DO WITH AS YOU PLEASE.
BUT HADES IS MINE.

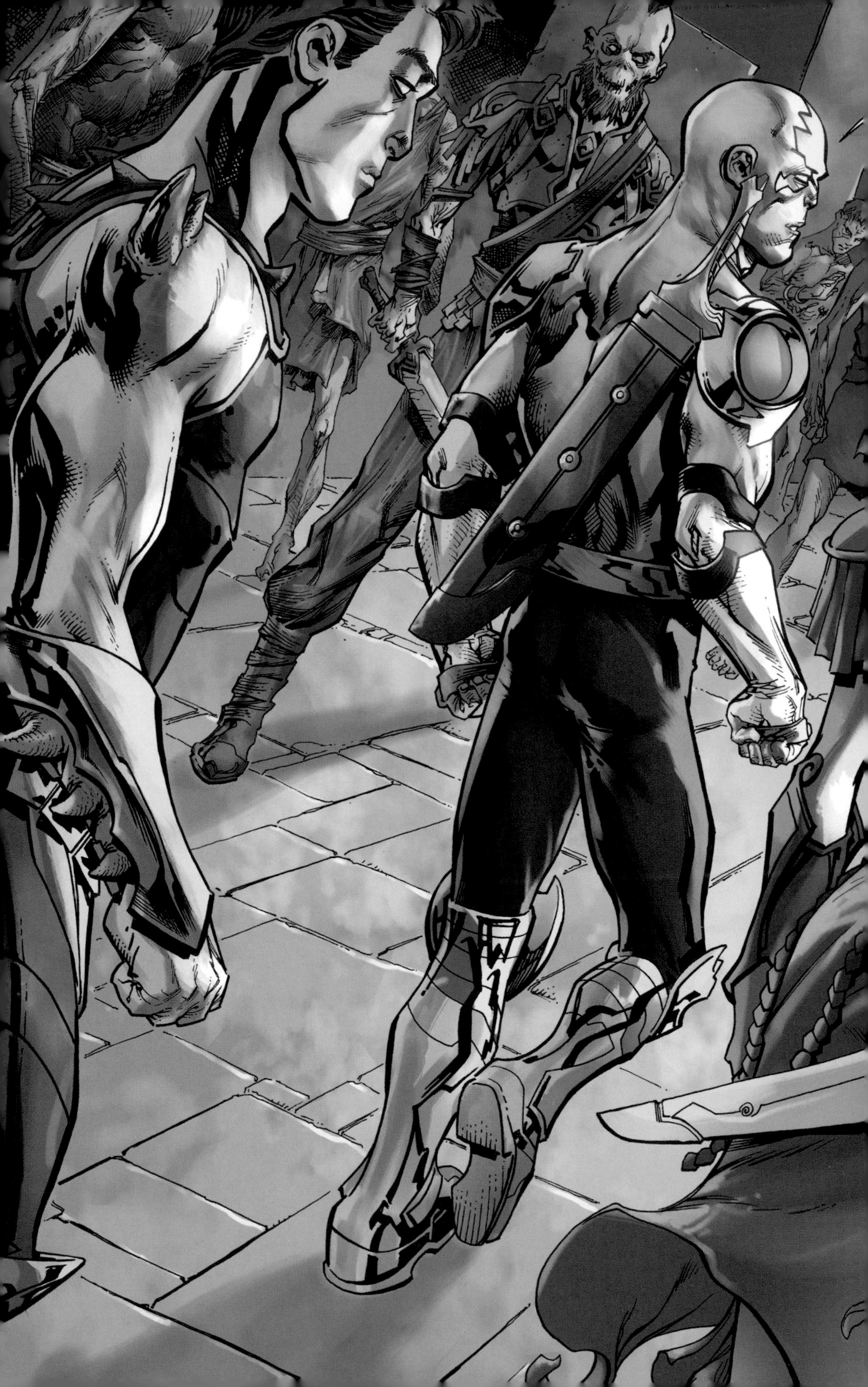

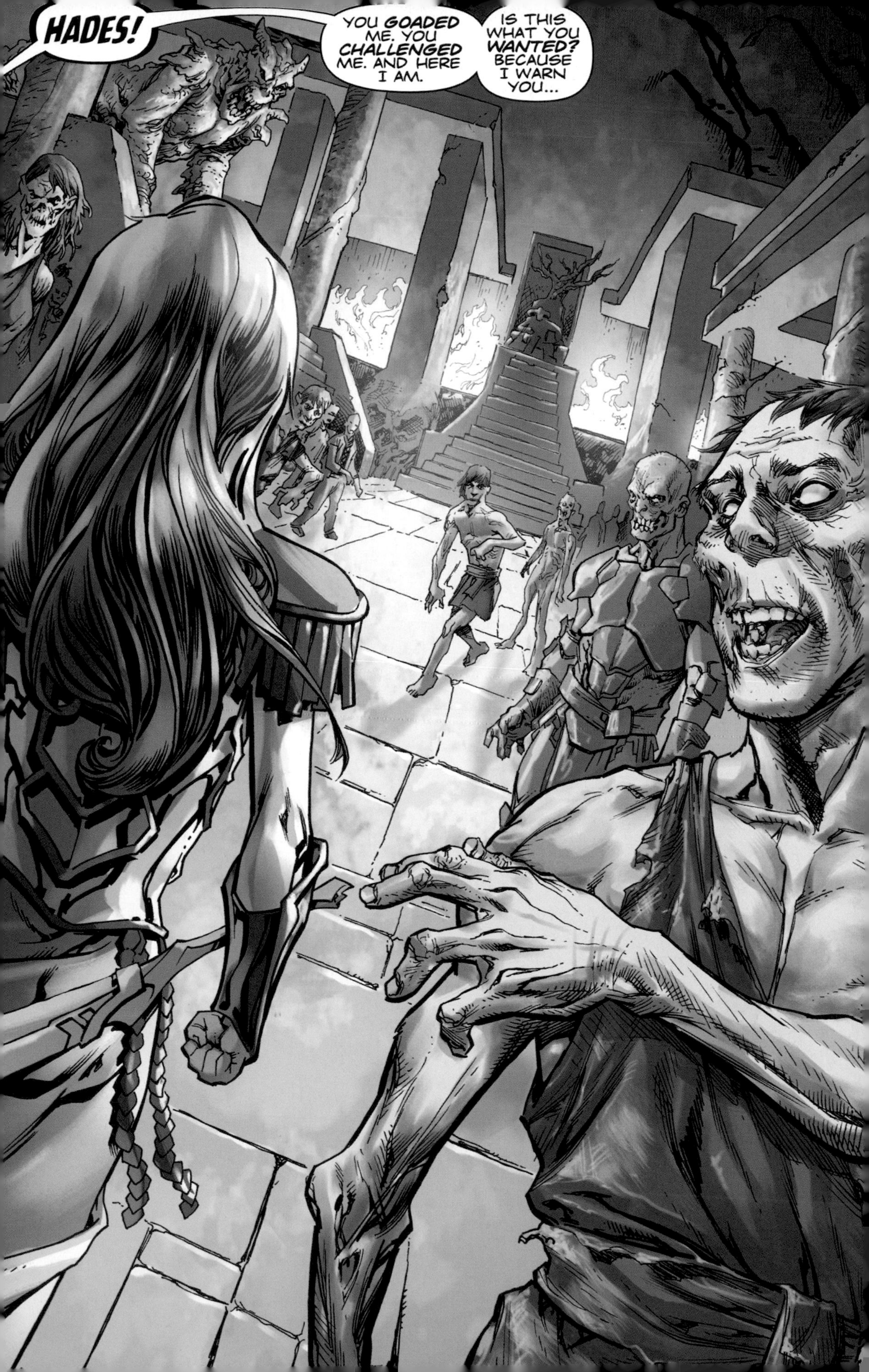
HADES!
YOU GOADED ME. YOU CHALLENGED ME. AND HERE I AM.
IS THIS WHAT YOU WANTED? BECAUSE I WARN YOU...

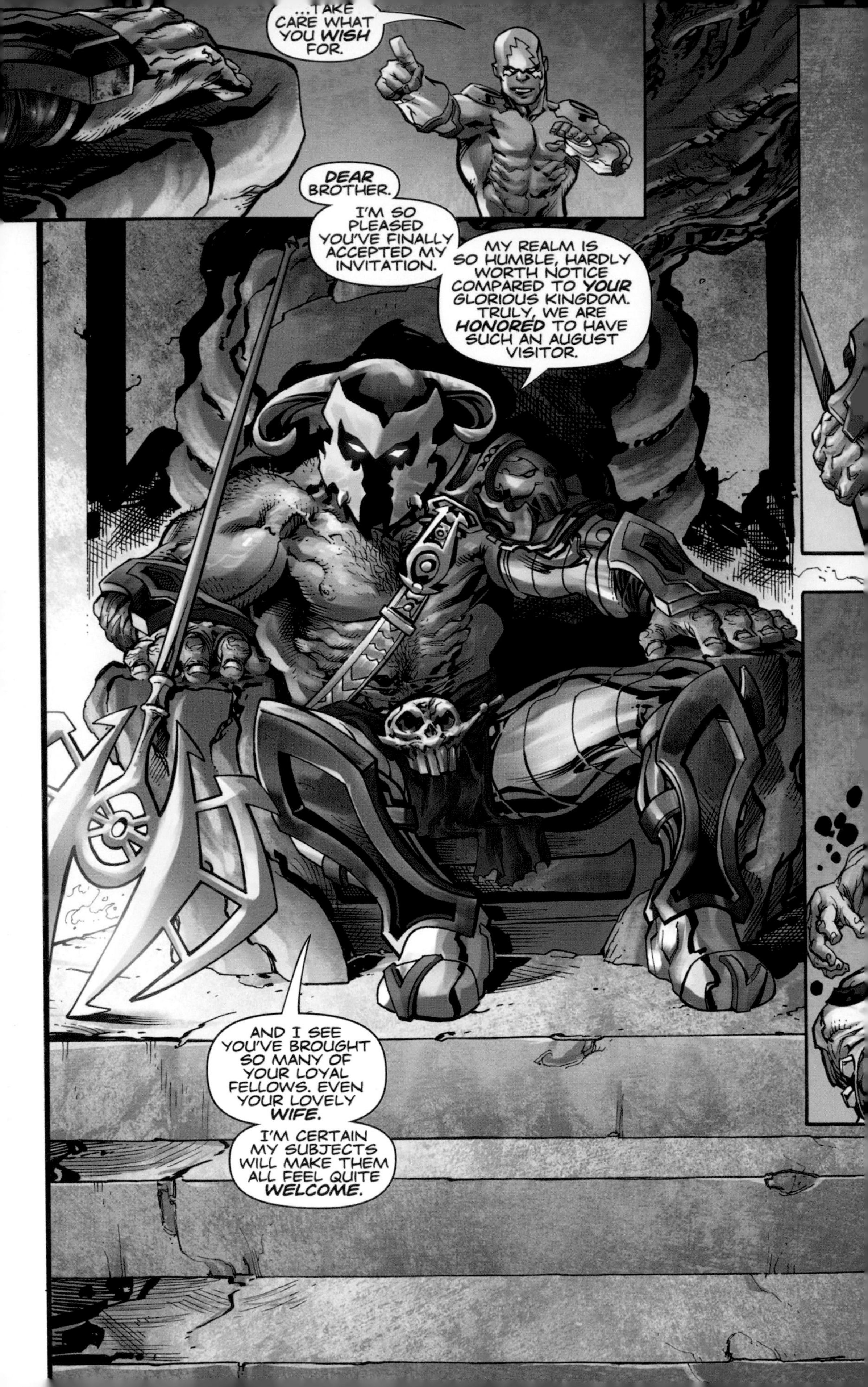
...TAKE CARE WHAT YOU WISH FOR.
DEAR BROTHER.
I'M SO PLEASED YOU'VE FINALLY ACCEPTED MY INVITATION.
MY REALM IS SO HUMBLE, HARDLY WORTH NOTICE COMPARED TO YOUR GLORIOUS KINGDOM. TRULY, WE ARE HONORED TO HAVE SUCH AN AUGUST VISITOR.
AND I SEE YOU'VE BROUGHT SO MANY OF YOUR LOYAL FELLOWS. EVEN YOUR LOVELY WIFE.
I'M CERTAIN MY SUBJECTS WILL MAKE THEM ALL FEEL QUITE WELCOME.

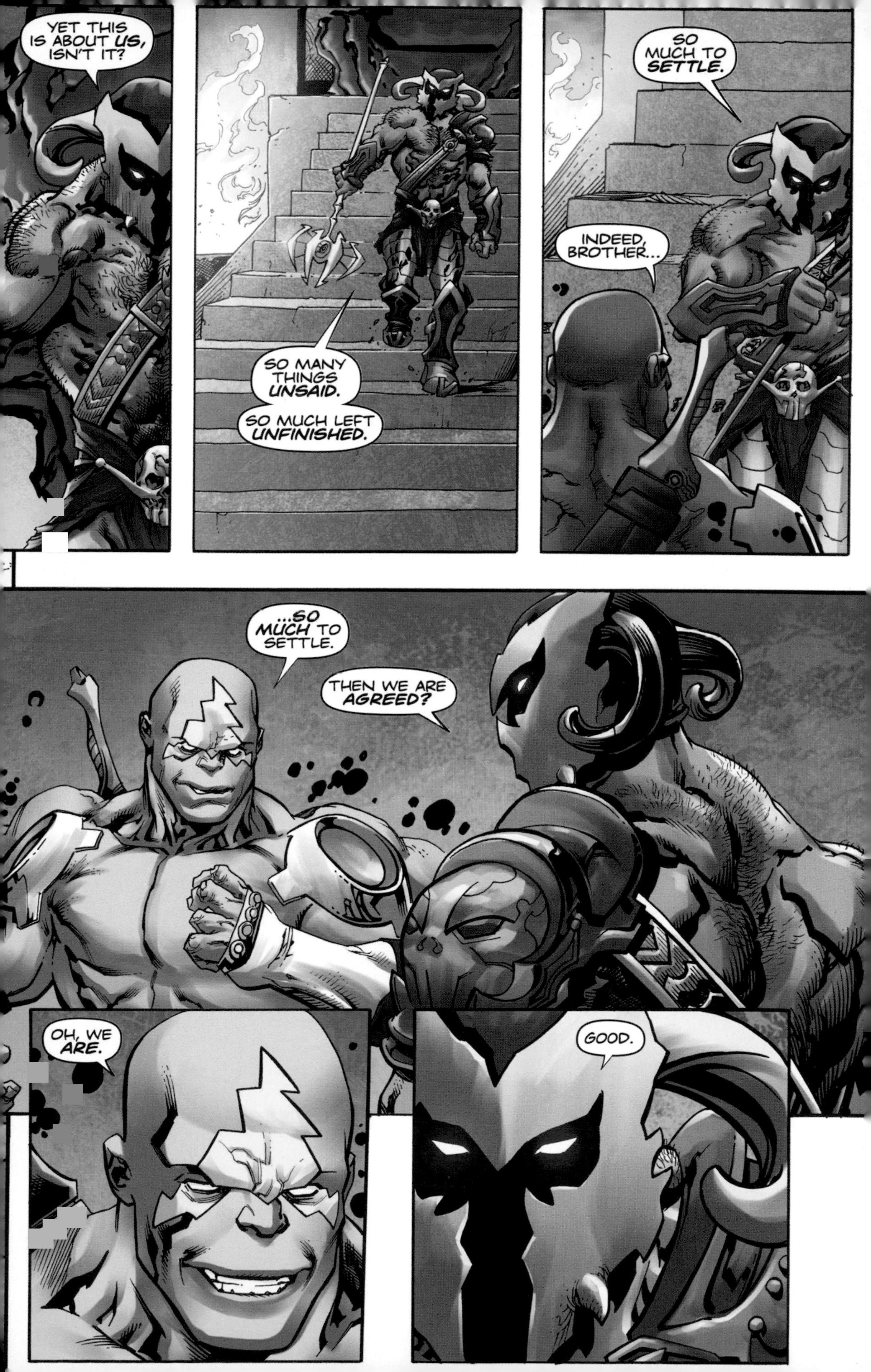
YET THIS IS ABOUT US, ISN'T IT?
SO MANY THINGS UNSAID.
SO MUCH LEFT UNFINISHED.
SO MUCH TO SETTLE.
INDEED, BROTHER...
...SO MUCH TO SETTLE.
THEN WE ARE AGREED?
OH, WE ARE.
GOOD.

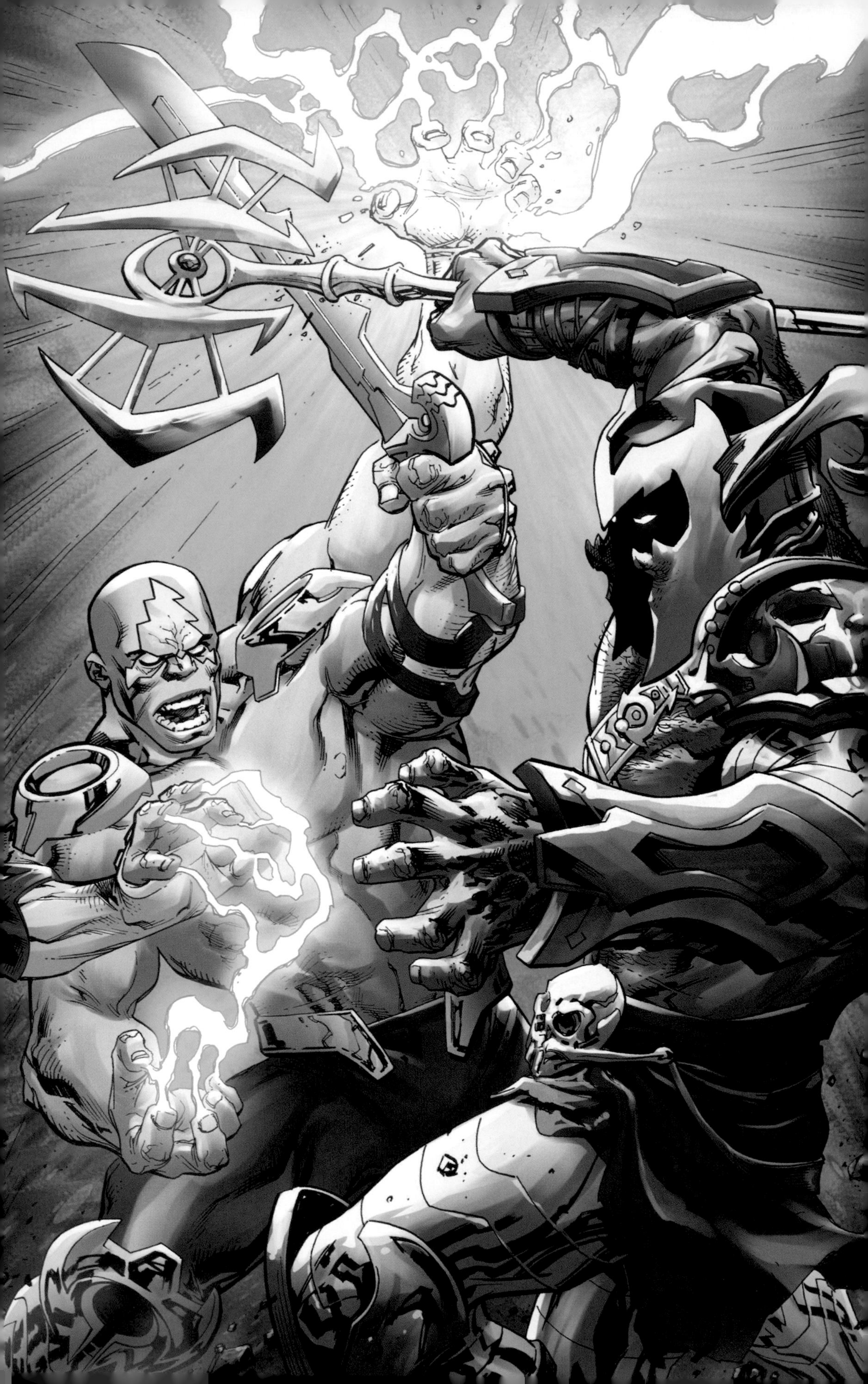

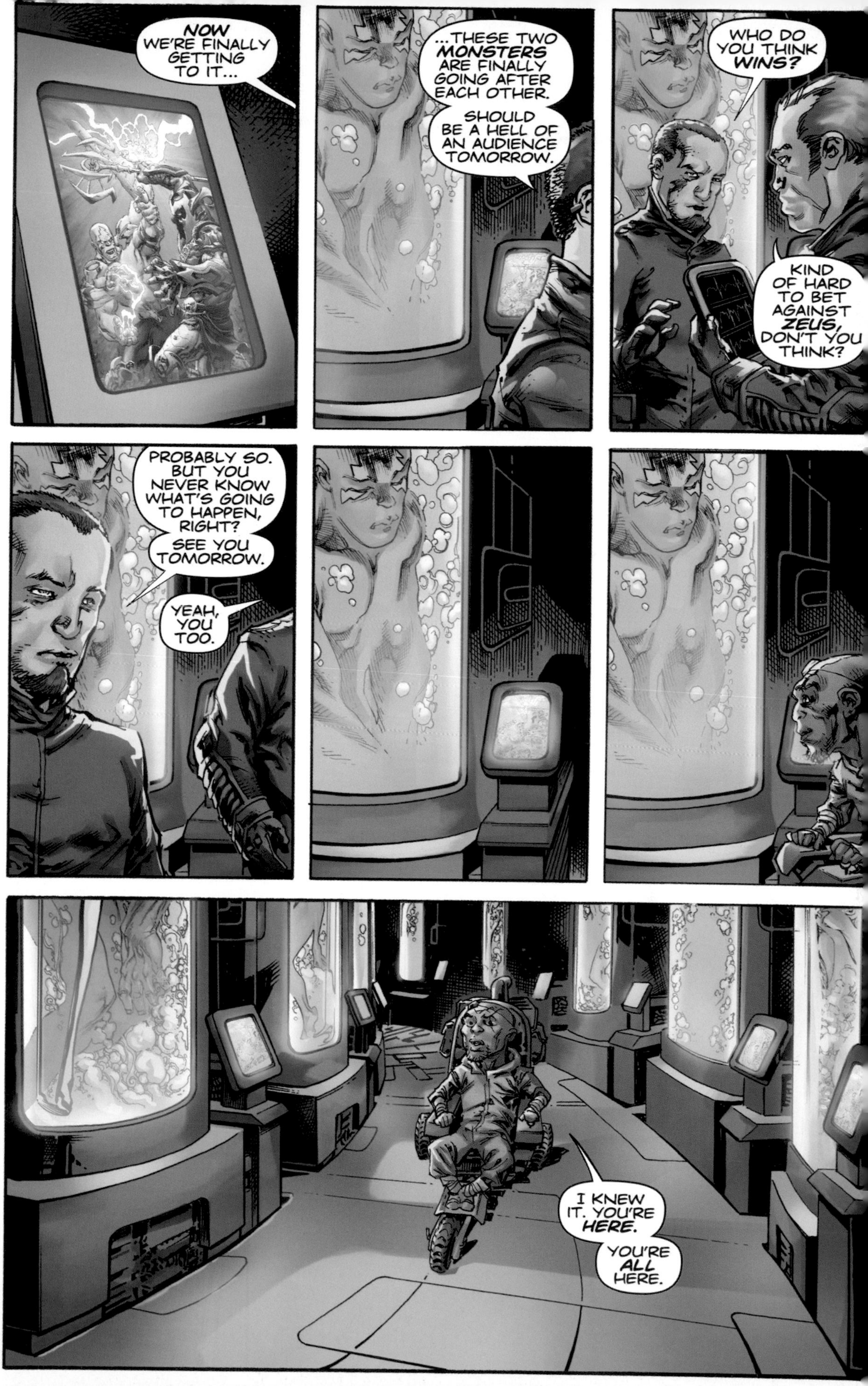

NOW WE'RE FINALLY GETTING TO IT...
...THESE TWO MONSTERS ARE FINALLY GOING AFTER EACH OTHER.
SHOULD BE A HELL OF AN AUDIENCE TOMORROW.
WHO DO YOU THINK WINS?
KIND OF HARD TO BET AGAINST ZEUS, DON'T YOU THINK?
PROBABLY SO. BUT YOU NEVER KNOW WHAT'S GOING TO HAPPEN, RIGHT?
SEE YOU TOMORROW.
YEAH, YOU TOO.
I KNEW IT. YOU'RE HERE.
YOU'RE ALL HERE.

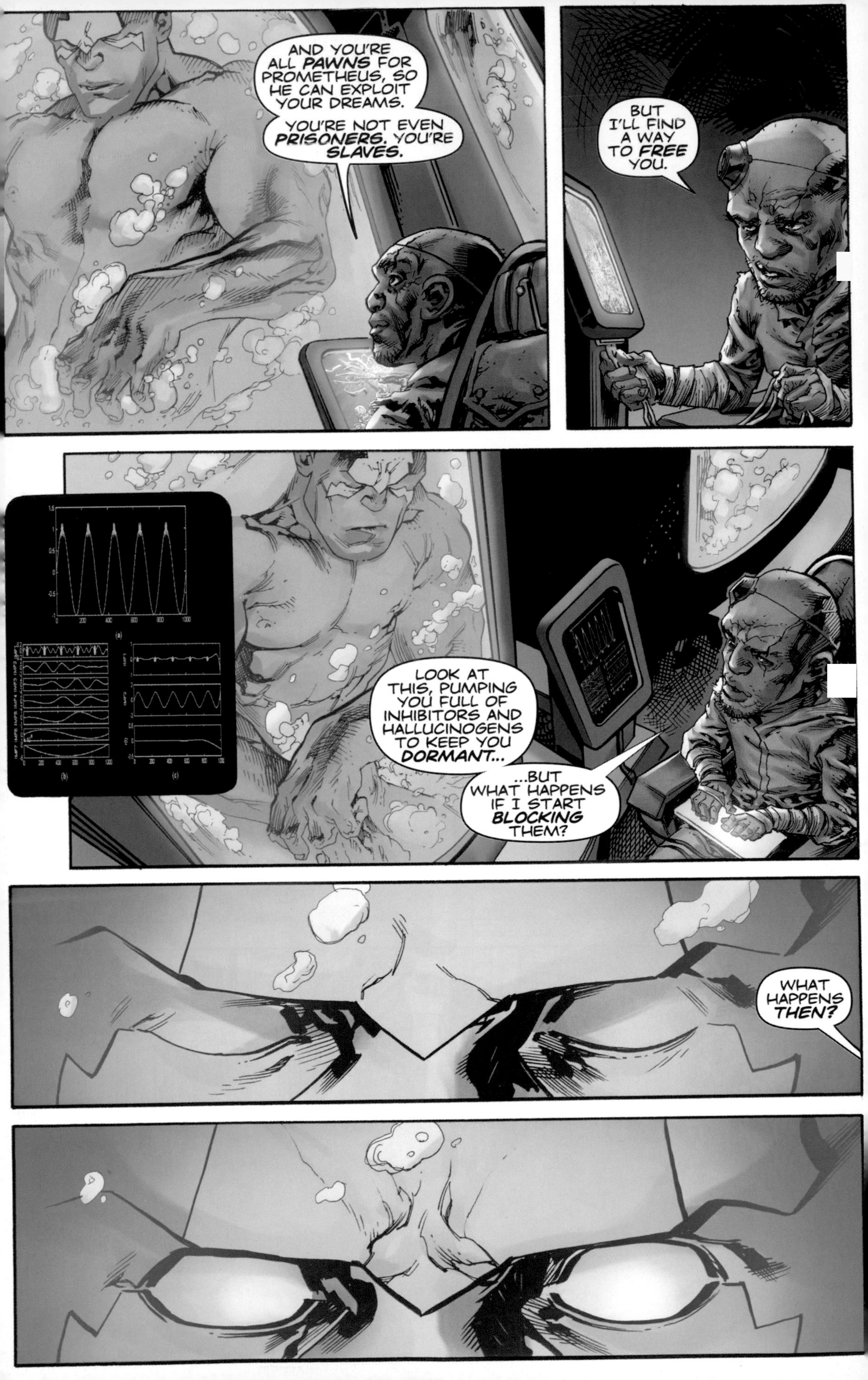
AND YOU'RE ALL PAWNS FOR PROMETHEUS, SO HE CAN EXPLOIT YOUR DREAMS.
YOU'RE NOT EVEN PRISONERS. YOU'RE SLAVES.
BUT I'LL FIND A WAY TO FREE YOU.
LOOK AT THIS, PUMPING YOU FULL OF INHIBITORS AND HALLUCINOGENS TO KEEP YOU DORMANT...
...BUT WHAT HAPPENS IF I START BLOCKING THEM?
WHAT HAPPENS THEN?

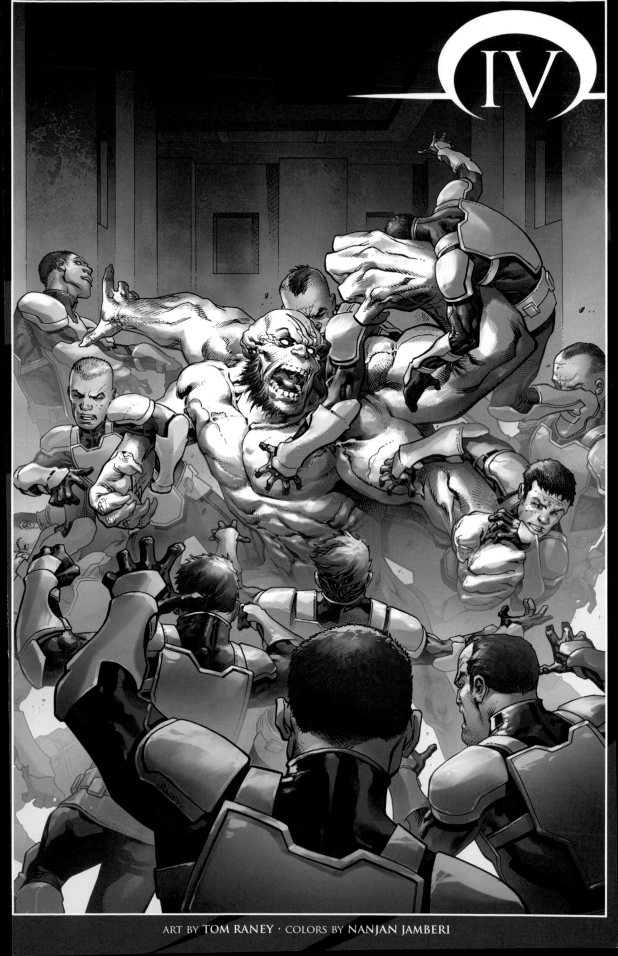

ART BY **TOM RANEY** · COLORS BY **NANJAN JAMBERI**

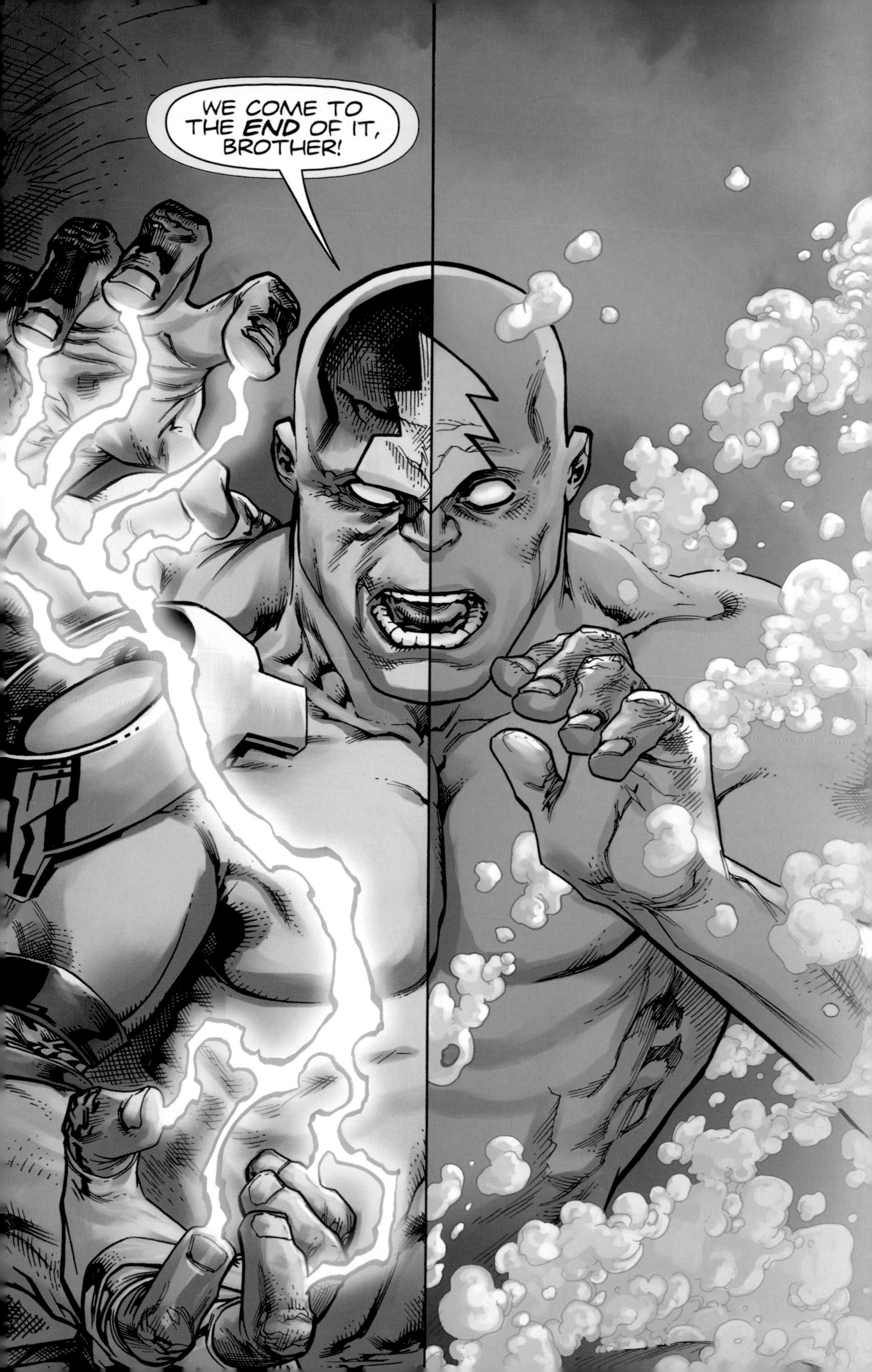
WE COME TO THE END OF IT, BROTHER!

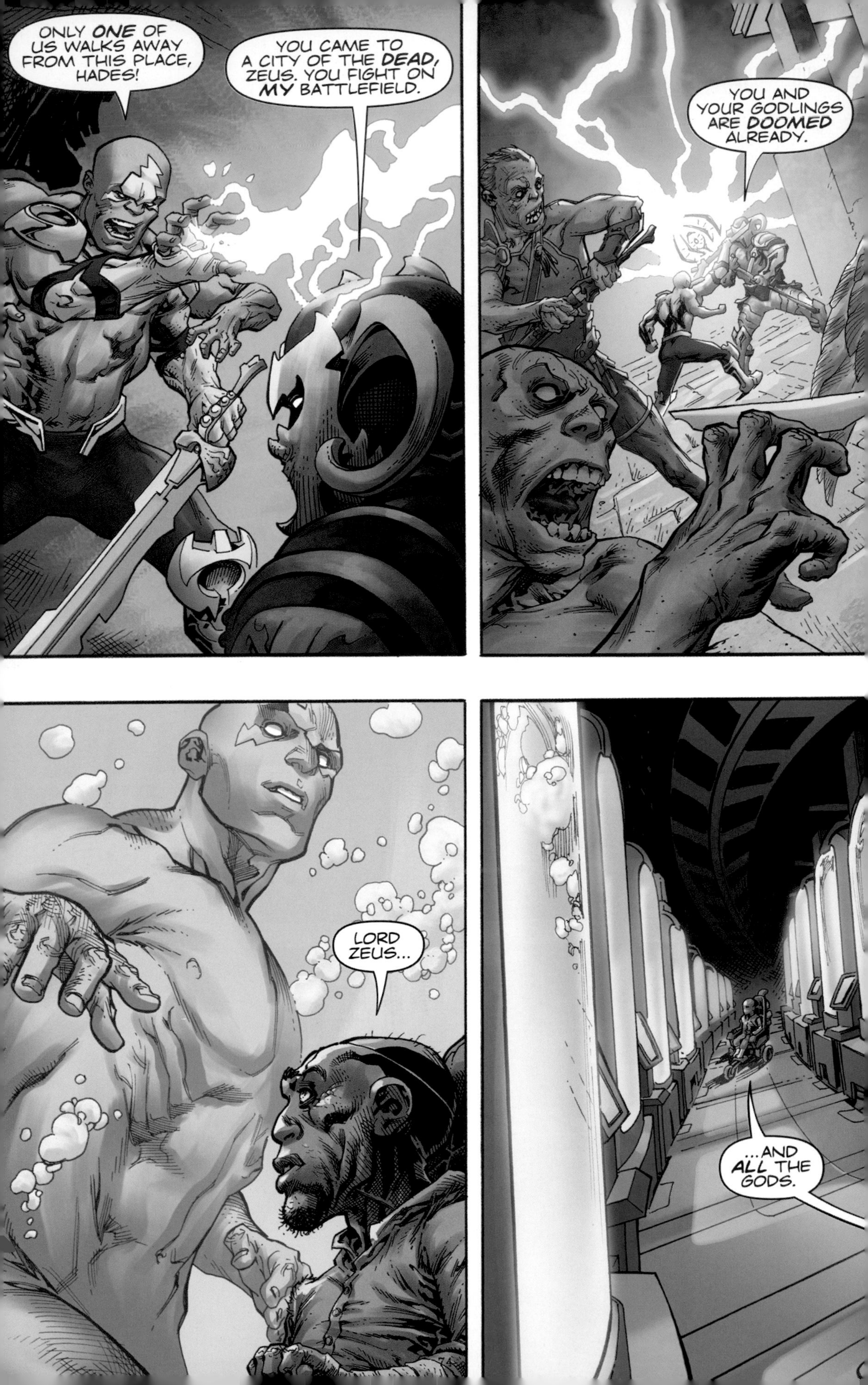
ONLY ONE OF US WALKS AWAY FROM THIS PLACE, HADES!
YOU CAME TO A CITY OF THE DEAD, ZEUS. YOU FIGHT ON MY BATTLEFIELD.
YOU AND YOUR GODLINGS ARE DOOMED ALREADY.
LORD ZEUS...
...AND ALL THE GODS.

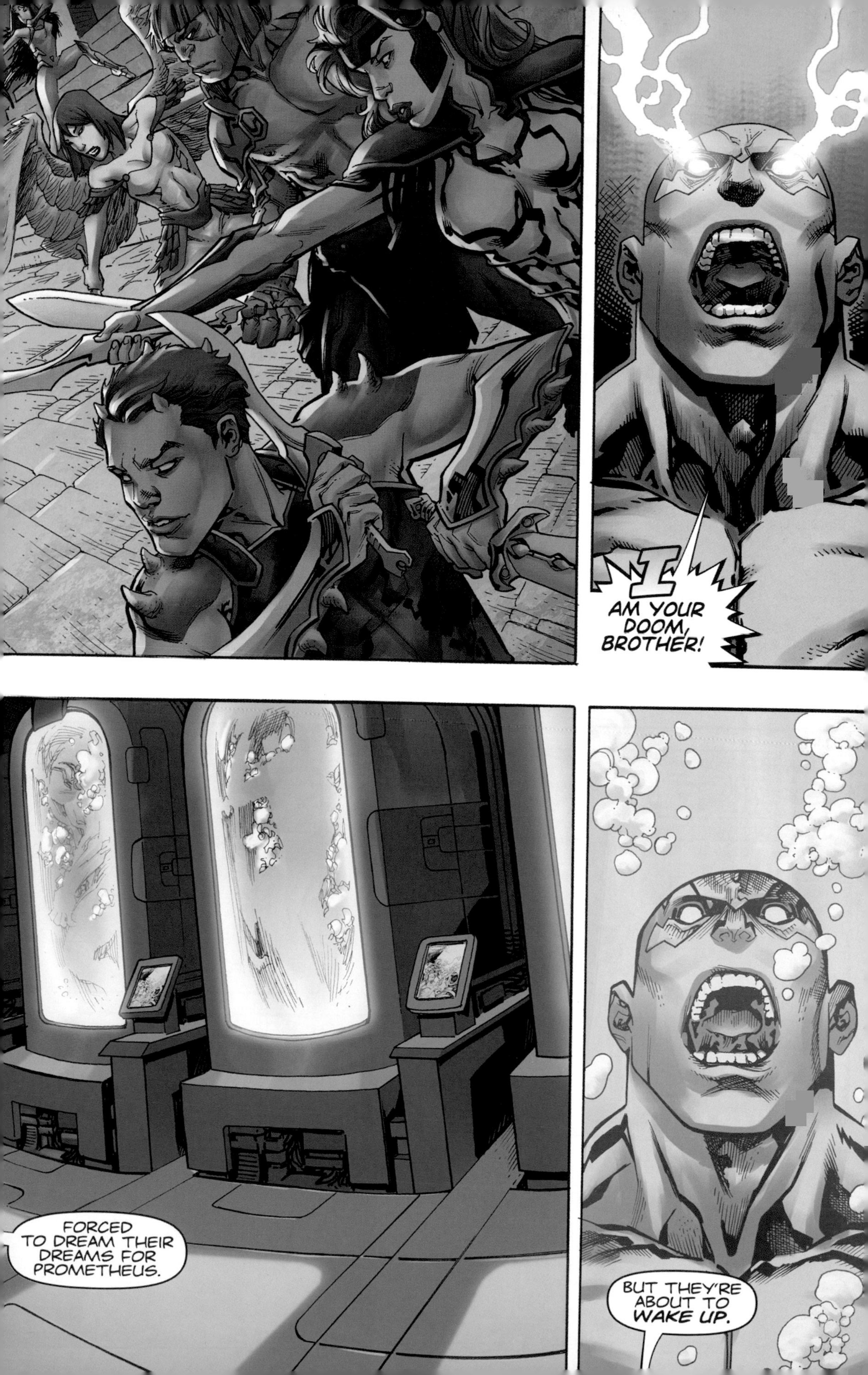
I AM YOUR DOOM, BROTHER!
FORCED TO DREAM THEIR DREAMS FOR PROMETHEUS.
BUT THEY'RE ABOUT TO WAKE UP.

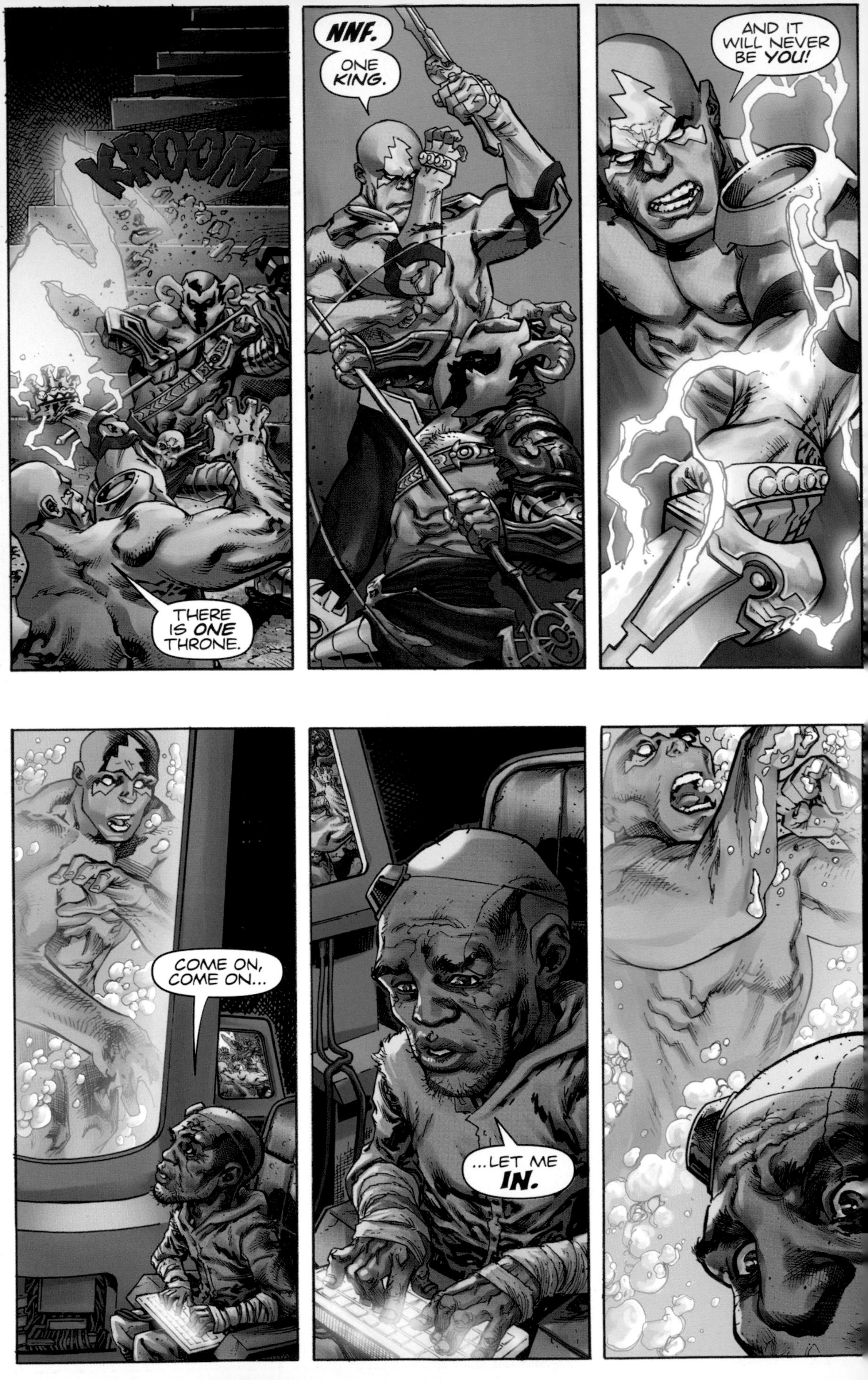
KROOM
THERE IS ONE THRONE.
NNF.
ONE KING.
AND IT WILL NEVER BE YOU!
COME ON, COME ON...
...LET ME IN.

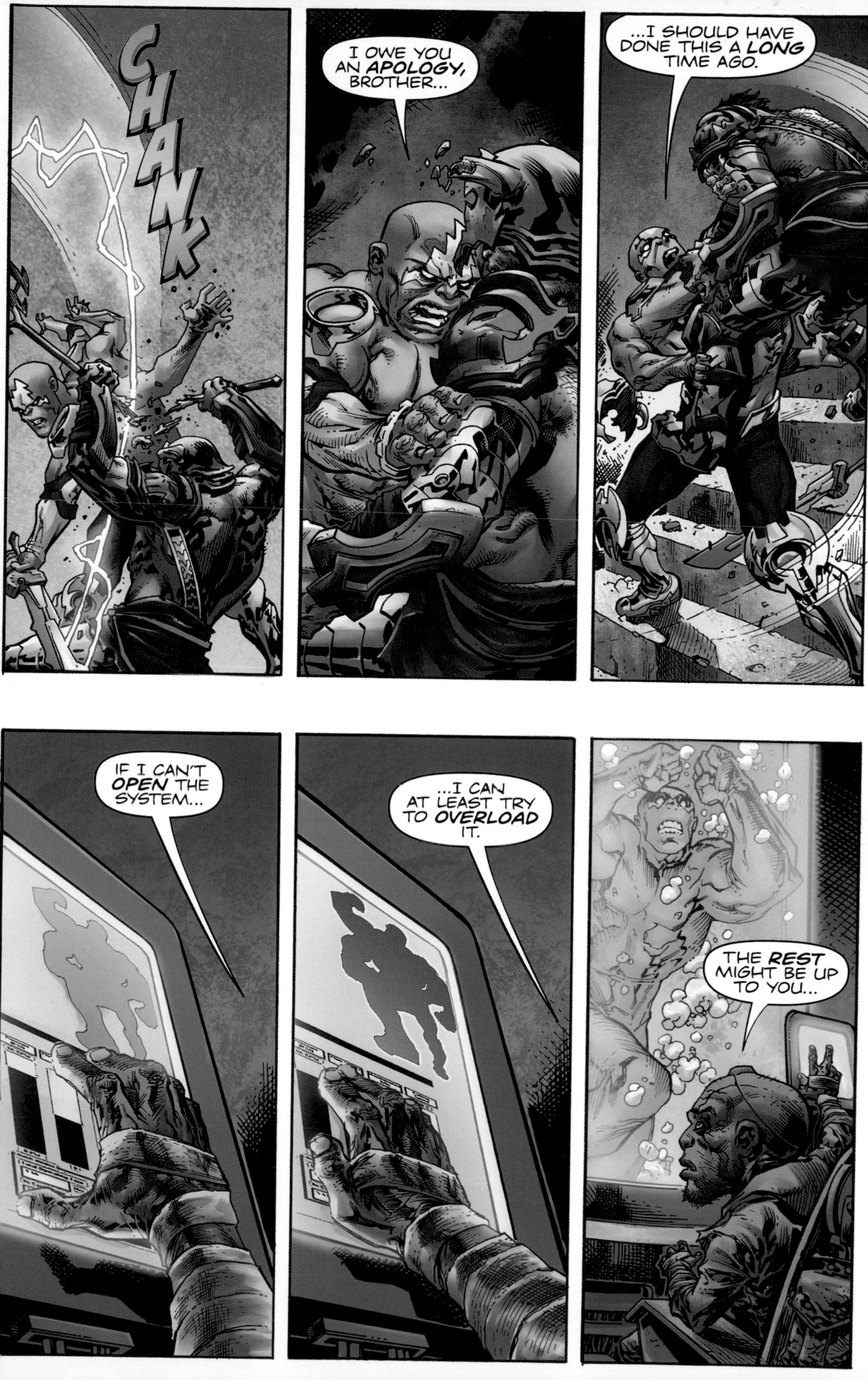
CHANK
I OWE YOU AN APOLOGY, BROTHER...
...I SHOULD HAVE DONE THIS A LONG TIME AGO.
IF I CAN'T OPEN THE SYSTEM...
...I CAN AT LEAST TRY TO OVERLOAD IT.
THE REST MIGHT BE UP TO YOU...

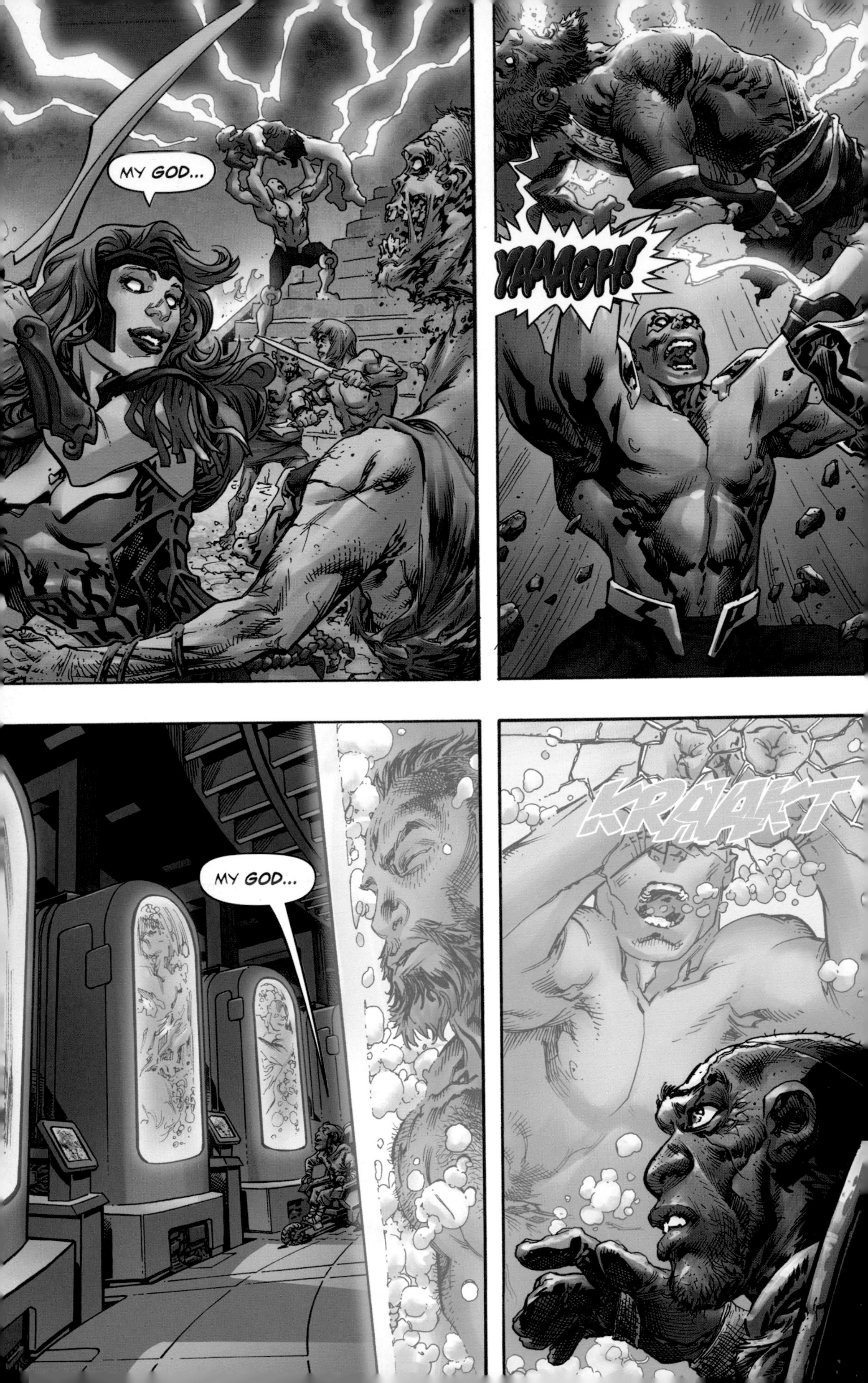
MY GOD...
YAAAGH!
MY GOD...
KRAAKT

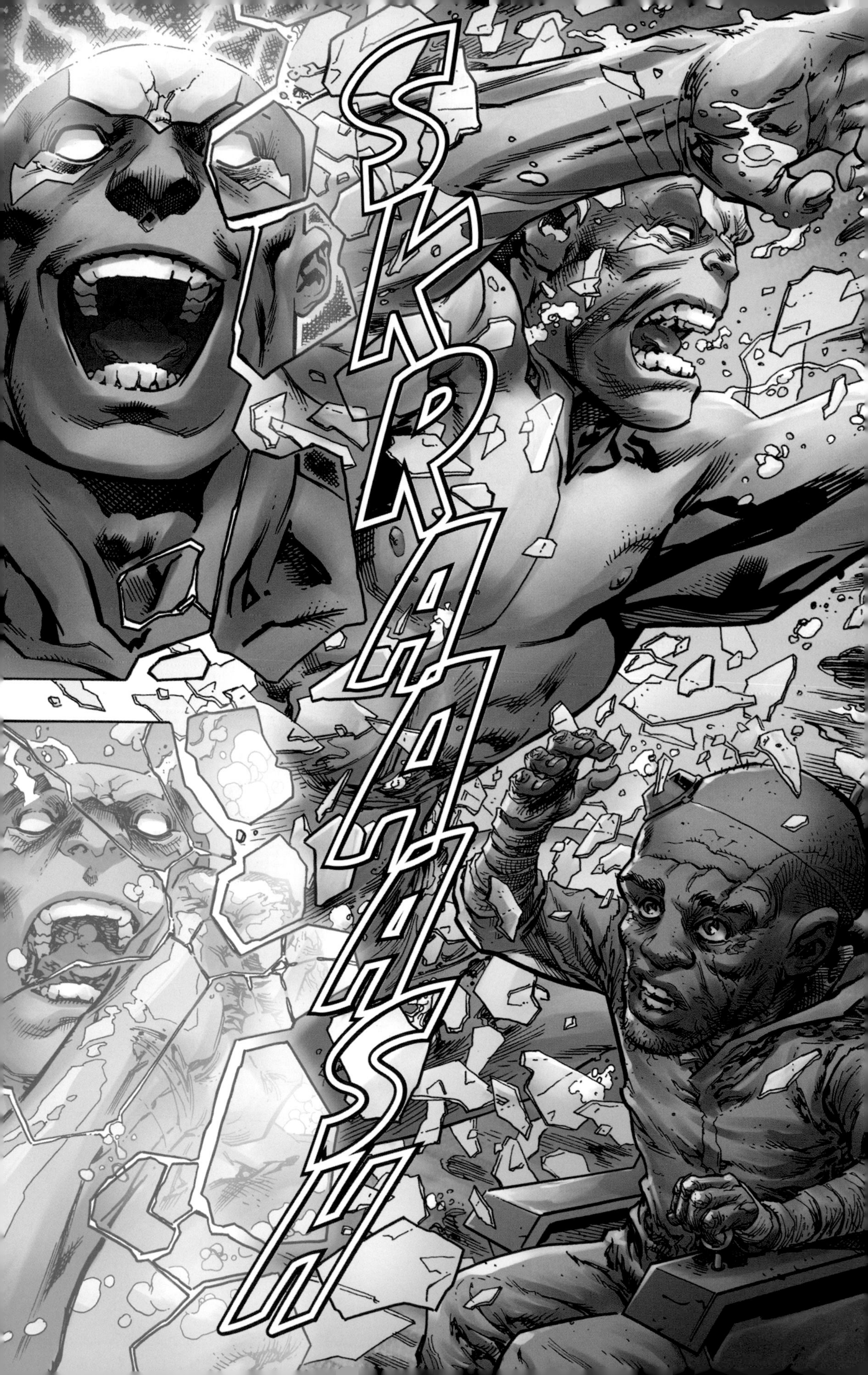
SKRAAASH

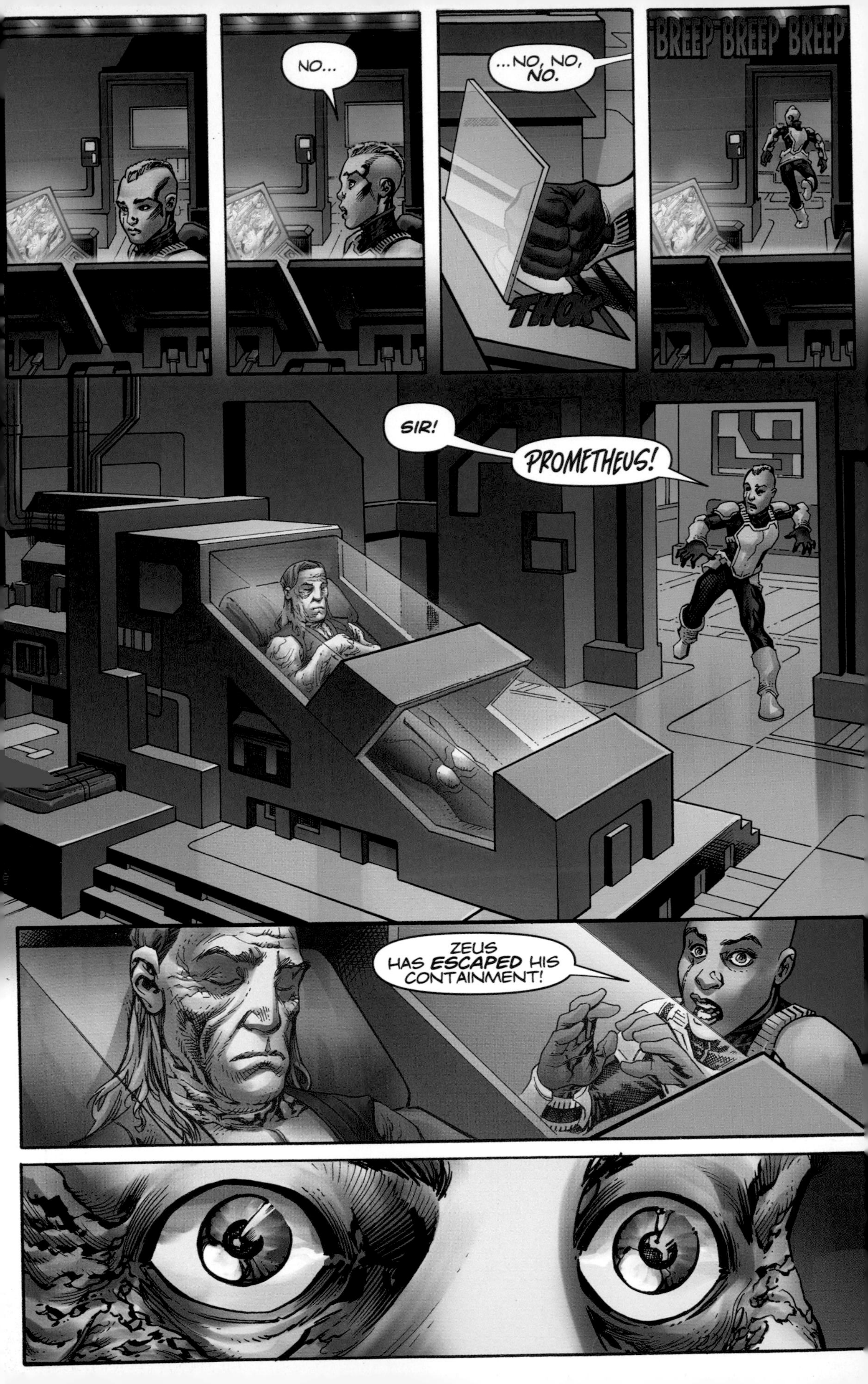

NO...
...NO, NO, NO.
THOK
BREEP BREEP BREEP
SIR!
PROMETHEUS!
ZEUS HAS ESCAPED HIS CONTAINMENT!

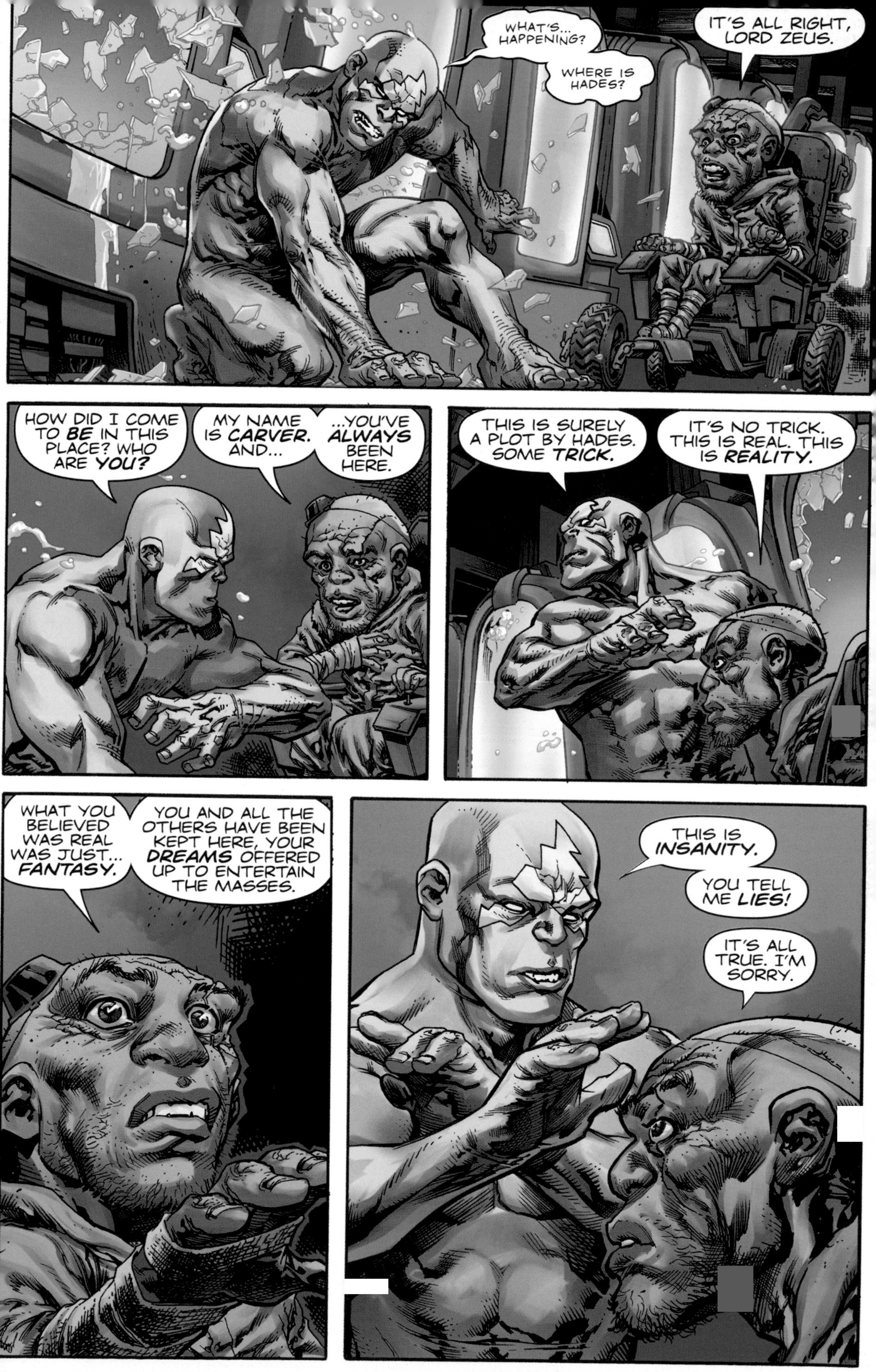
WHAT'S... HAPPENING?
WHERE IS HADES?
IT'S ALL RIGHT, LORD ZEUS.
HOW DID I COME TO BE IN THIS PLACE? WHO ARE YOU?
MY NAME IS CARVER. AND...
...YOU'VE ALWAYS BEEN HERE.
THIS IS SURELY A PLOT BY HADES. SOME TRICK.
IT'S NO TRICK. THIS IS REAL. THIS IS REALITY.
WHAT YOU BELIEVED WAS REAL WAS JUST... FANTASY.
YOU AND ALL THE OTHERS HAVE BEEN KEPT HERE, YOUR DREAMS OFFERED UP TO ENTERTAIN THE MASSES.
THIS IS INSANITY.
YOU TELL ME LIES!
IT'S ALL TRUE. I'M SORRY.

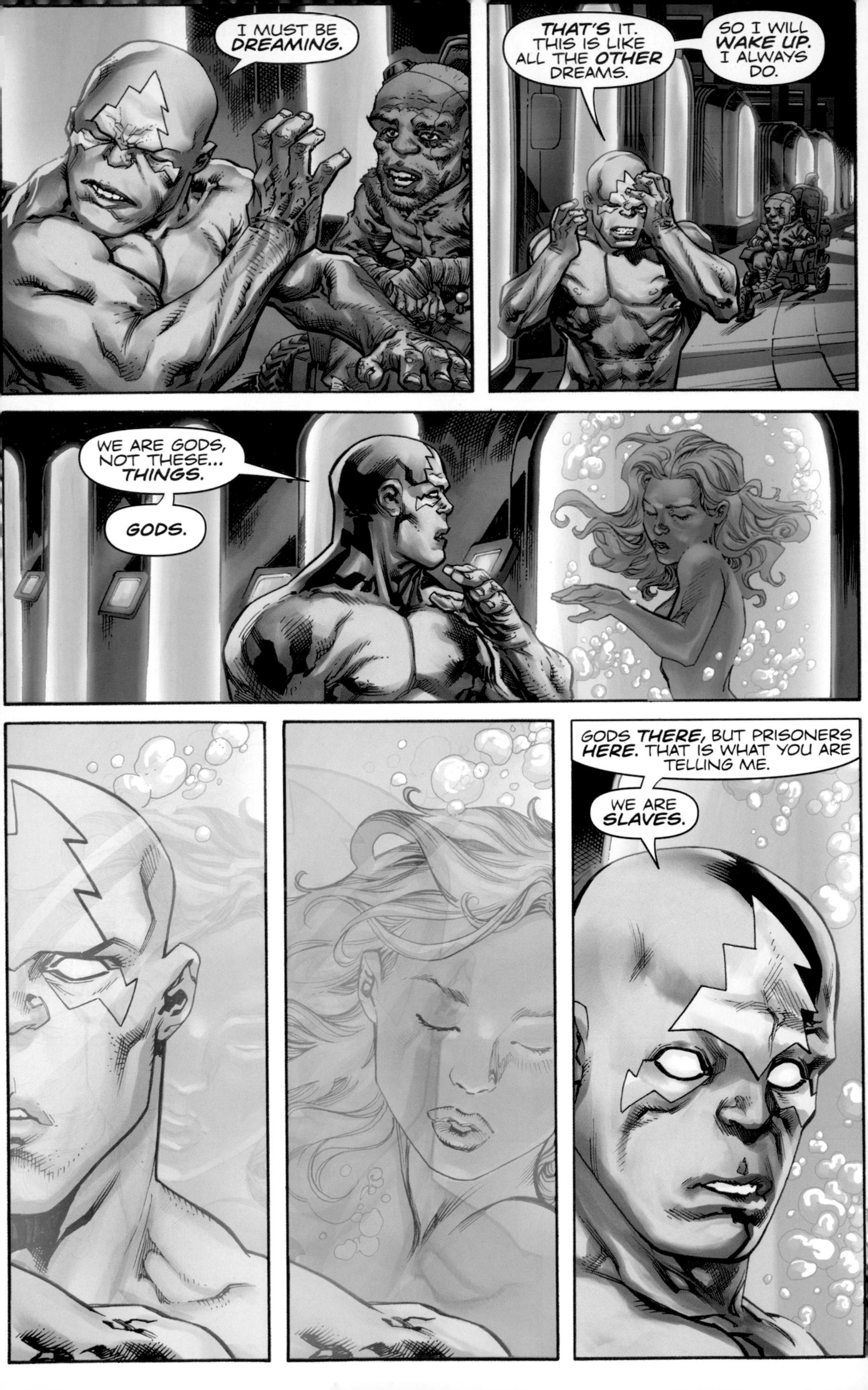
I MUST BE DREAMING.
THAT'S IT. THIS IS LIKE ALL THE OTHER DREAMS.
SO I WILL WAKE UP. I ALWAYS DO.
WE ARE GODS, NOT THESE... THINGS.
GODS.
GODS THERE, BUT PRISONERS HERE. THAT IS WHAT YOU ARE TELLING ME.
WE ARE SLAVES.

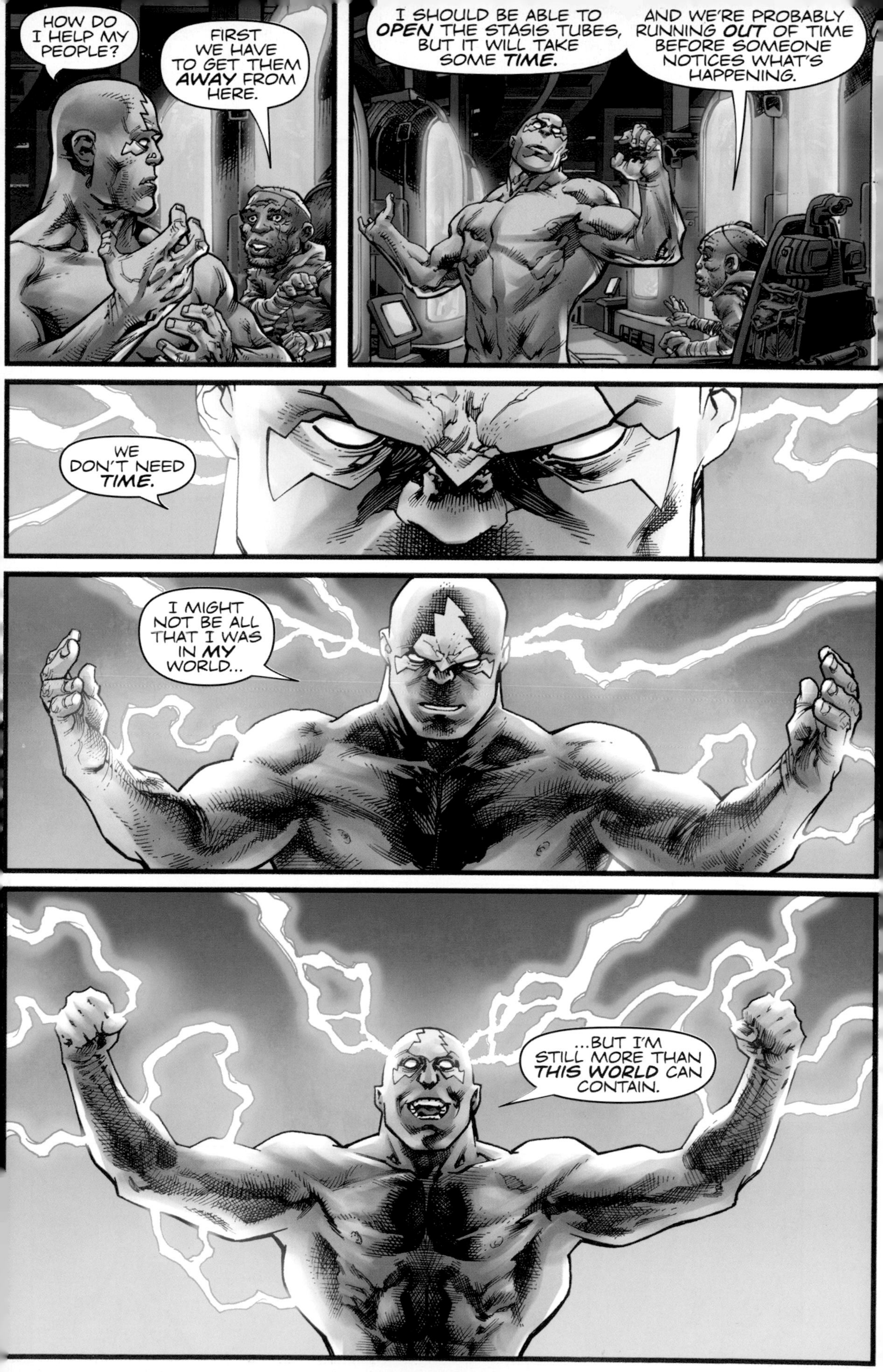
HOW DO I HELP MY PEOPLE?
FIRST WE HAVE TO GET THEM AWAY FROM HERE.
I SHOULD BE ABLE TO OPEN THE STASIS TUBES, BUT IT WILL TAKE SOME TIME.
AND WE'RE PROBABLY RUNNING OUT OF TIME BEFORE SOMEONE NOTICES WHAT'S HAPPENING.
WE DON'T NEED TIME.
I MIGHT NOT BE ALL THAT I WAS IN MY WORLD...
...BUT I'M STILL MORE THAN THIS WORLD CAN CONTAIN.

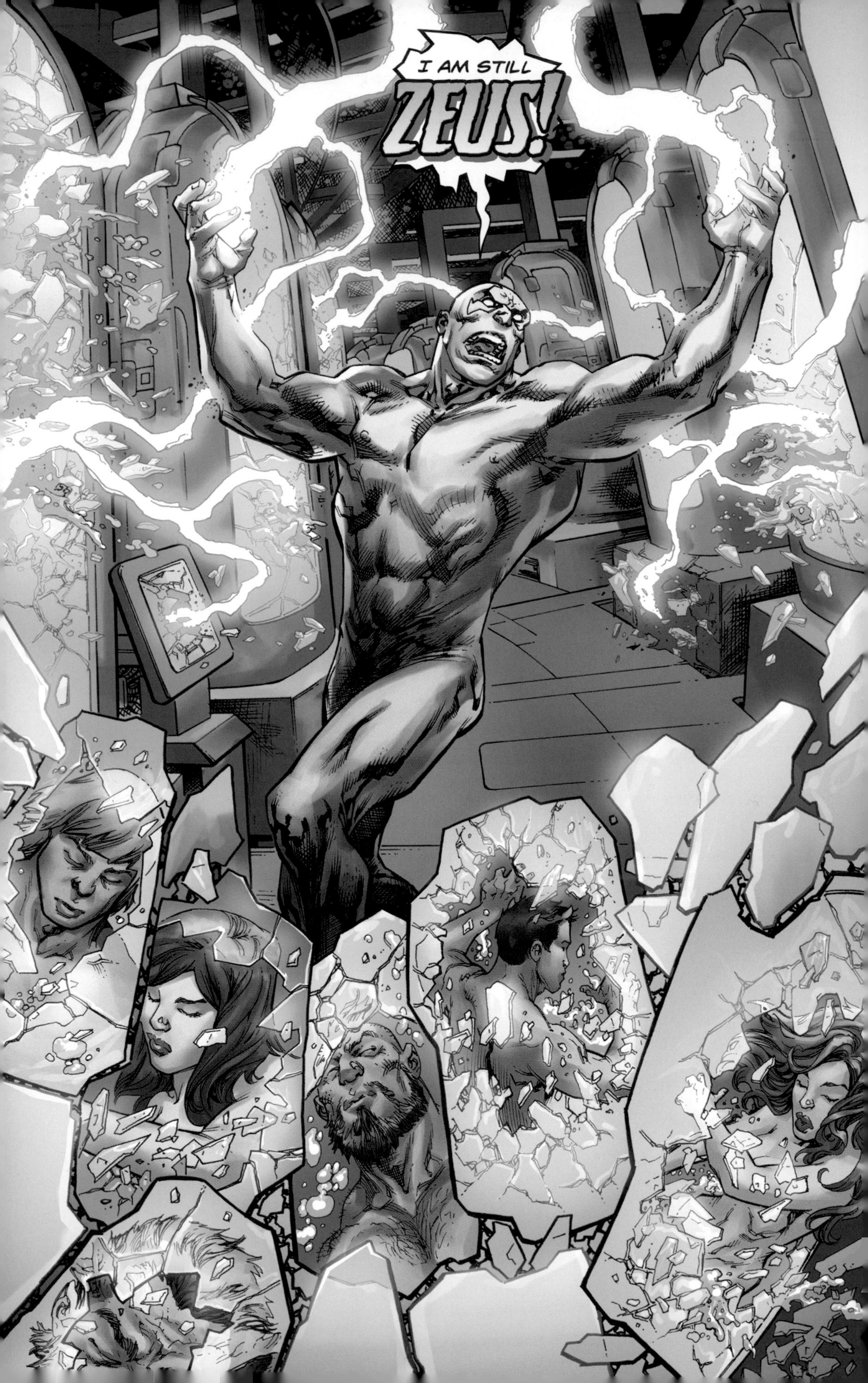
I AM STILL
ZEUS!

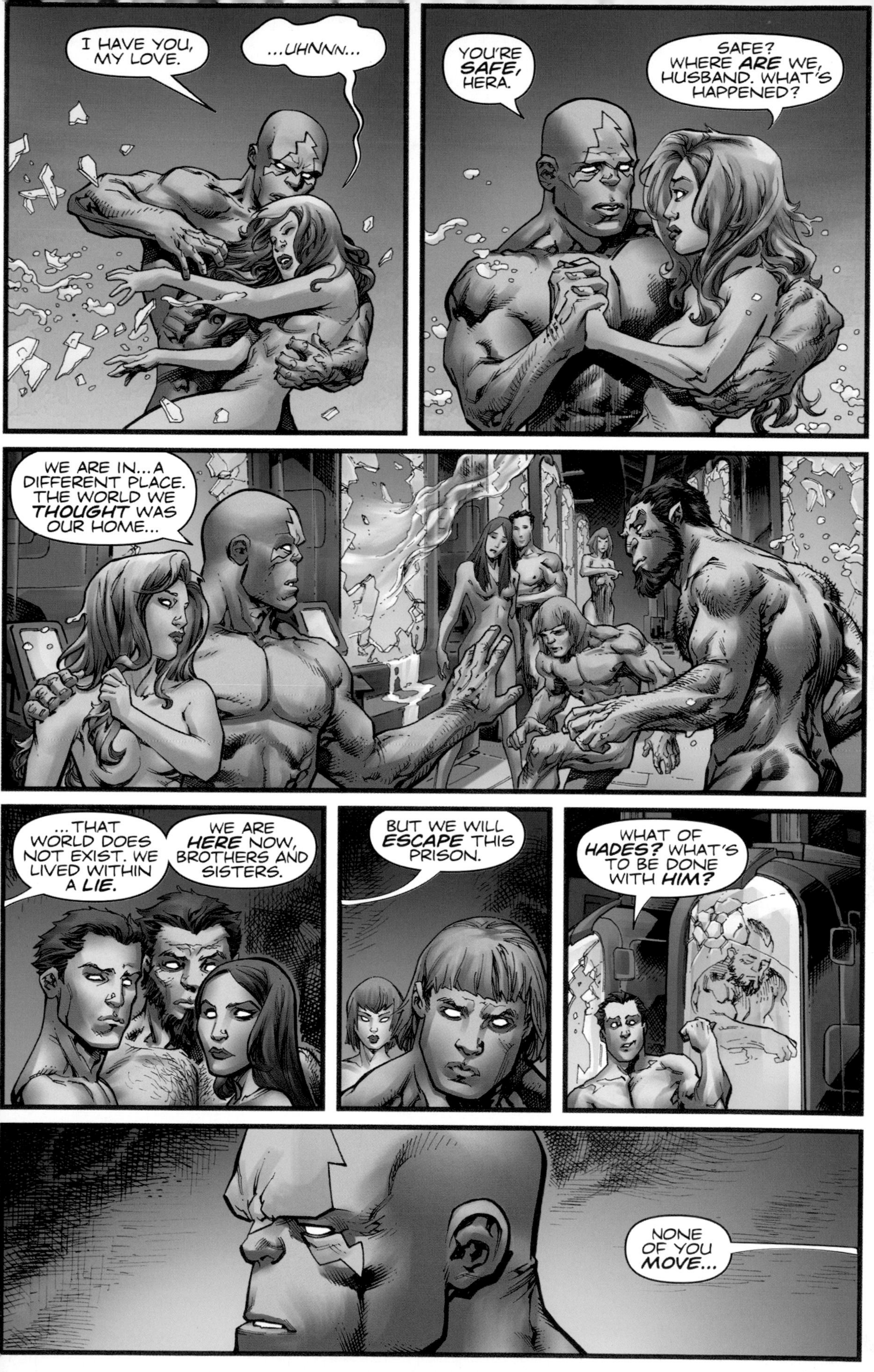
I HAVE YOU, MY LOVE.
...UHNNN...
YOU'RE **SAFE,** HERA.
SAFE? WHERE **ARE** WE, HUSBAND. WHAT'S HAPPENED?
WE ARE IN... A DIFFERENT PLACE. THE WORLD WE **THOUGHT** WAS OUR HOME...
...THAT WORLD DOES NOT EXIST. WE LIVED WITHIN A **LIE.**
WE ARE **HERE** NOW, BROTHERS AND SISTERS.
BUT WE WILL **ESCAPE** THIS PRISON.
WHAT OF **HADES?** WHAT'S TO BE DONE WITH **HIM?**
NONE OF YOU **MOVE...**

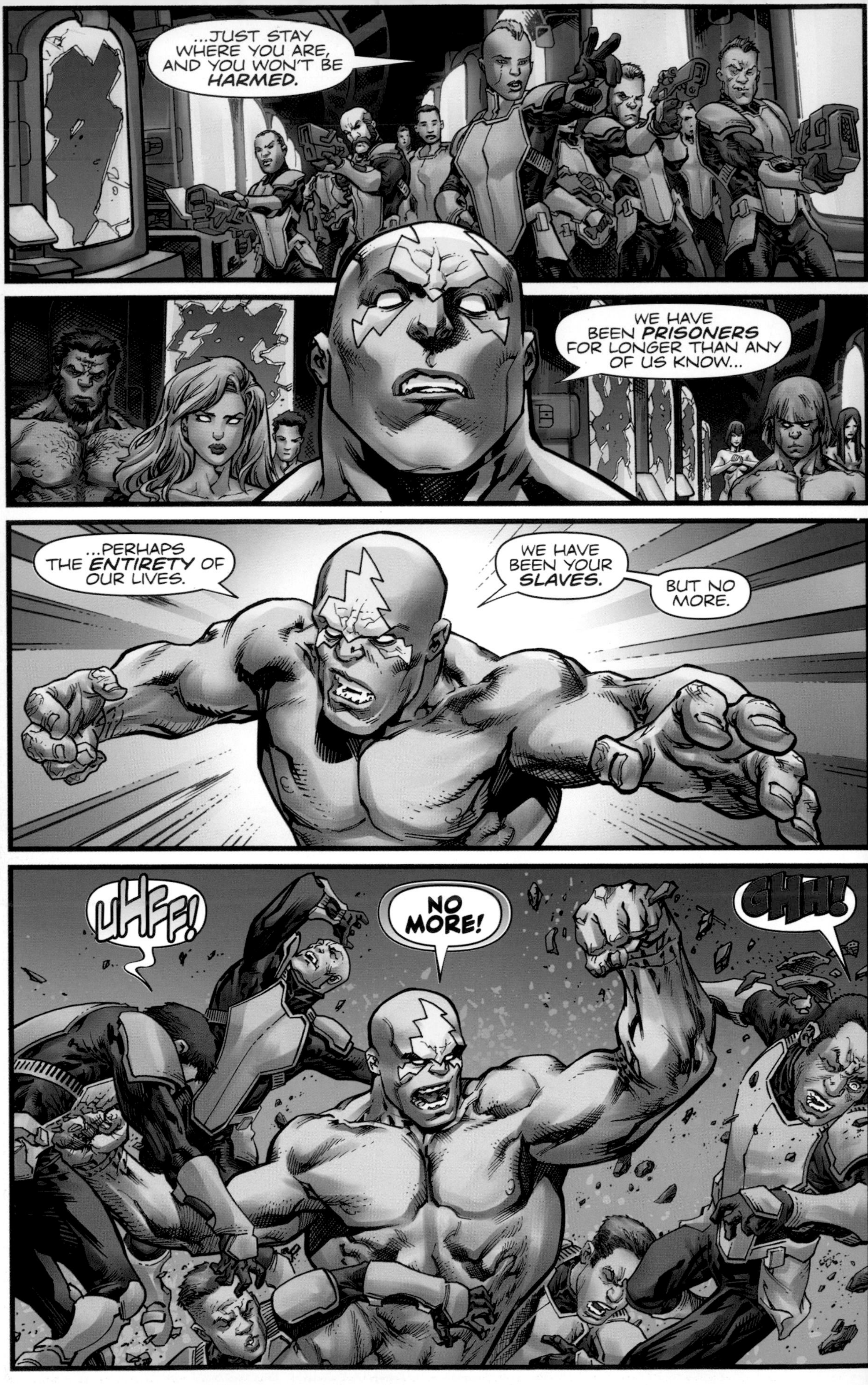

...JUST STAY WHERE YOU ARE, AND YOU WON'T BE HARMED.
WE HAVE BEEN PRISONERS FOR LONGER THAN ANY OF US KNOW...
...PERHAPS THE ENTIRETY OF OUR LIVES.
WE HAVE BEEN YOUR SLAVES.
BUT NO MORE.
UHFF!
NO MORE!
GHH!

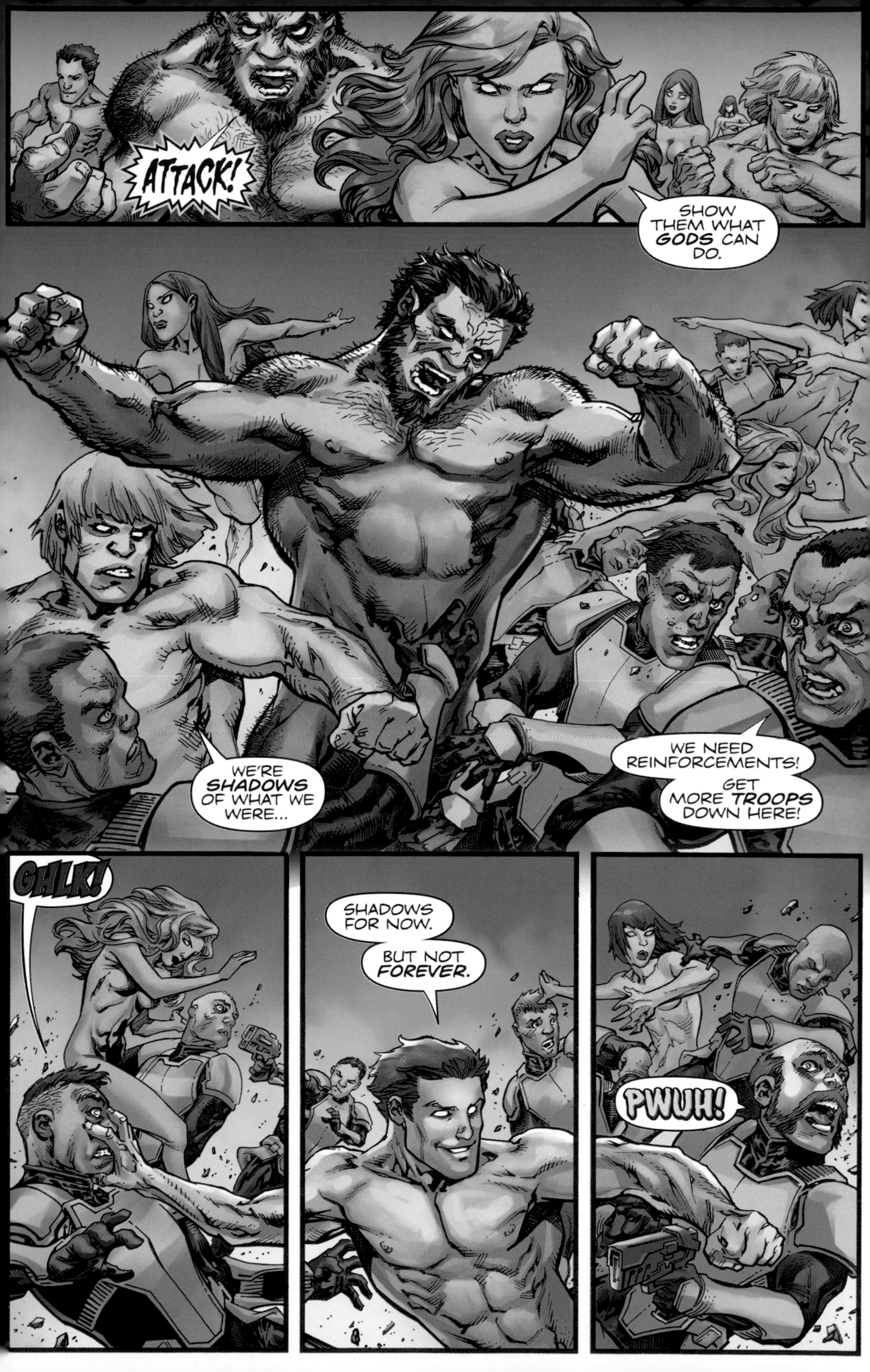
ATTACK!
SHOW THEM WHAT GODS CAN DO.
WE'RE SHADOWS OF WHAT WE WERE...
WE NEED REINFORCEMENTS!
GET MORE TROOPS DOWN HERE!
GHLK!
SHADOWS FOR NOW.
BUT NOT FOREVER.
PWUH!

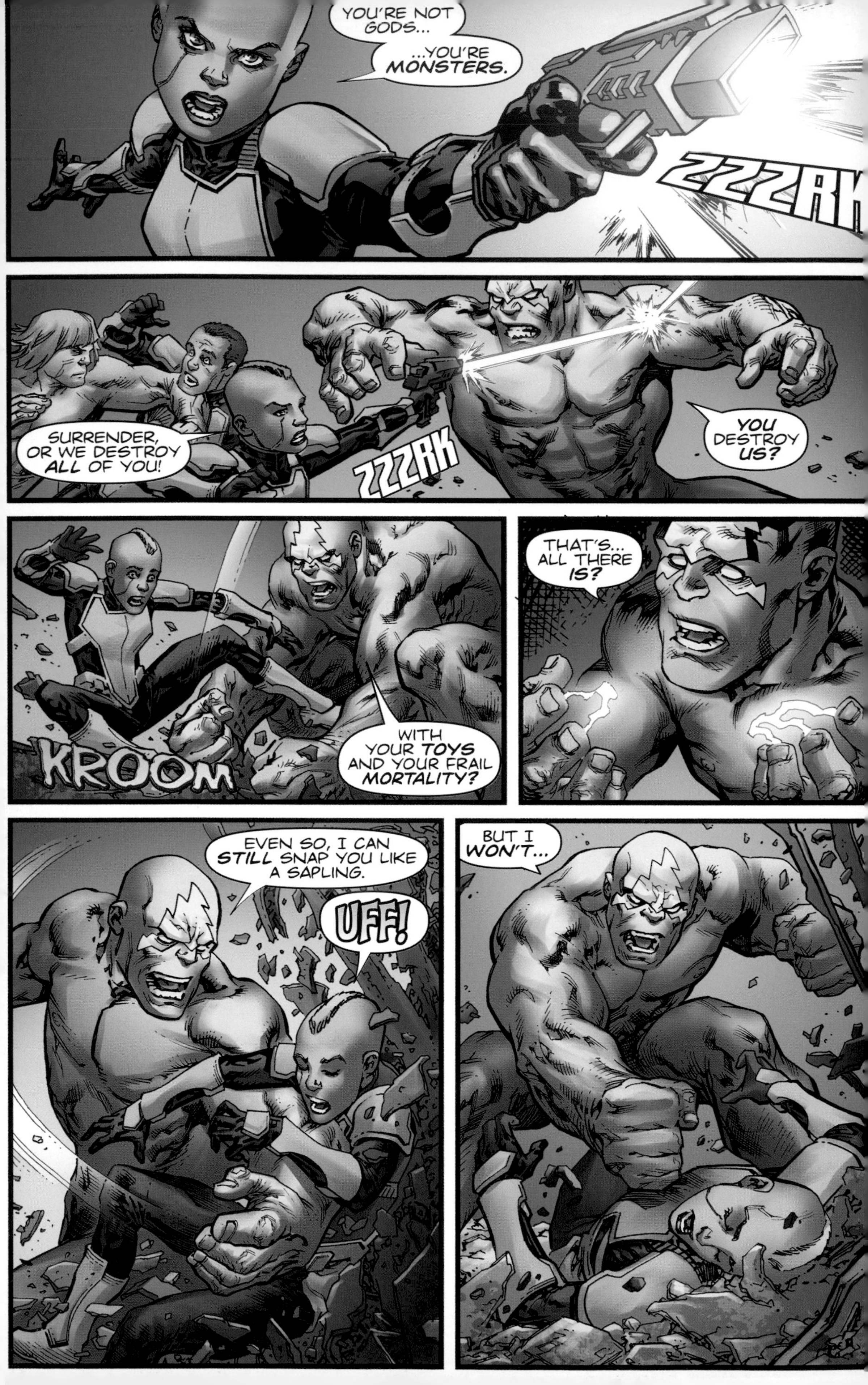

YOU'RE NOT GODS...
...YOU'RE MONSTERS.
ZZZRK
SURRENDER, OR WE DESTROY ALL OF YOU!
ZZZRK
YOU DESTROY US?
KROOM
WITH YOUR TOYS AND YOUR FRAIL MORTALITY?
THAT'S... ALL THERE IS?
EVEN SO, I CAN STILL SNAP YOU LIKE A SAPLING.
UFF!
BUT I WON'T...

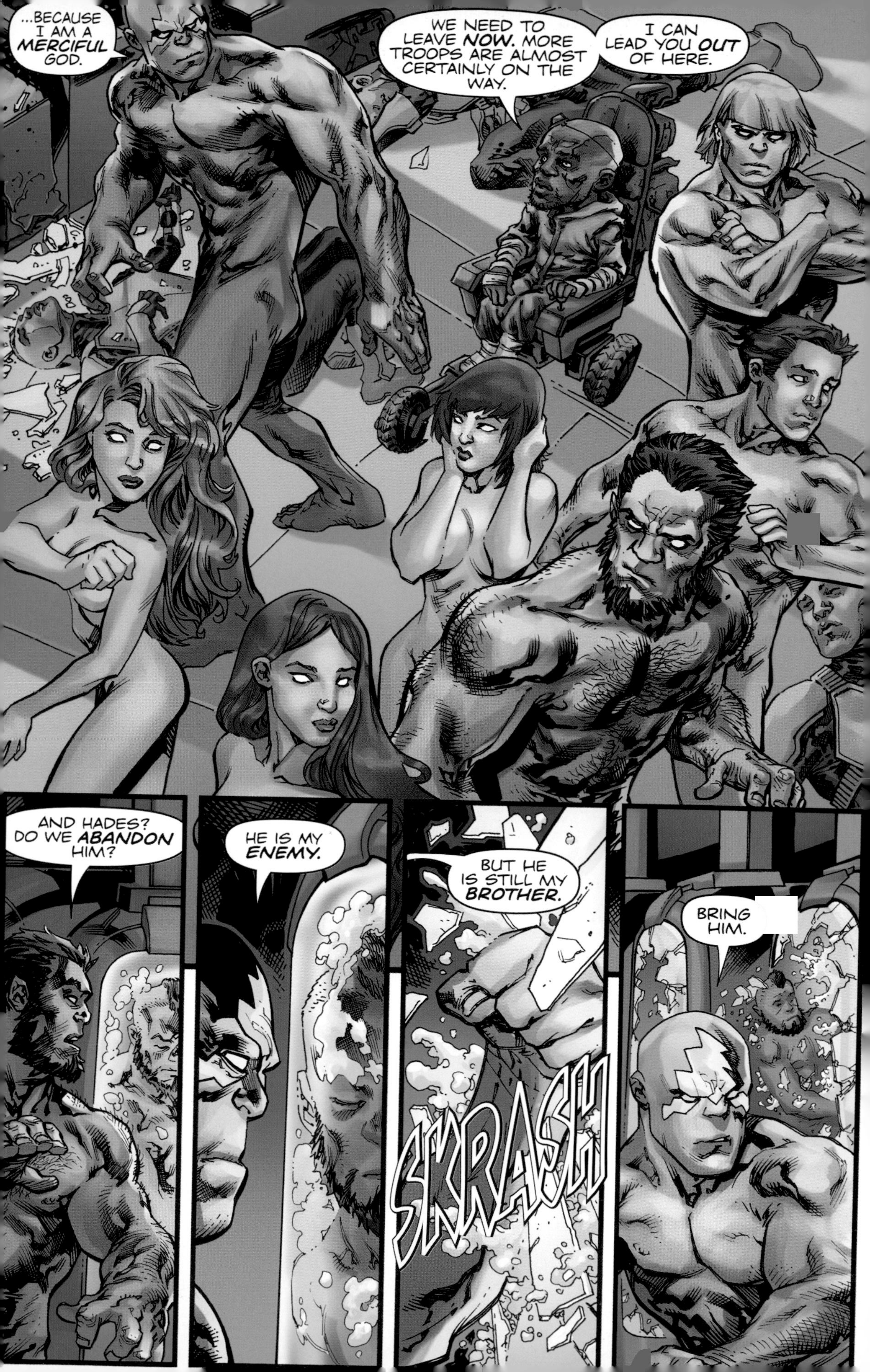
...BECAUSE I AM A MERCIFUL GOD.
WE NEED TO LEAVE NOW. MORE TROOPS ARE ALMOST CERTAINLY ON THE WAY.
I CAN LEAD YOU OUT OF HERE.
AND HADES? DO WE ABANDON HIM?
HE IS MY ENEMY.
BUT HE IS STILL MY BROTHER.
SKRASH
BRING HIM.

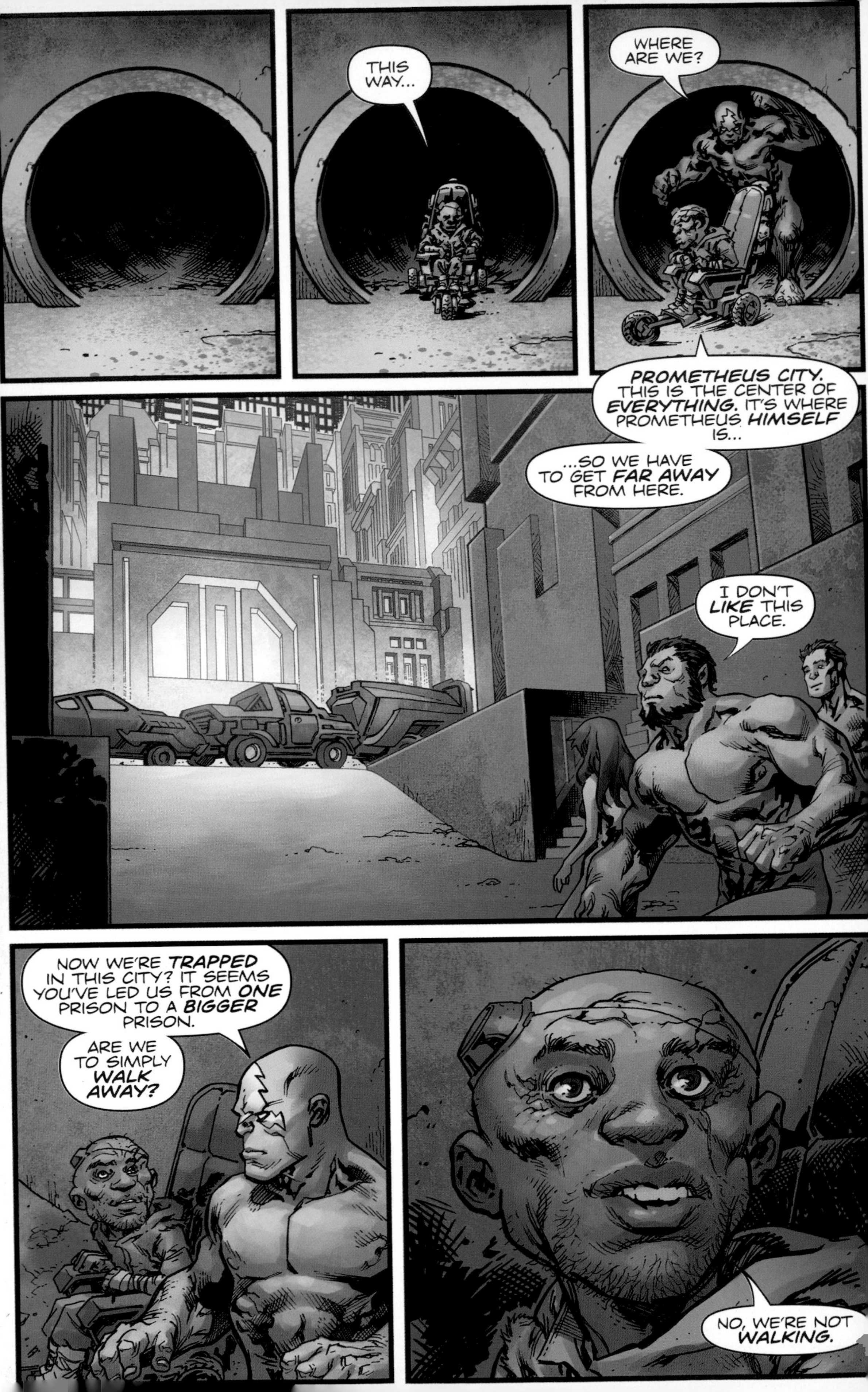

THIS WAY...
WHERE ARE WE?
PROMETHEUS CITY. THIS IS THE CENTER OF EVERYTHING. IT'S WHERE PROMETHEUS HIMSELF IS...
...SO WE HAVE TO GET FAR AWAY FROM HERE.
I DON'T LIKE THIS PLACE.
NOW WE'RE TRAPPED IN THIS CITY? IT SEEMS YOU'VE LED US FROM ONE PRISON TO A BIGGER PRISON.
ARE WE TO SIMPLY WALK AWAY?
NO, WE'RE NOT WALKING.

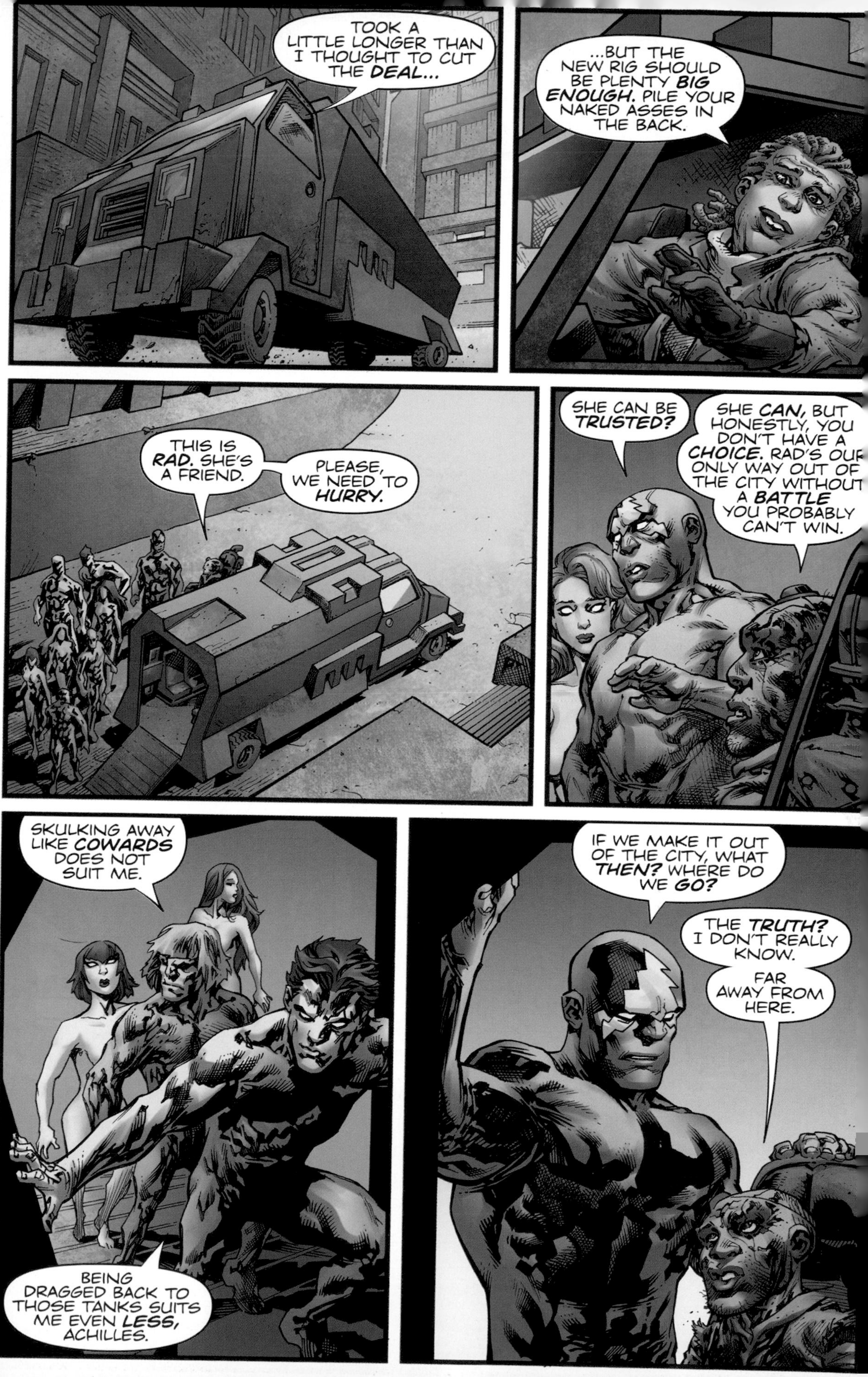

TOOK A LITTLE LONGER THAN I THOUGHT TO CUT THE DEAL...
...BUT THE NEW RIG SHOULD BE PLENTY BIG ENOUGH. PILE YOUR NAKED ASSES IN THE BACK.
THIS IS RAD. SHE'S A FRIEND.
PLEASE, WE NEED TO HURRY.
SHE CAN BE TRUSTED?
SHE CAN, BUT HONESTLY, YOU DON'T HAVE A CHOICE. RAD'S OUR ONLY WAY OUT OF THE CITY WITHOUT A BATTLE YOU PROBABLY CAN'T WIN.
SKULKING AWAY LIKE COWARDS DOES NOT SUIT ME.
BEING DRAGGED BACK TO THOSE TANKS SUITS ME EVEN LESS, ACHILLES.
IF WE MAKE IT OUT OF THE CITY, WHAT THEN? WHERE DO WE GO?
THE TRUTH? I DON'T REALLY KNOW.
FAR AWAY FROM HERE.

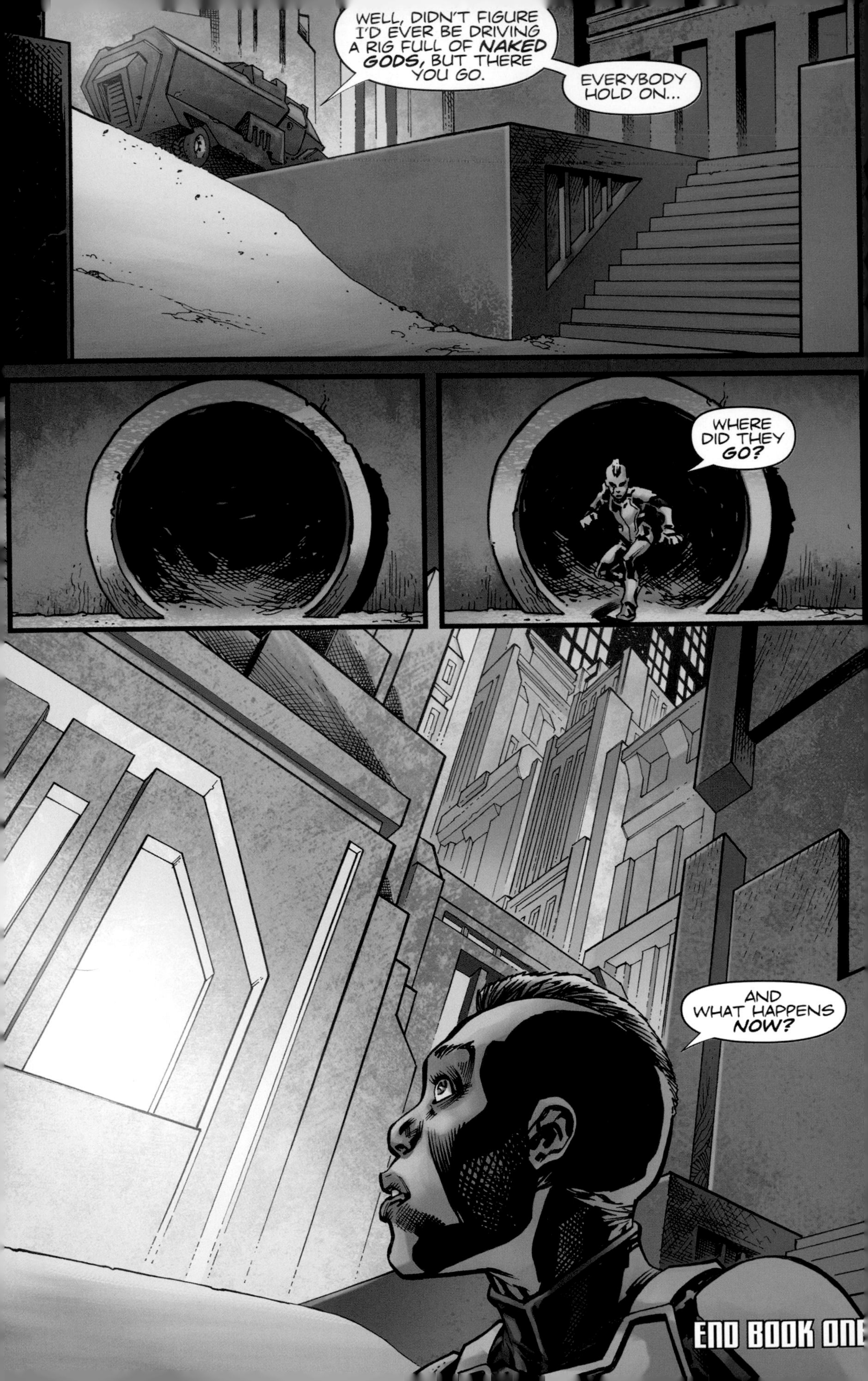
WELL, DIDN'T FIGURE I'D EVER BE DRIVING A RIG FULL OF **NAKED GODS,** BUT THERE YOU GO.
EVERYBODY HOLD ON...
WHERE DID THEY ***GO?***
AND WHAT HAPPENS ***NOW?***
END BOOK ONE

COVER
GALLERY

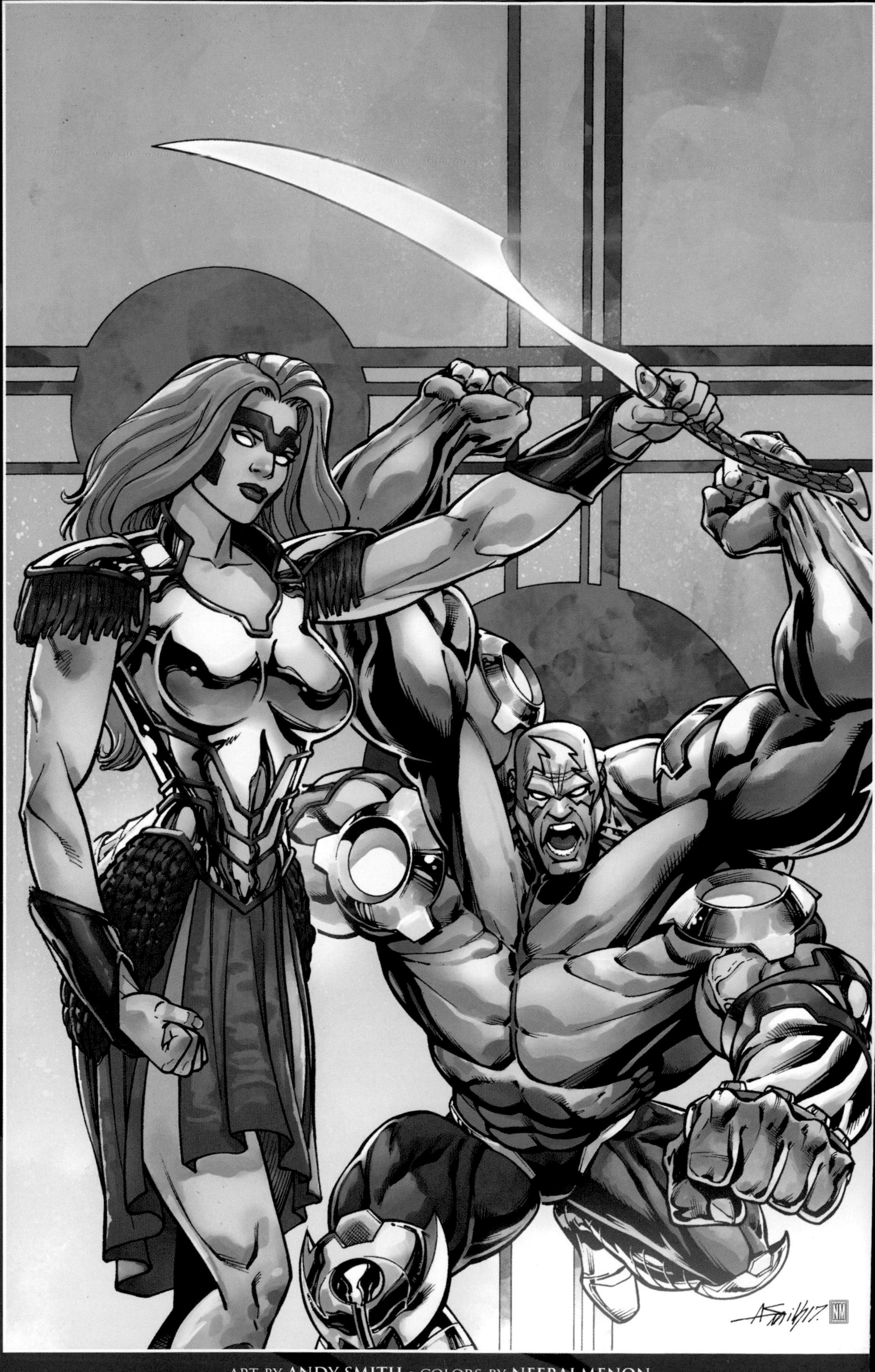

ART BY **ANDY SMITH** · COLORS BY **NEERAJ MENON**

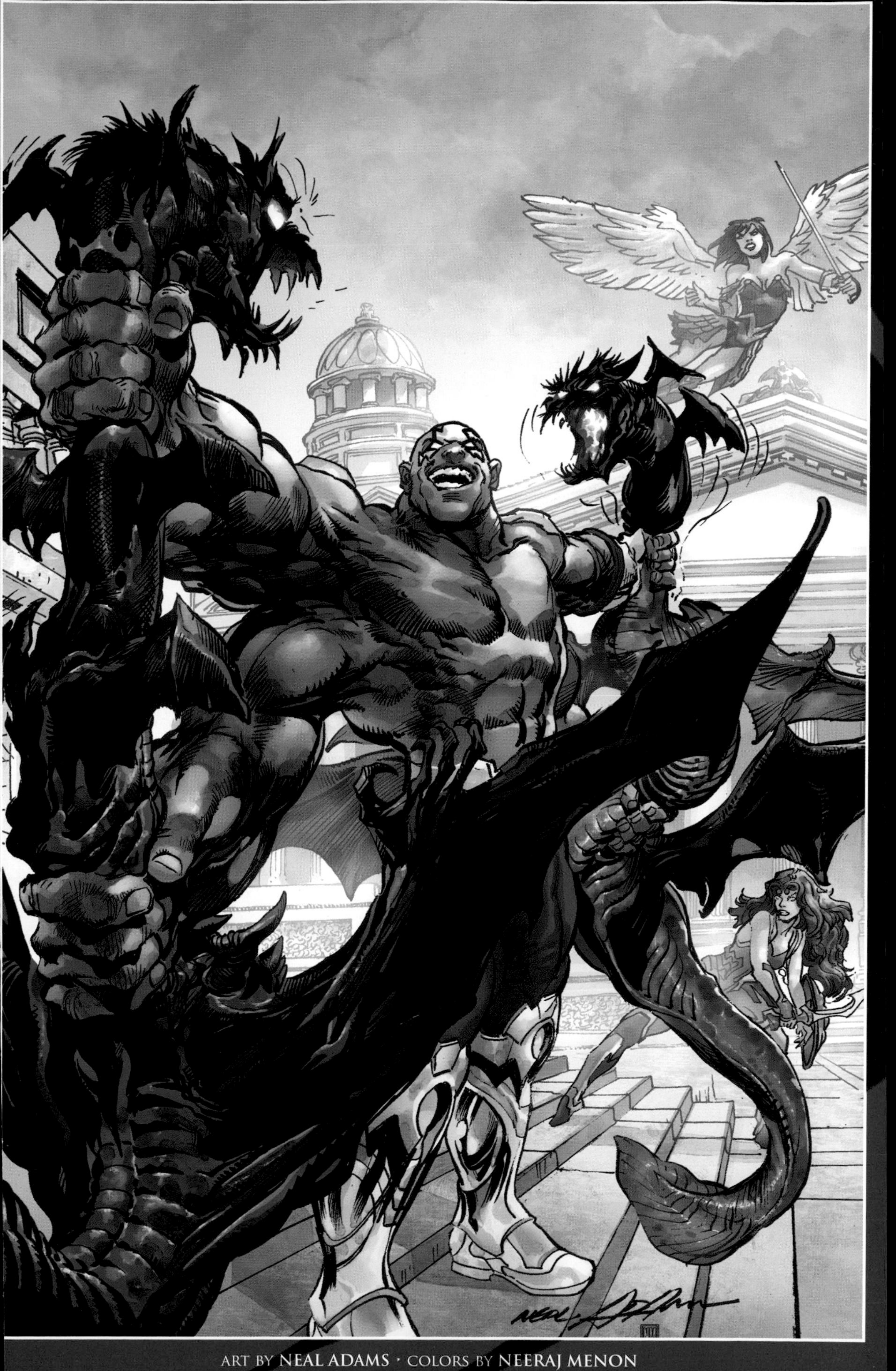

ART BY **NEAL ADAMS** · COLORS BY **NEERAJ MENON**

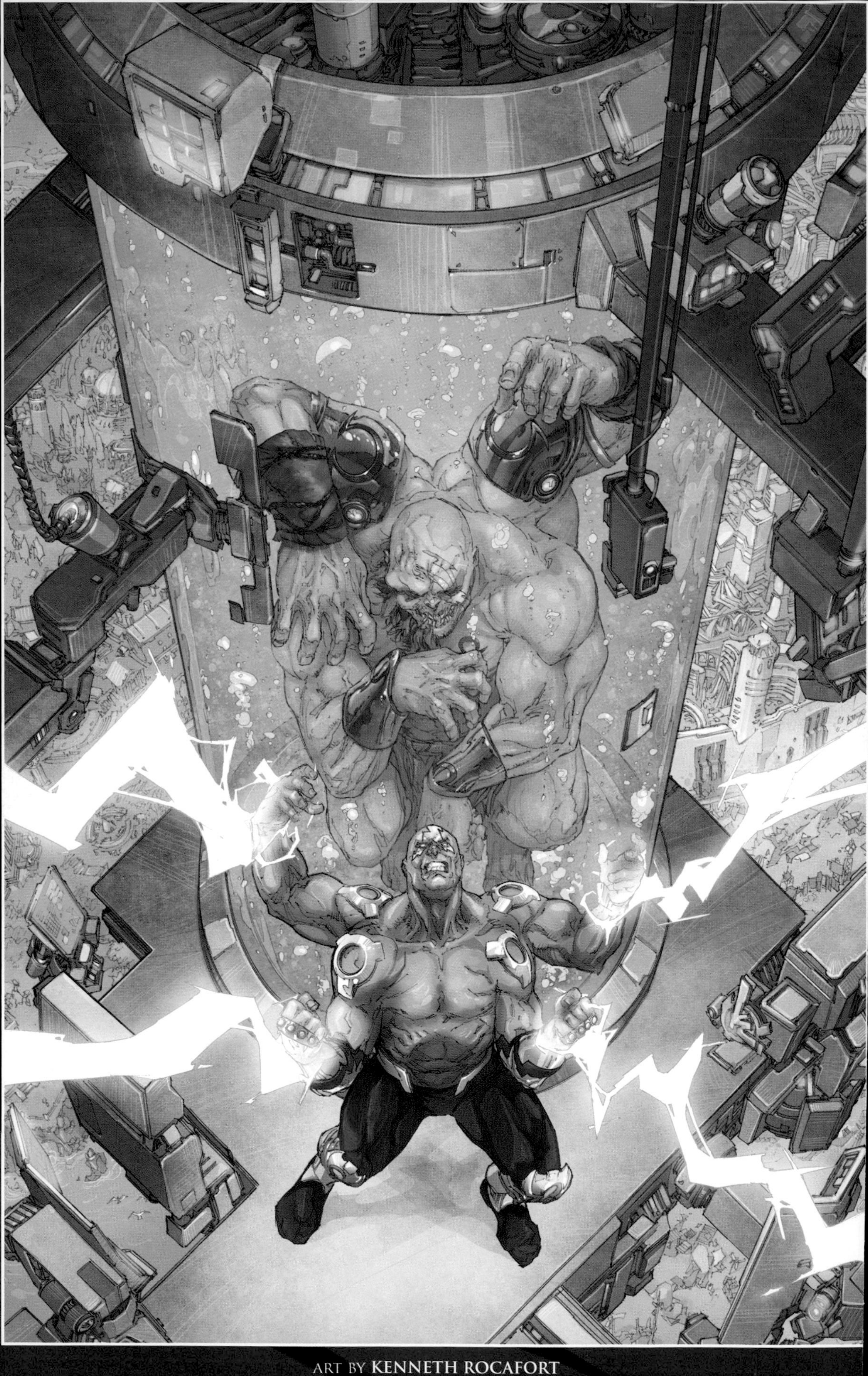

ART BY KENNETH ROCAFORT

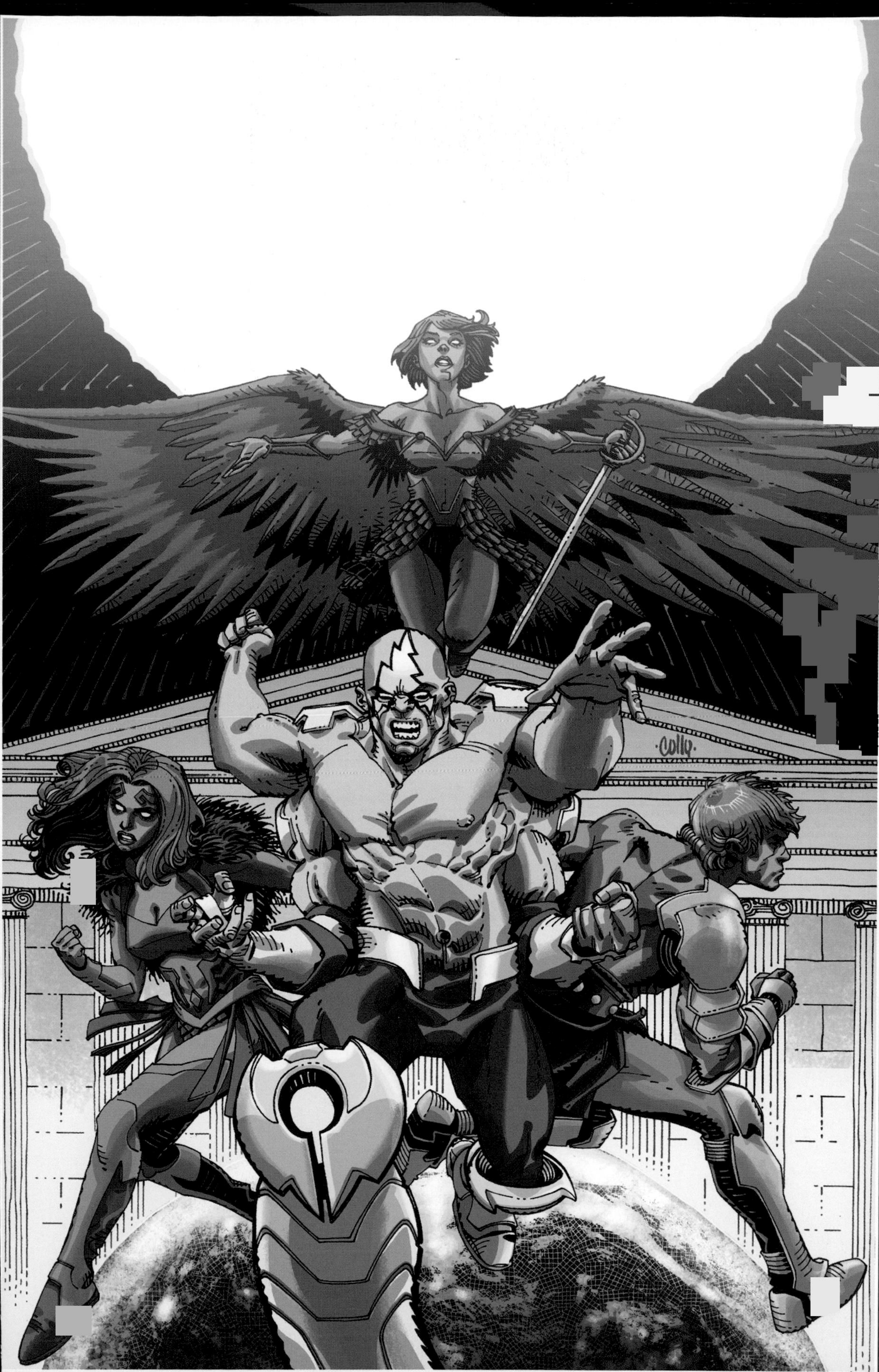

ART BY **CULLY HAMNER**

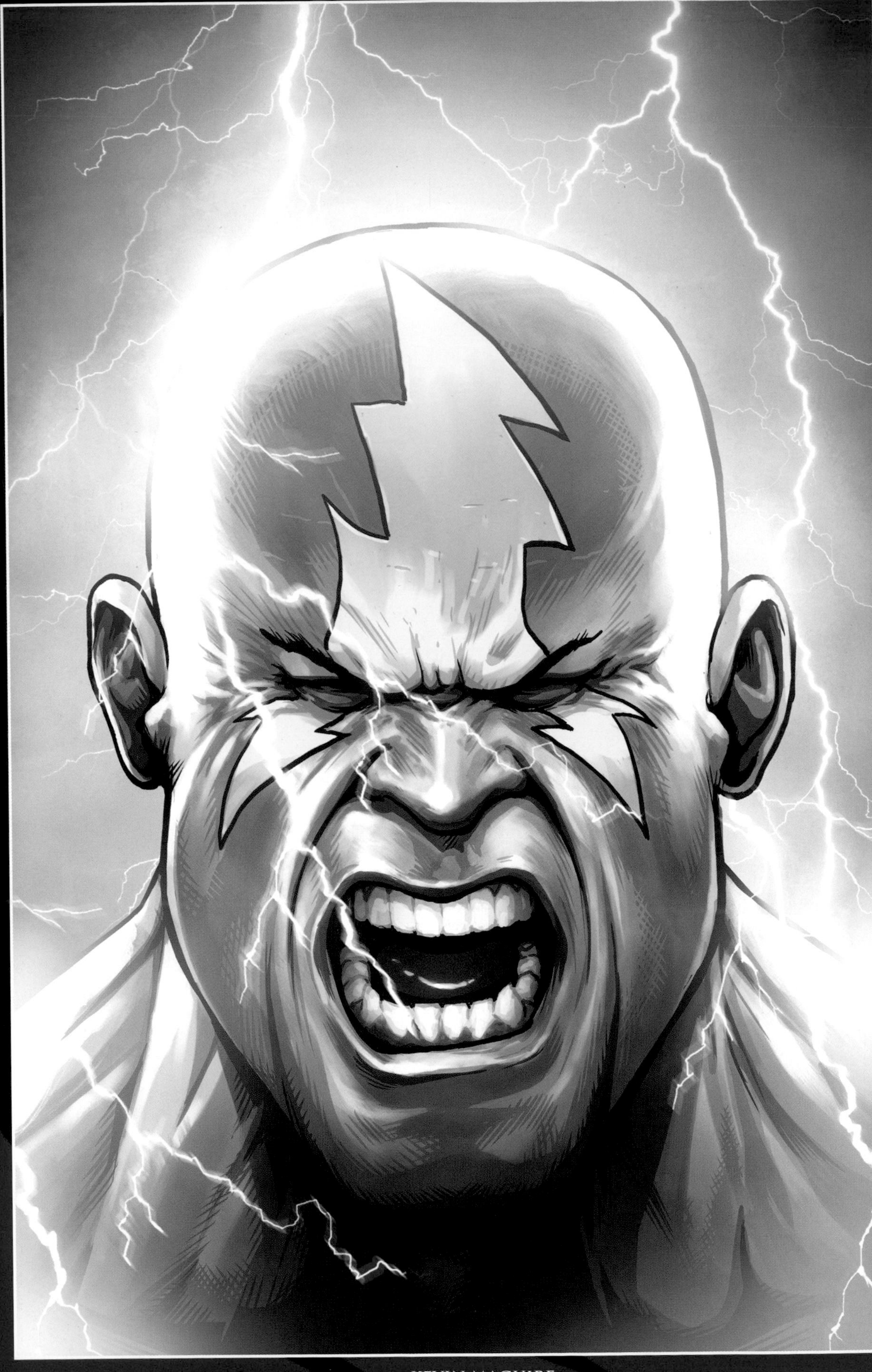

ART BY KEVIN MAGUIRE

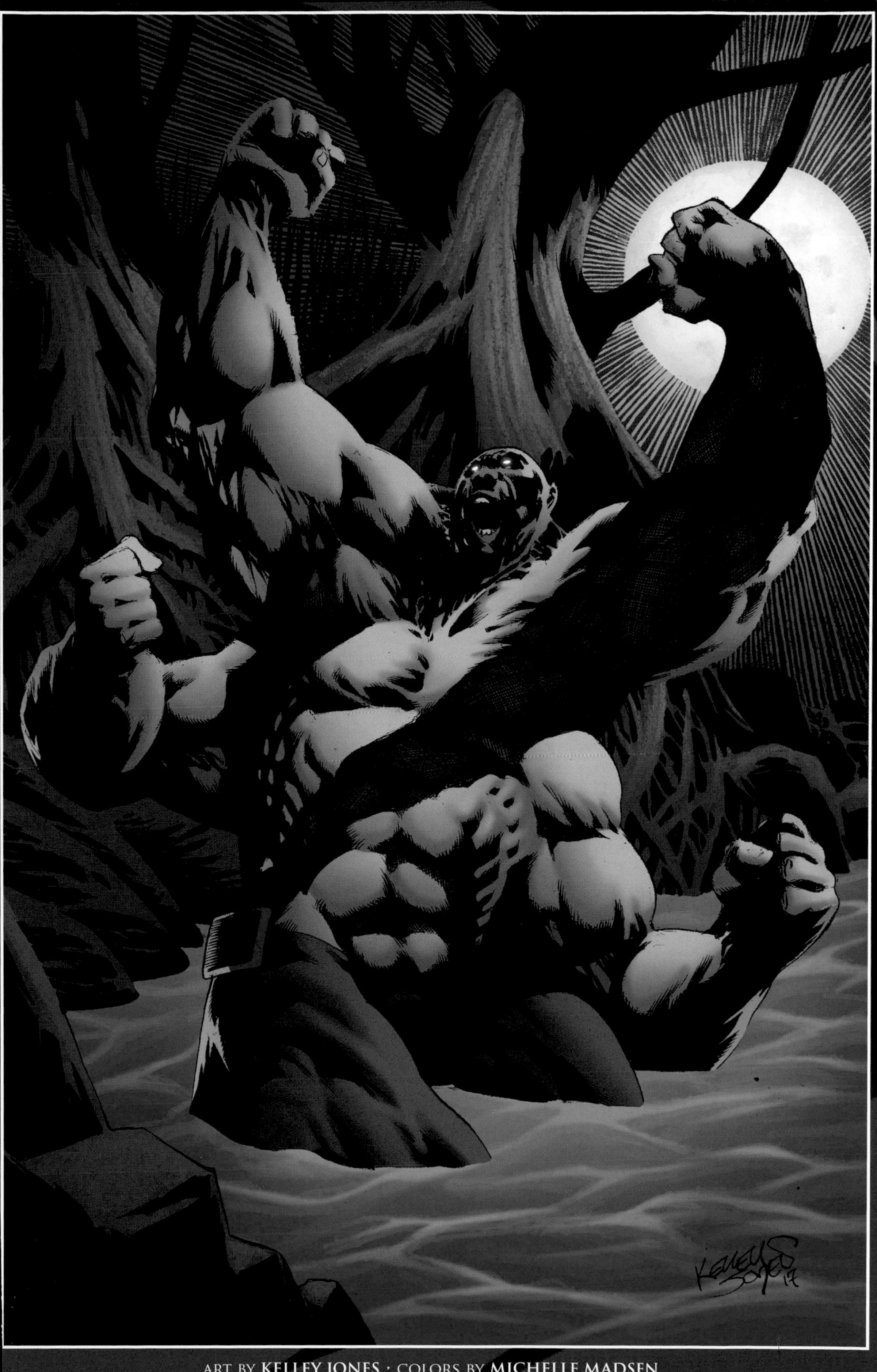

ART BY **KELLEY JONES** · COLORS BY **MICHELLE MADSEN**

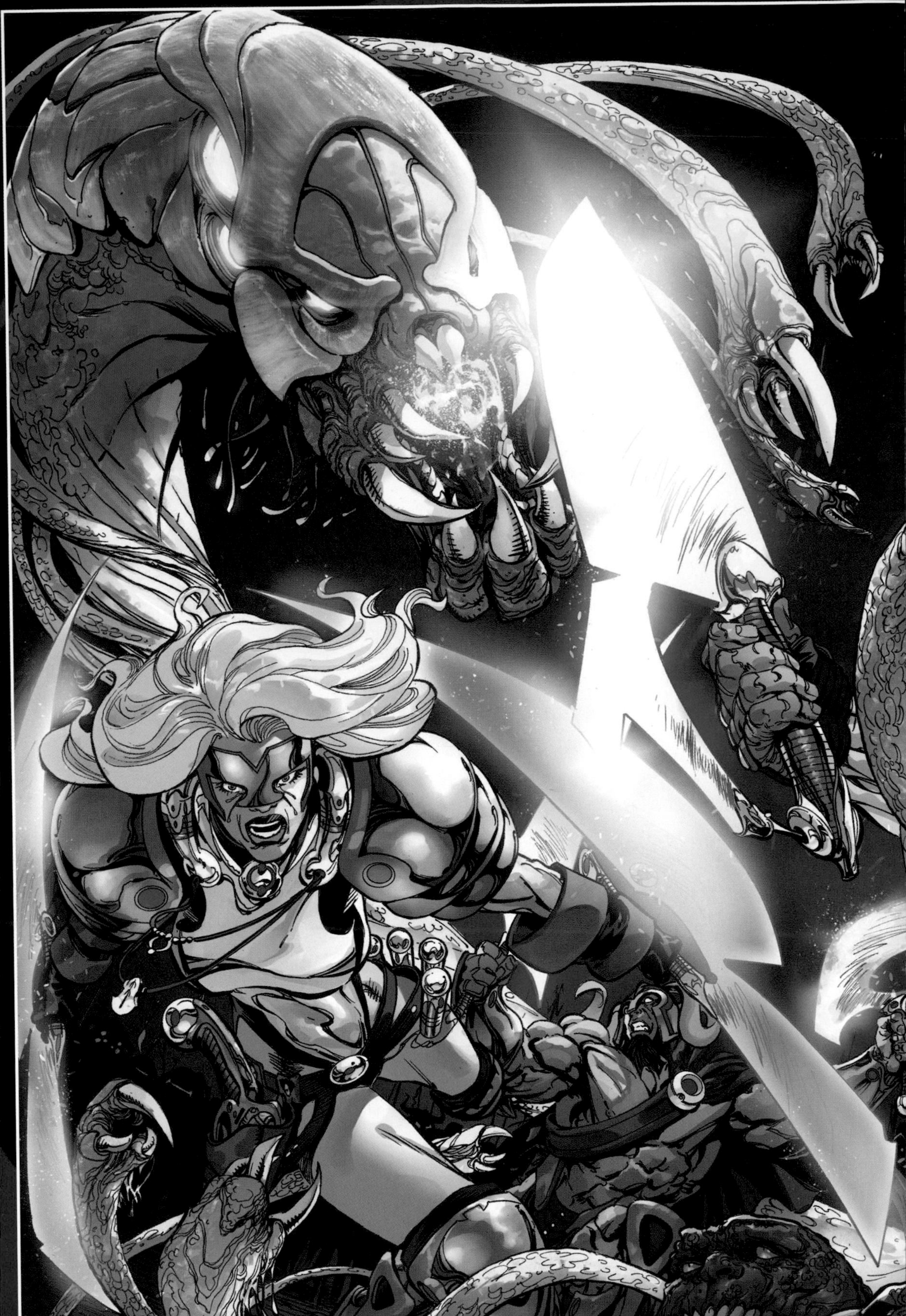

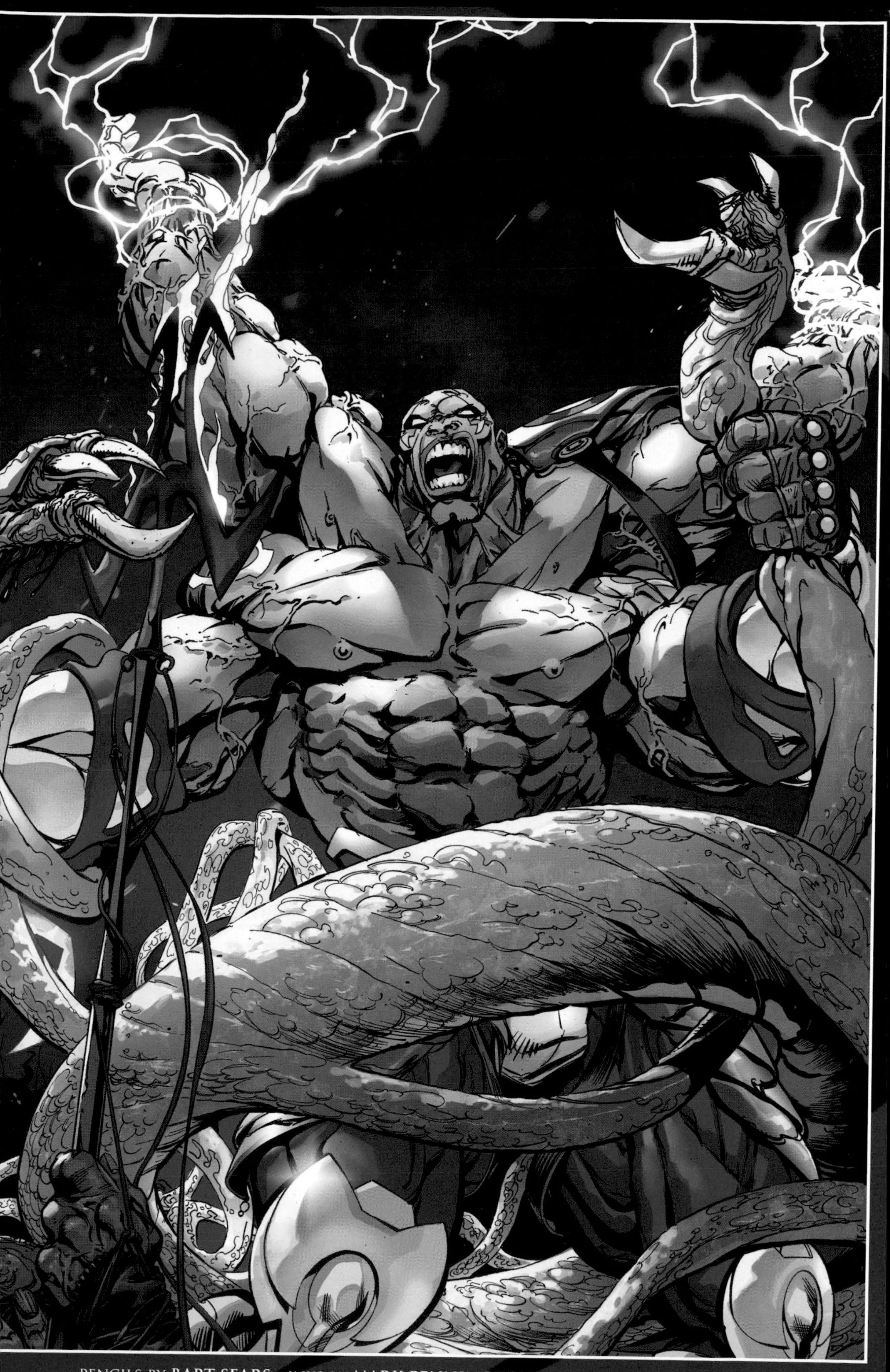

PENCILS BY **BART SEARS** · INKS BY **MARK PENNINGTON** · COLORS BY **NEERAJ MENON**

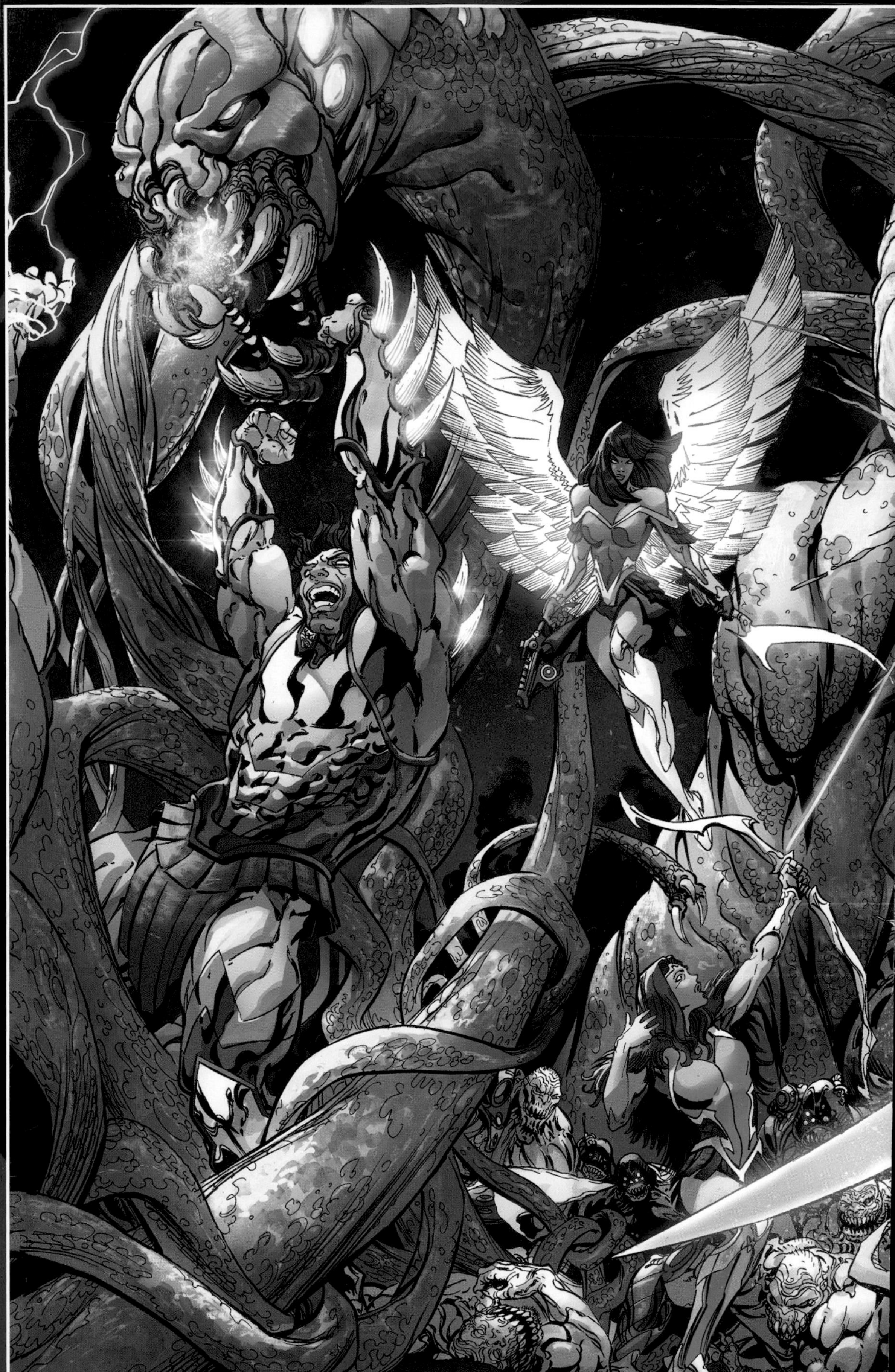

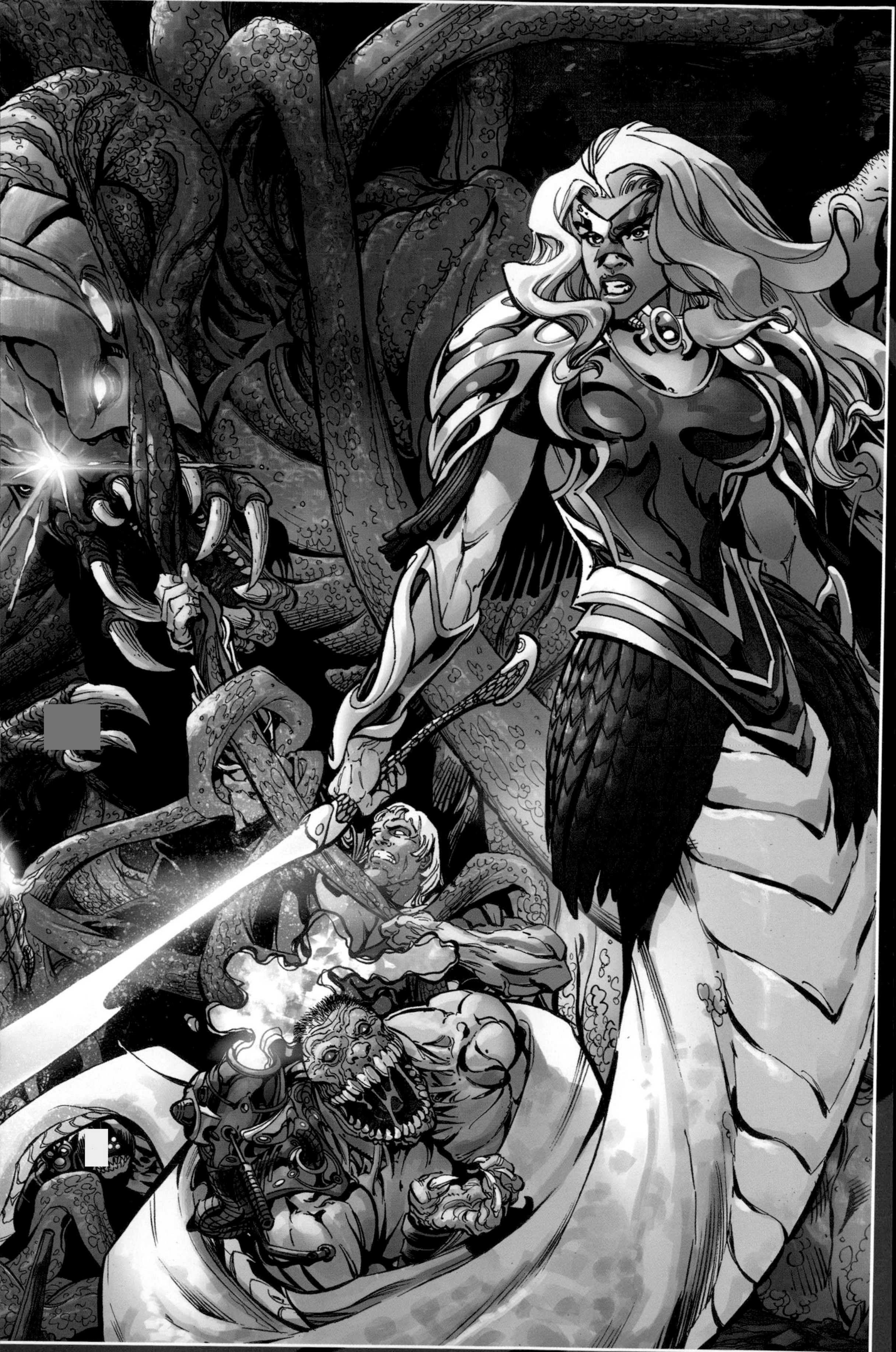

PENCILS BY **BART SEARS** · INKS BY **MARK PENNINGTON** · COLORS BY **NEERAJ MENON**

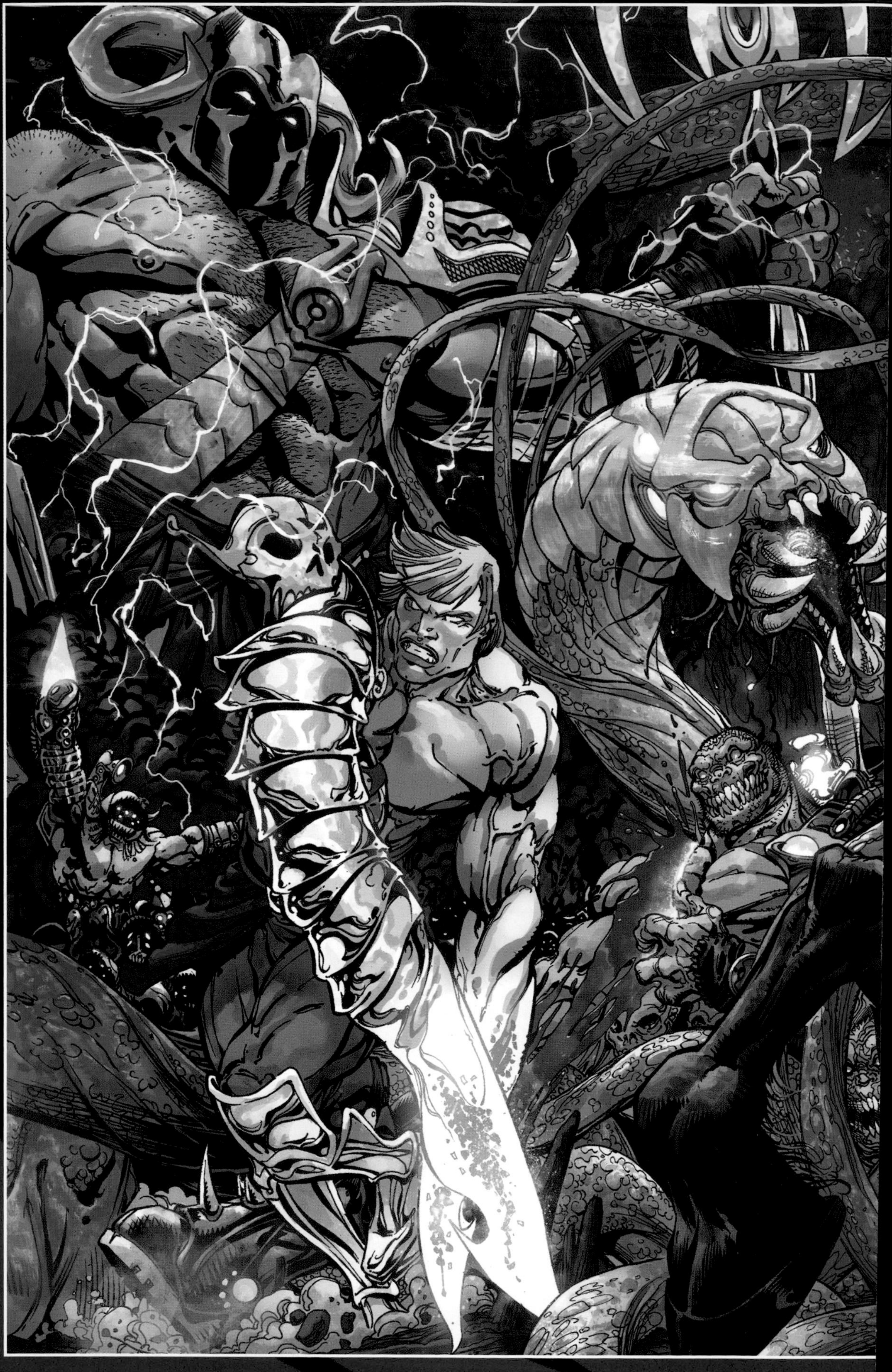

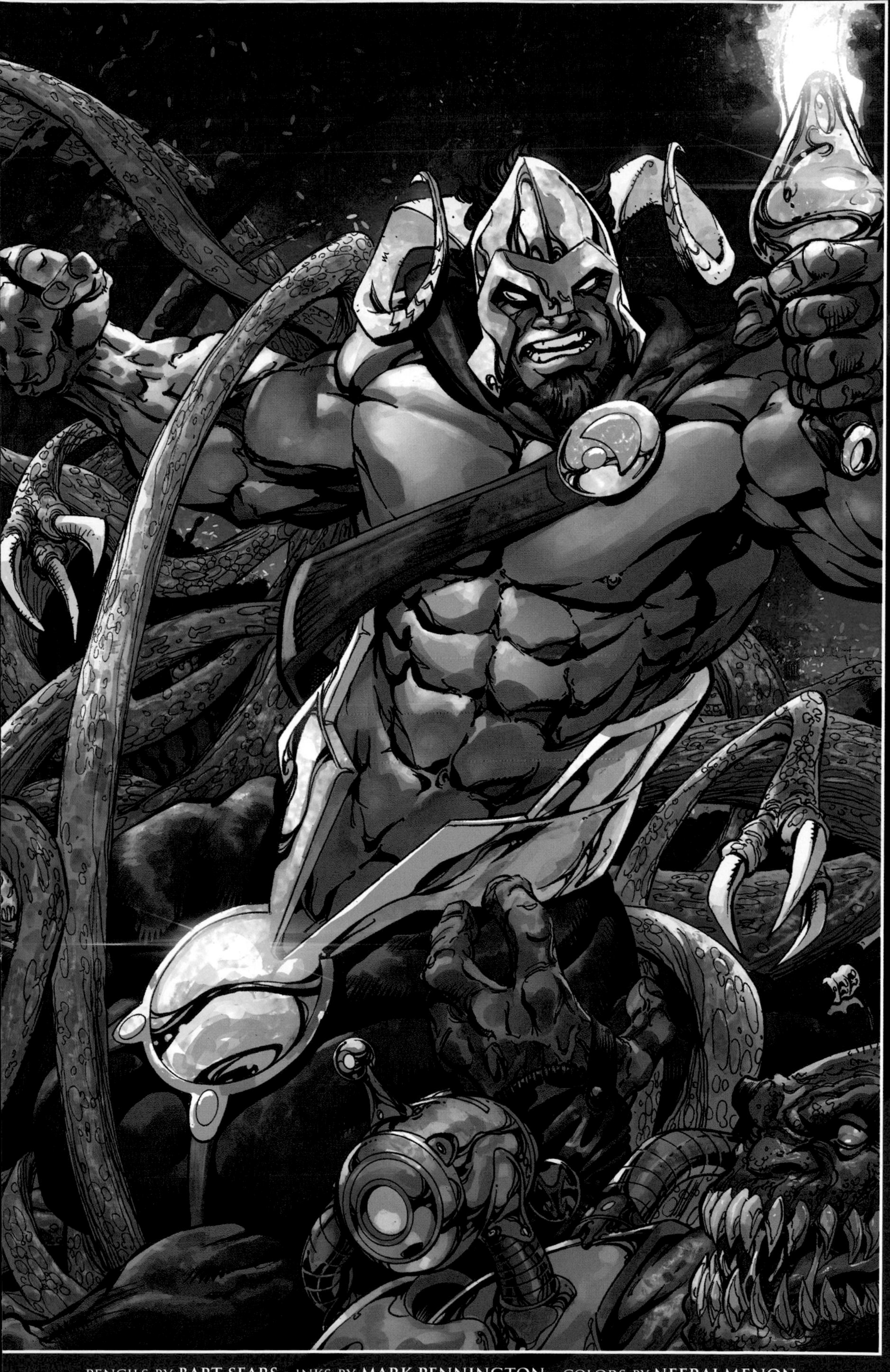

PENCILS BY **BART SEARS** · INKS BY **MARK PENNINGTON** · COLORS BY **NEERAJ MENON**

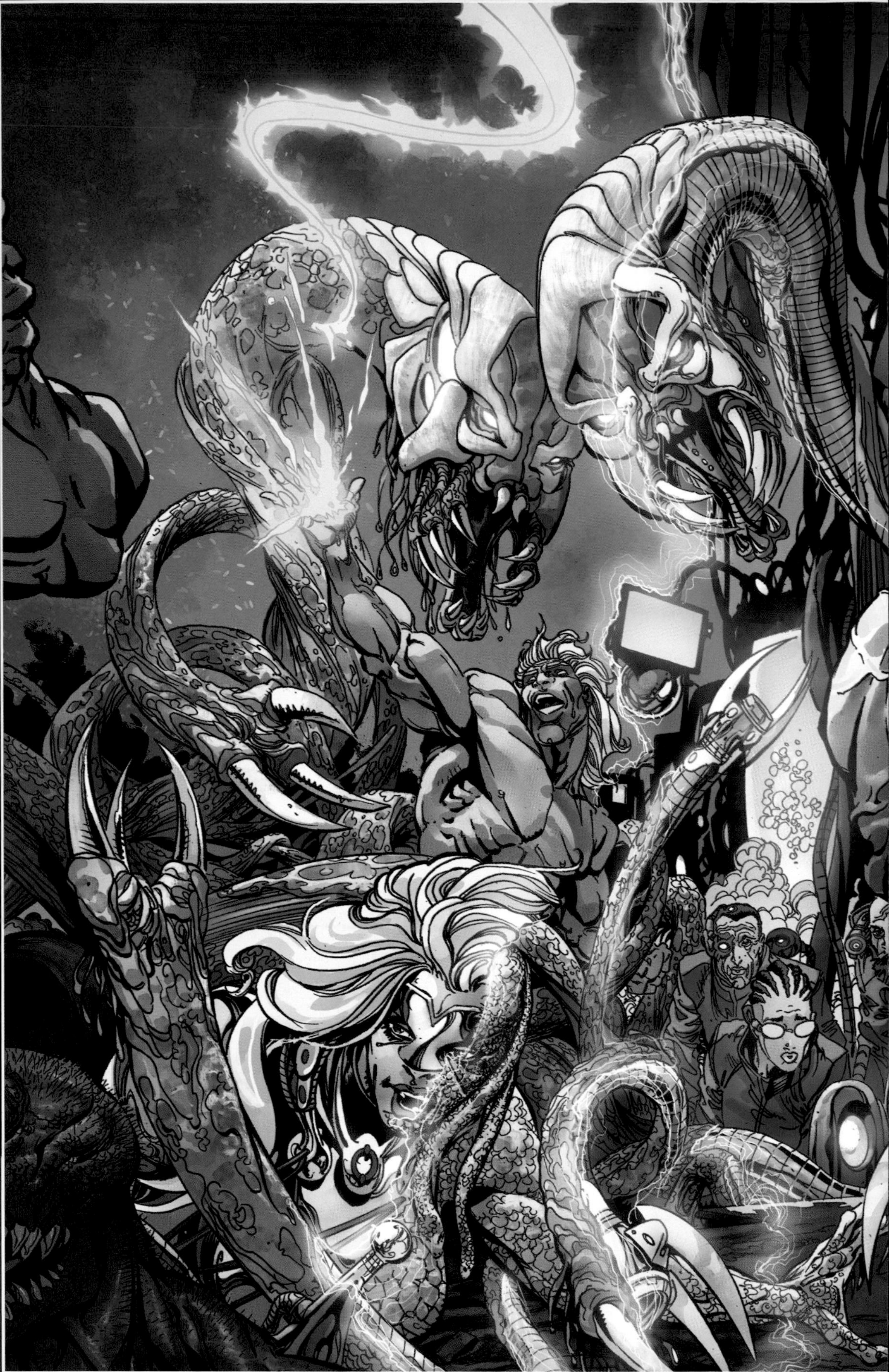

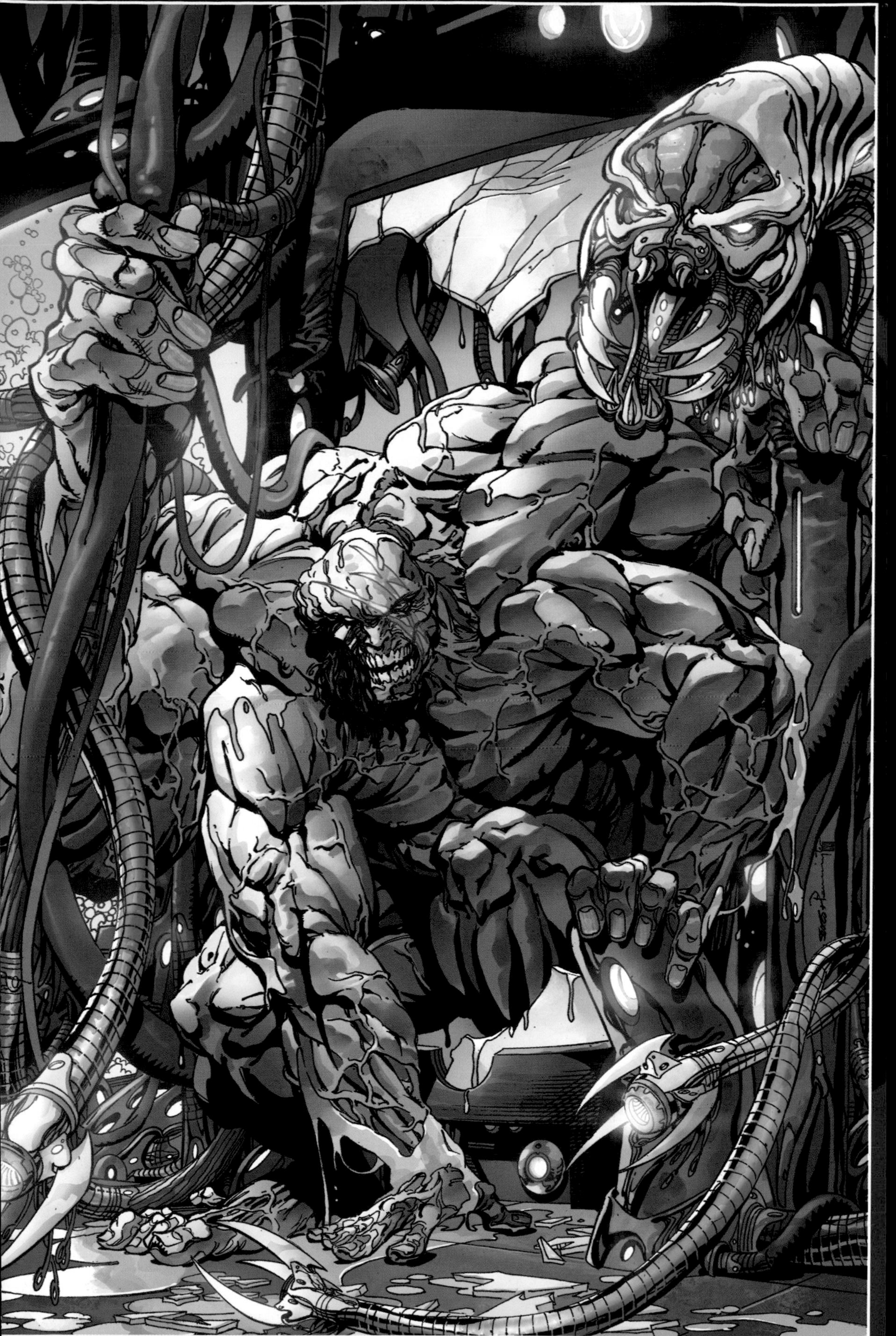

PENCILS BY **BART SEARS** · INKS BY **MARK PENNINGTON** · COLORS BY **NEERAJ MENON**

DESIGN & SKETCH GALLERY

BY TOM RANEY

BOOK Issue# Page# Art:

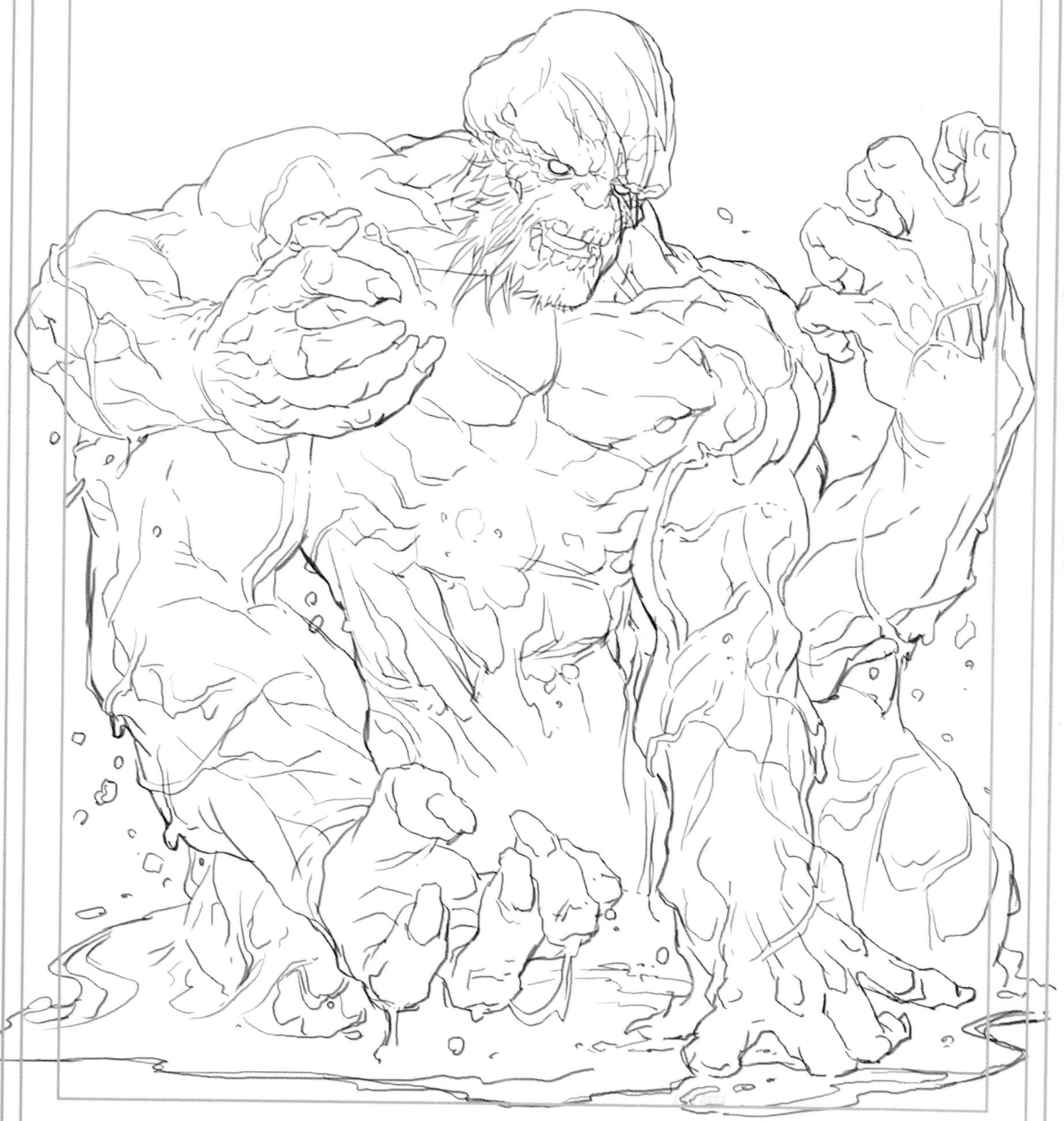

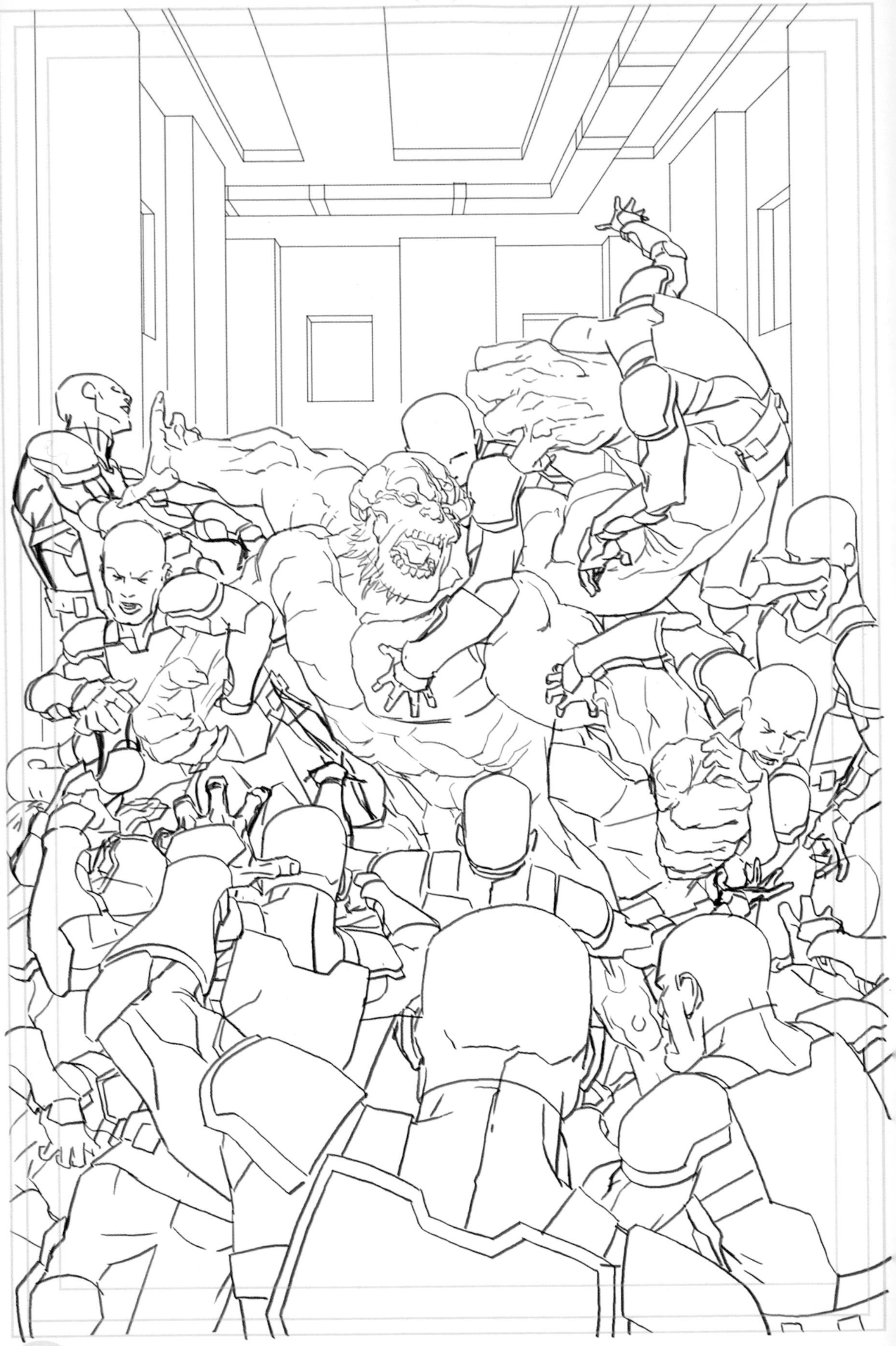

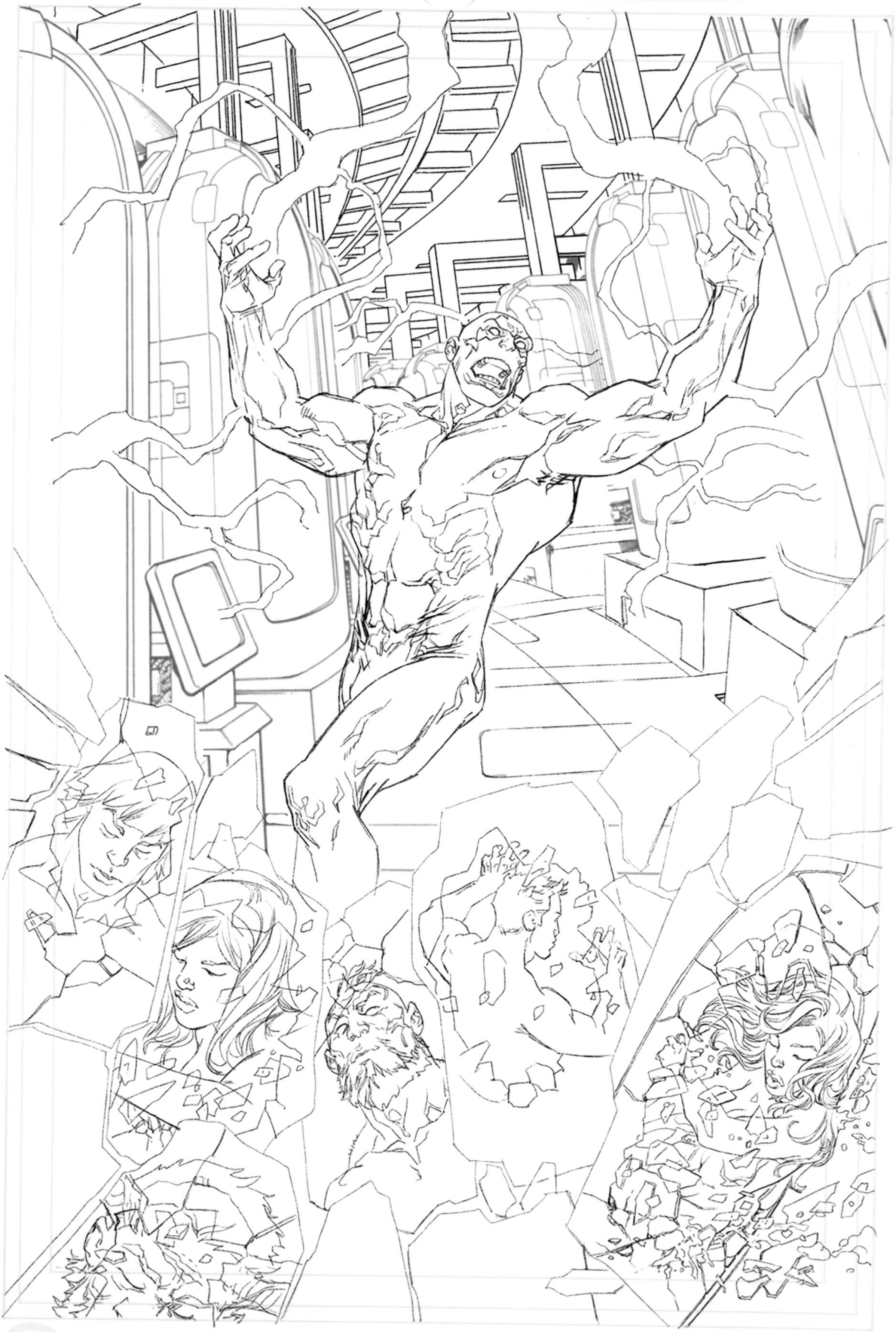

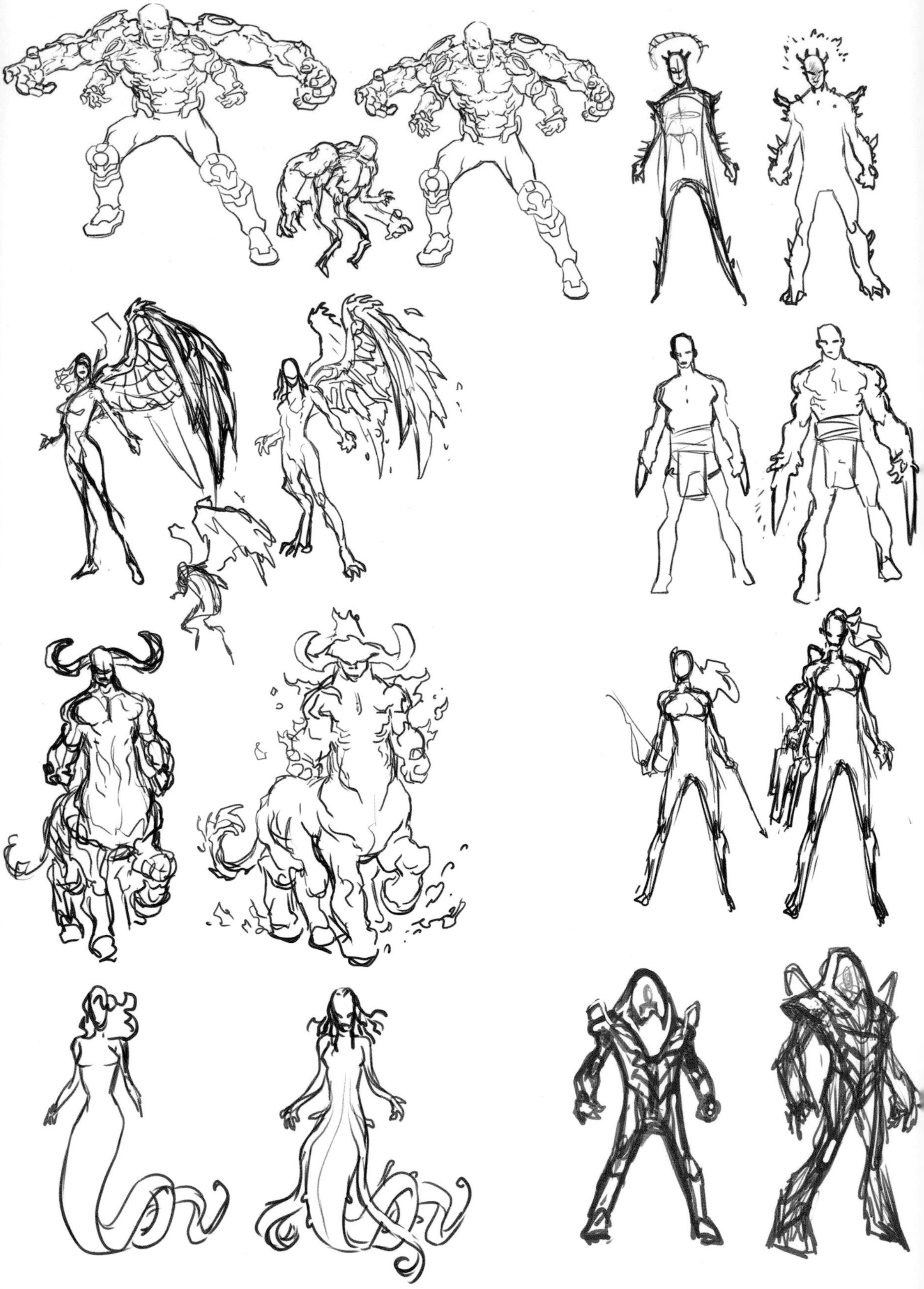

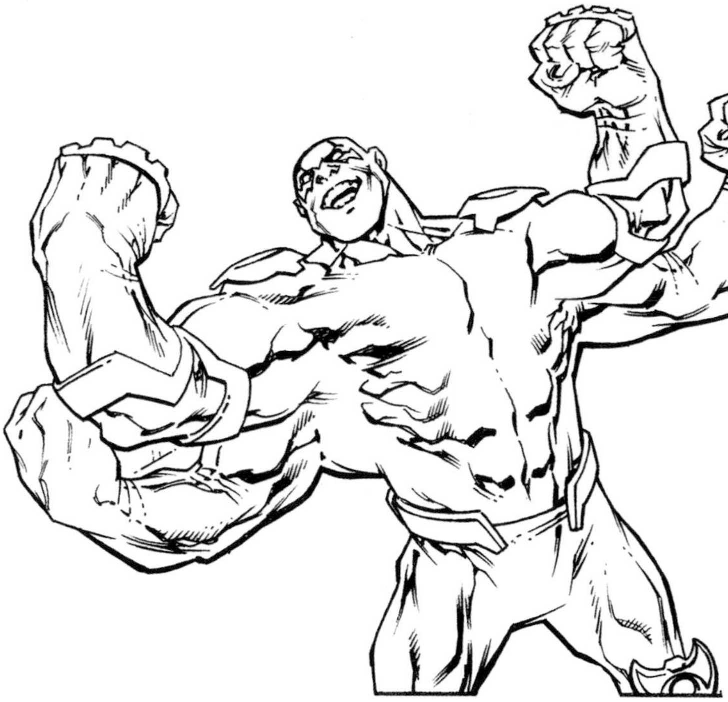
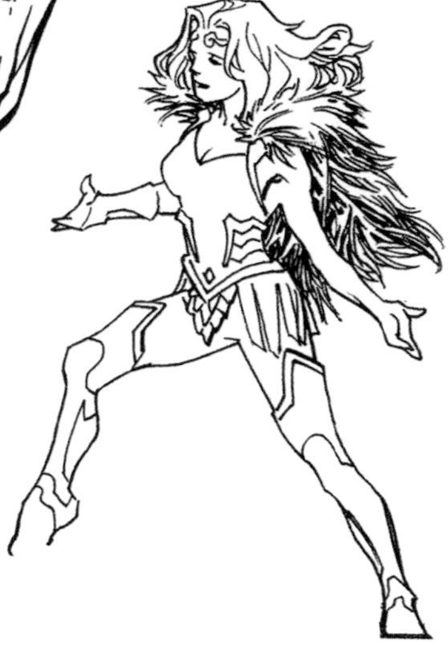
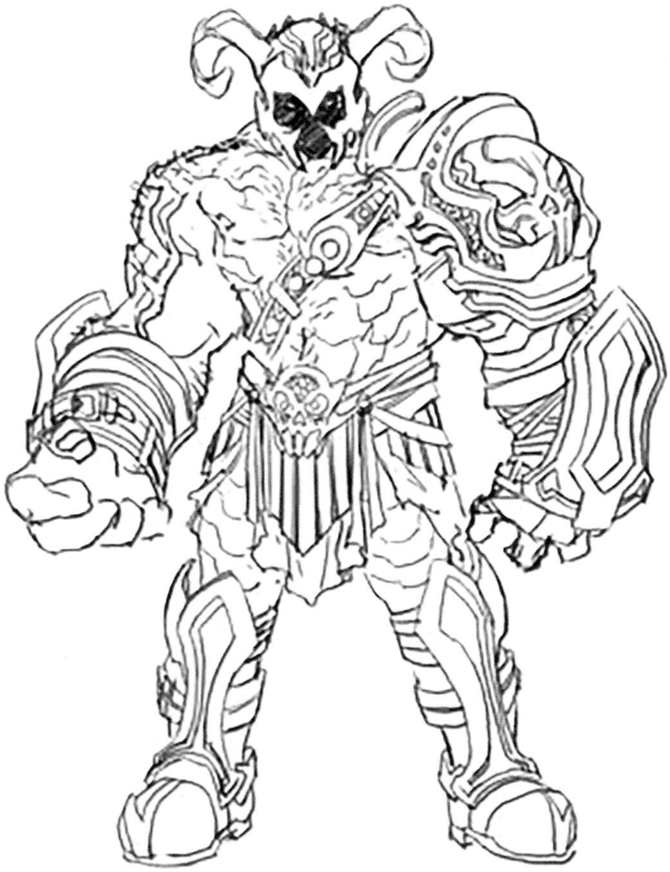
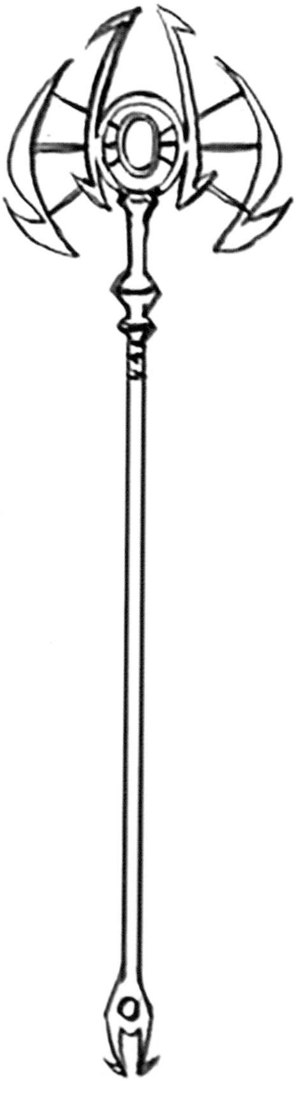

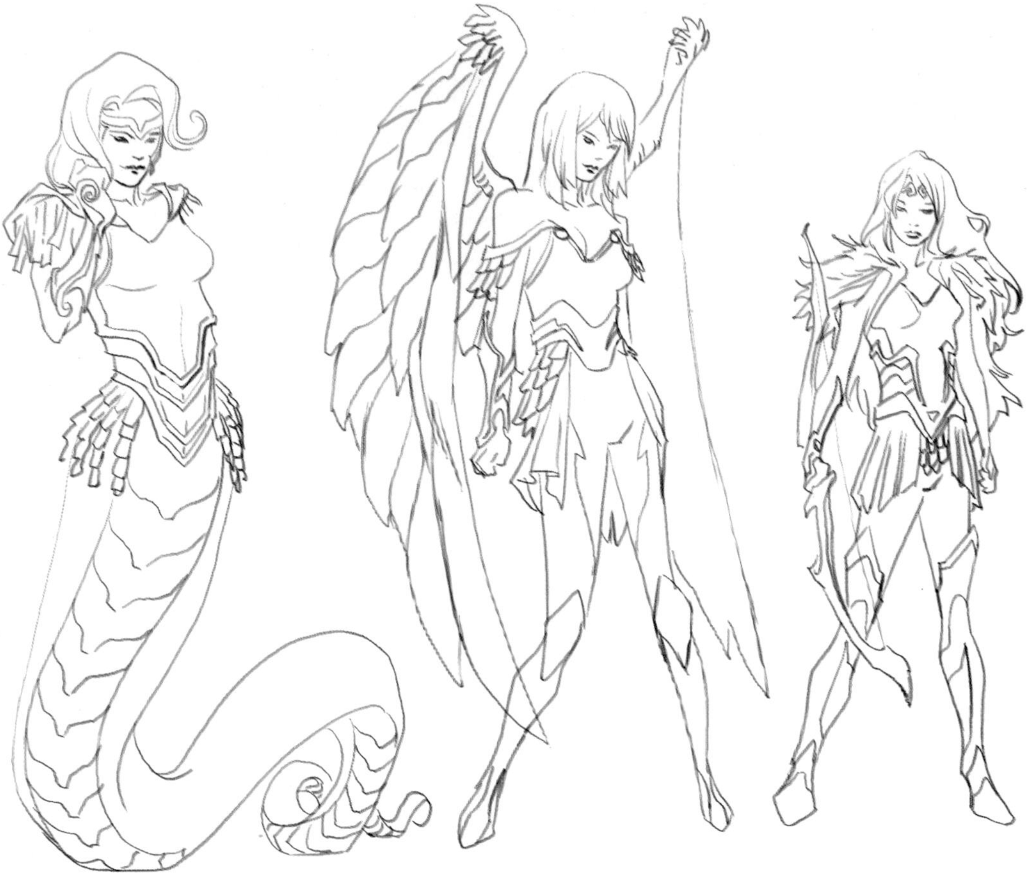

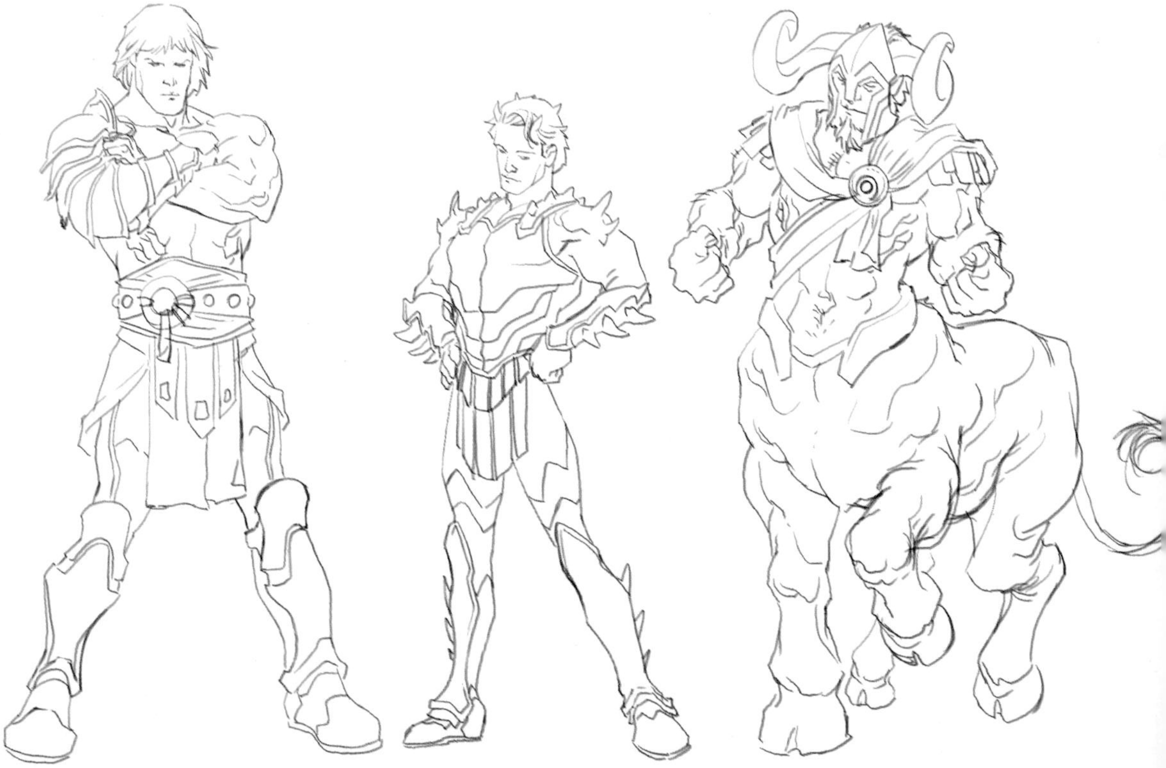

BOOK Issue# Page# Art:

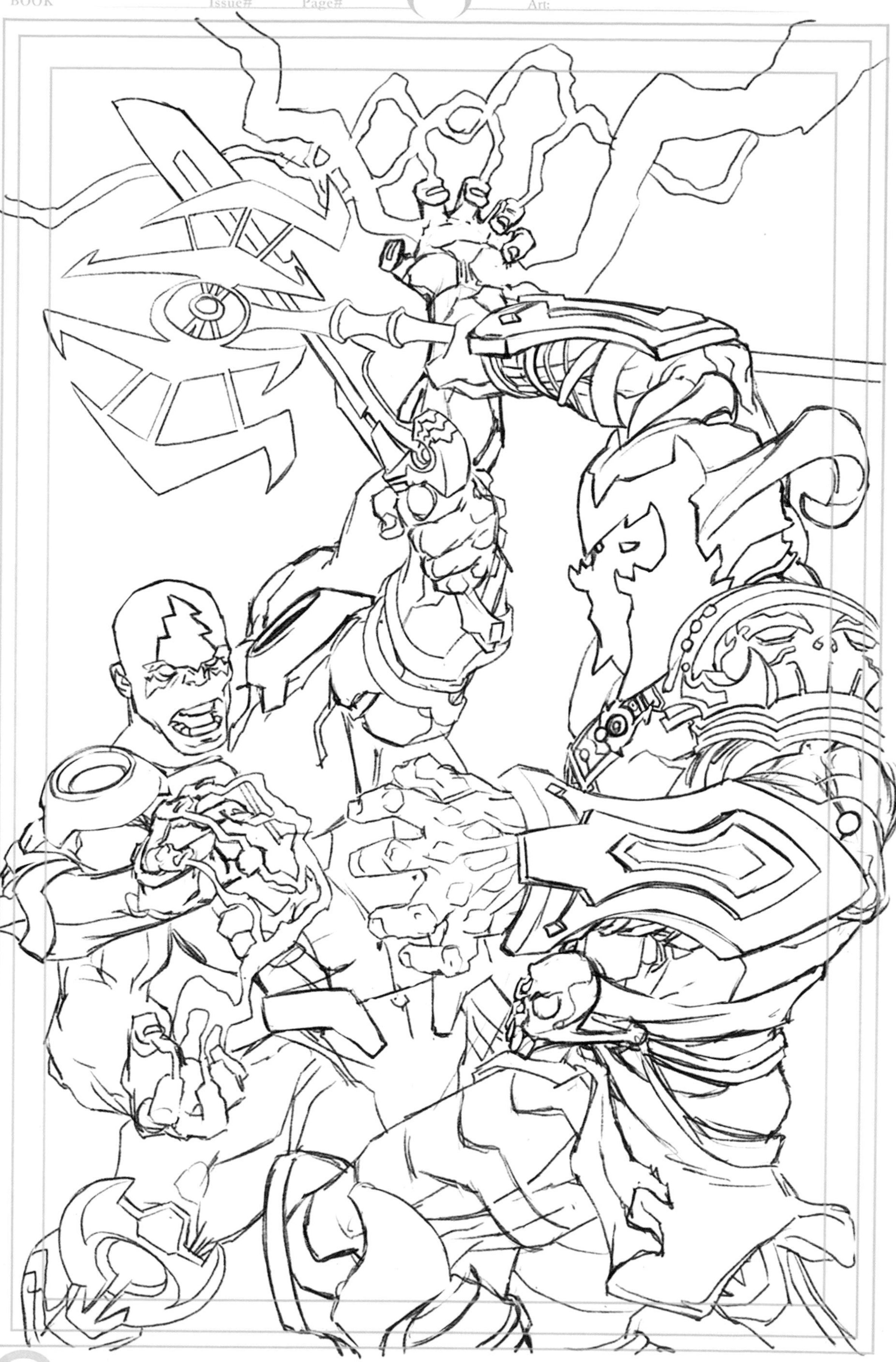

BOOK Issue# Page# Art:

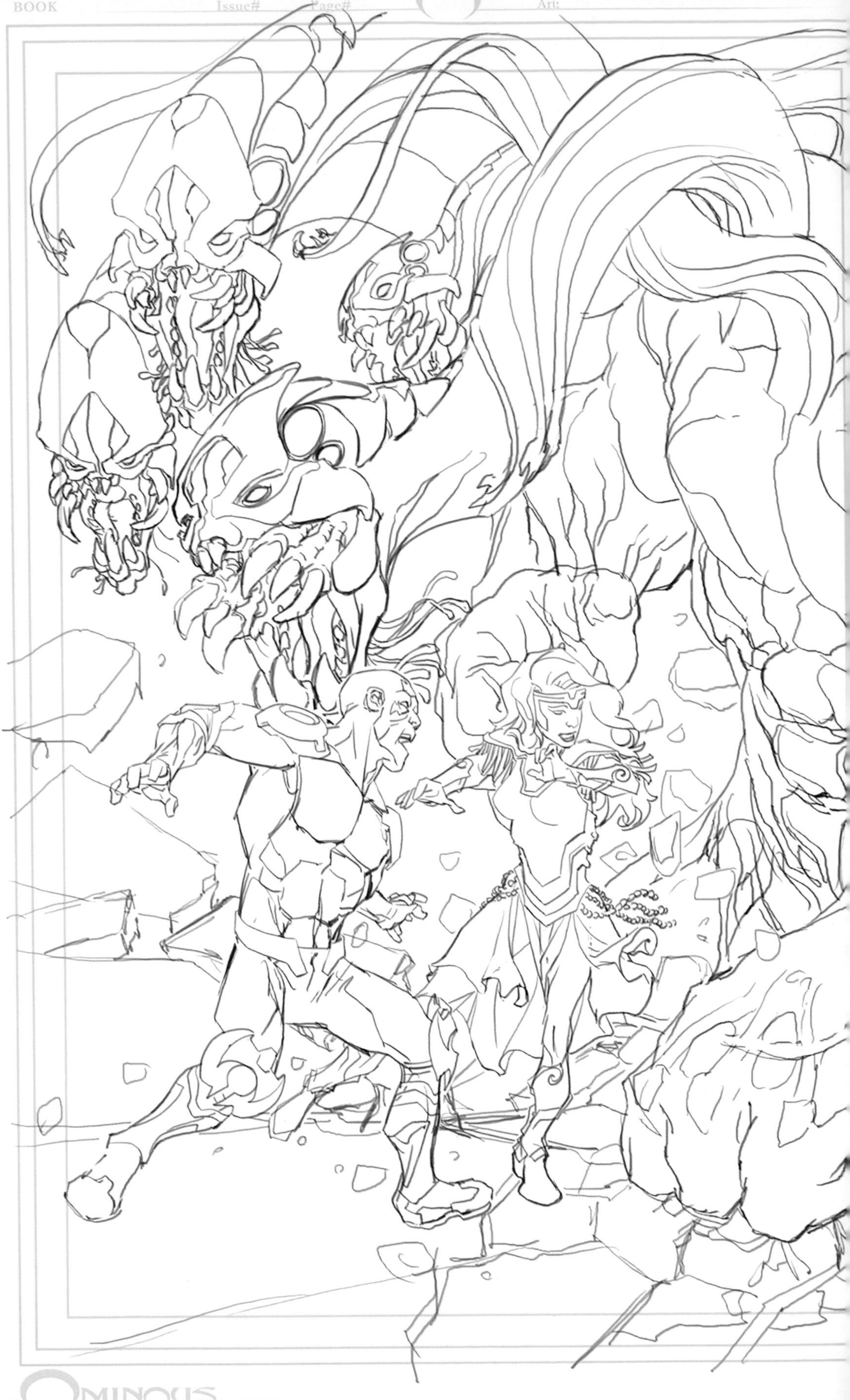

Issue# Page# Art:

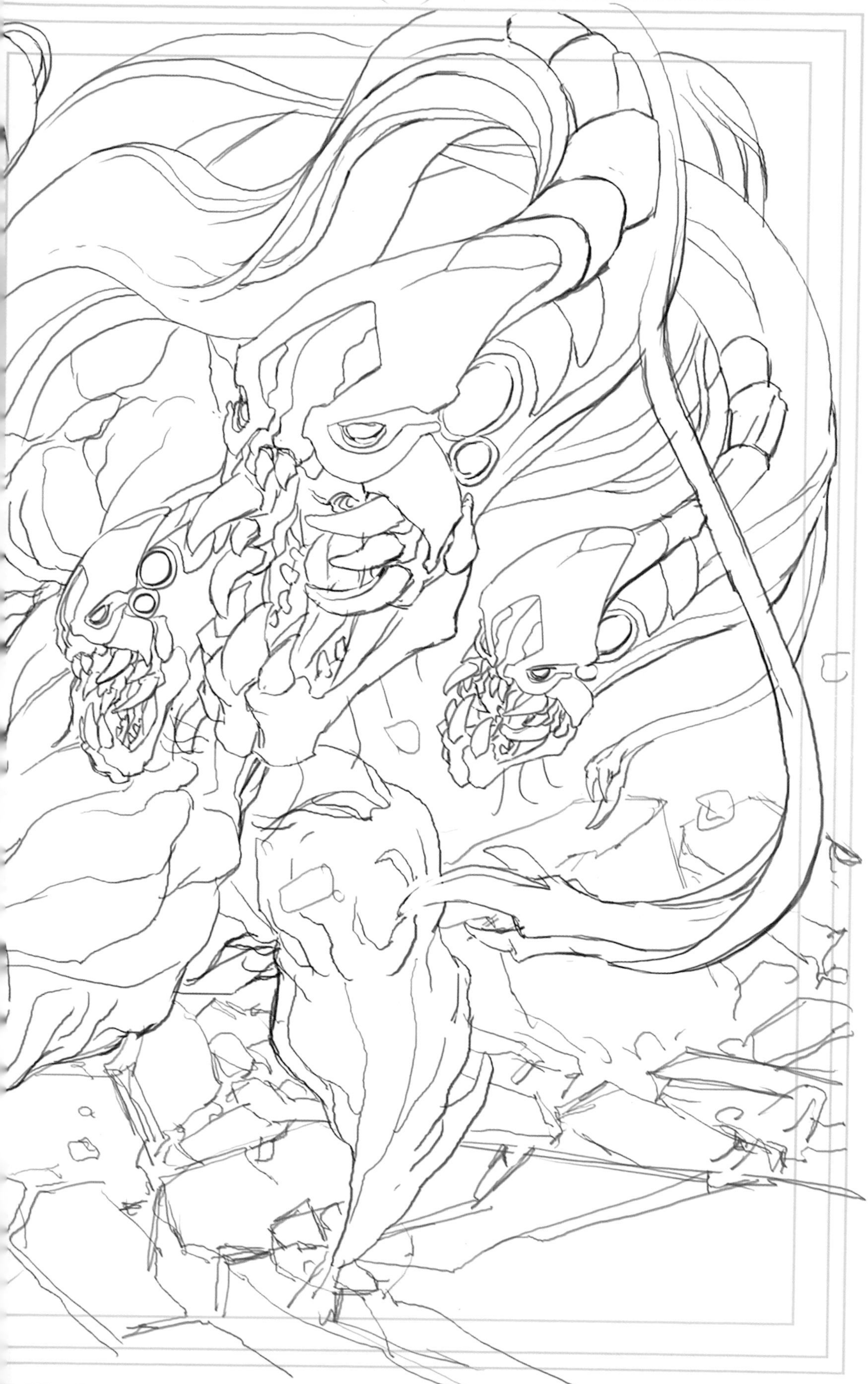

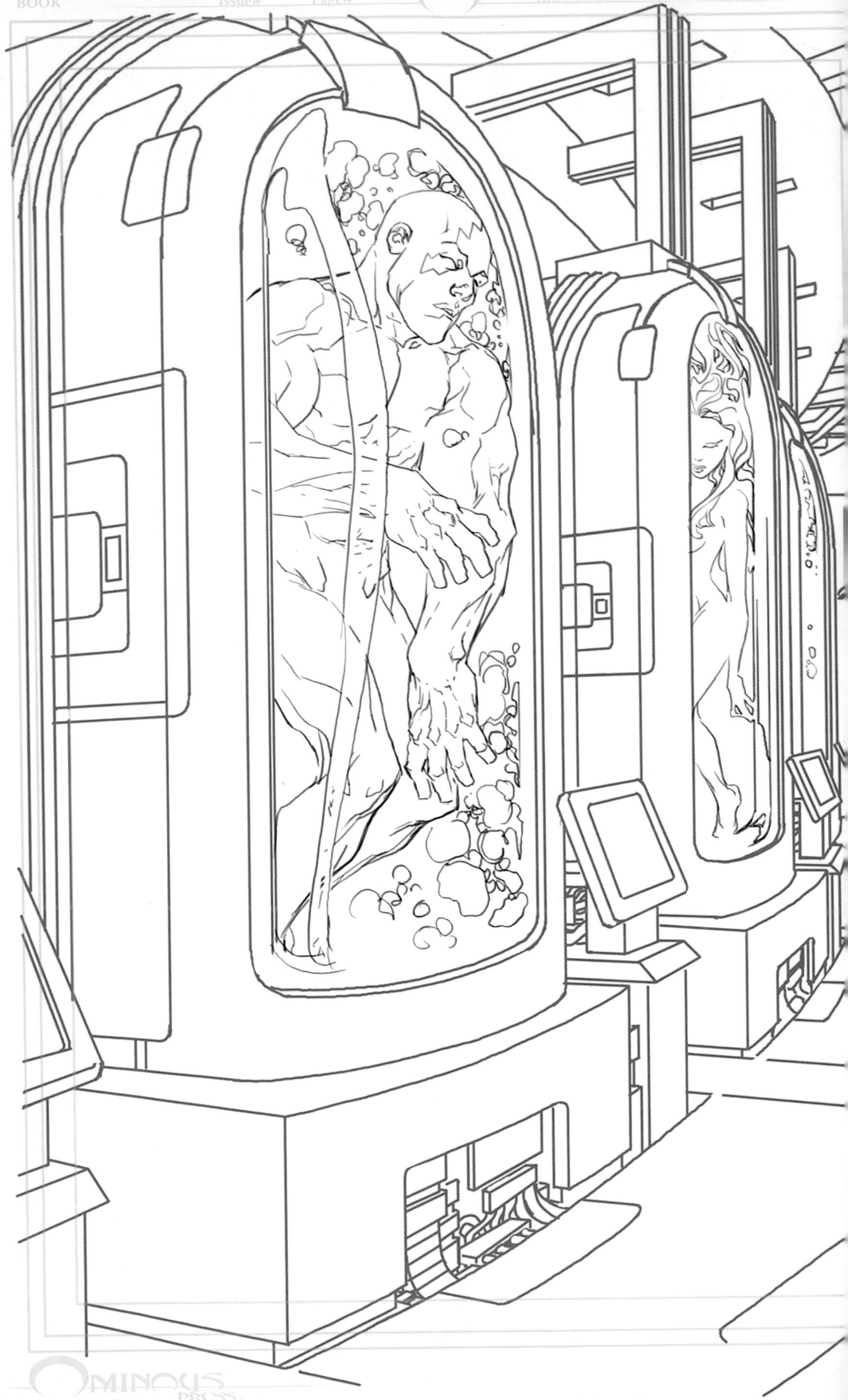

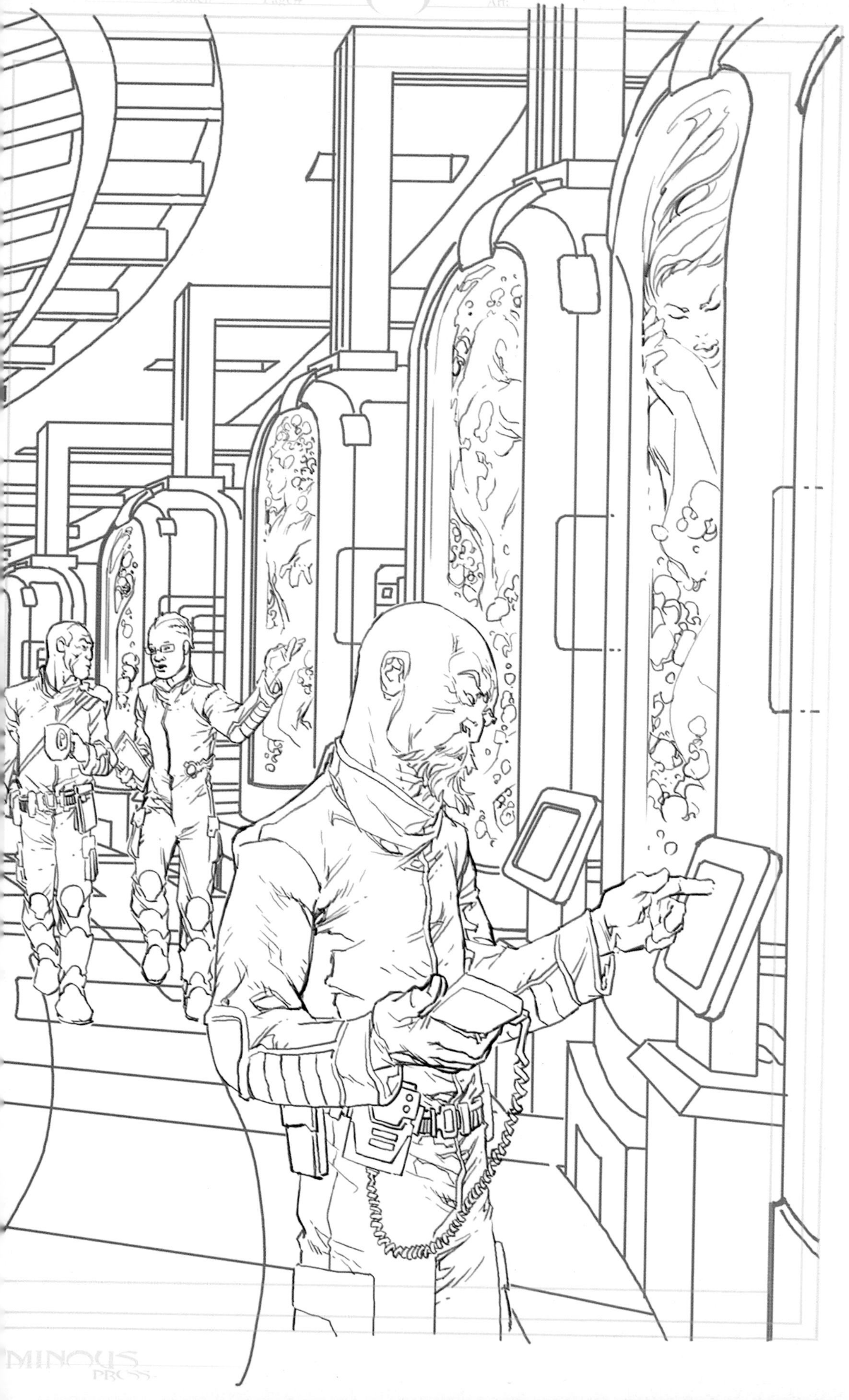

DREAD GODS™
WILL RETURN